KAIJU: DEADFALL

JE GURLEY

ISBN: 978-1-925225-28-0

1

Wednesday, August 8, 2018   5:30 a.m. (PDT)   San Francisco, California –

If he had known he was going to die, Miles Candicott still probably wouldn't have changed his routine, but he might have enjoyed his last morning on Earth more deeply. He was a habitual early riser, not for the opportunity to watch the sun rising over Eureka Peak, but to beat the early morning traffic. As on any other day, he left his Outer Sunset two-bedroom, 1950's bungalow on Noriega Street at five in the morning and jogged to the Great Highway along the coast. From there, his trek would take him one mile north to Golden Gate Park, returning home for a shower and breakfast before leaving for his law office in downtown San Francisco.

He had unfailingly performed this morning ritual for five years. At forty-one, he thought himself in better shape than when he turned twenty-five. He was single, enjoyed a full life both in and outside the gay community, and his salary was in the comfortable upper six-figure range. He embraced his lifestyle with gusto. As a native San Franciscan, he wished to be no other place in the world.

The park was his favorite leg of the route. He relished the two mile jog along the deserted park trails. A light mist had rolled in from the ocean hiding the sidewalk, but he knew the path by heart. The streetlights created undulating pools of brightness. The nearby trees floated on a luminescent cloud. When the tops of the trees began to glow with reflected light, Miles glanced upwards to find the entire eastern sky aglow. Confused, he stopped to check his watch – 5:30 a.m. As he watched dumfounded, the sun grew brighter. *Not the sun*, he surmised. *A meteor, a large one. Make a wish.*

The falling star moved quickly, growing larger as it approached, crossing the night sky like a herald of the morning to follow. His heart raced, not from the vigor of his run, but from the fear that he was the target of a celestial object that seemed to be zeroing in on him. Night turned to day, as the object lit up the sky overhead. He held his breath, fighting a growing panic, as the meteor shot overhead at a distance of less than a mile. The warmth of its heat touched his upturned face. A trail of smoke and flame followed the fireball as it descended. When the sonic boom it produced slammed into him, he clapped his hands over his ears and grimaced from the pain. Car alarms began wailing in the nearby neighborhoods. Dogs howled.

Mouth open in awe, blinking his eyes against the bright glare, he watched mutely, as the fireball struck the water near the Farallon Islands some twenty-seven miles distant. Its impact illuminated the ocean, sending a plume of steam skyward, as millions of gallons of seawater vaporized in an instant. Seconds later, the cloud of steam turned to glowing vaporized rock as the object buried into the seabed. Just as the glow died, the ground began to tremble, a low rumble at first, but steadily growing stronger until the tremor knocked him to his knees. He braced himself with his hands. The leaves rustled as the trees around him shook violently. The sidewalk cracked beneath him; then buckled. He had experienced mild 4.0 tremors in his lifetime, and this one was much worse, a 5.0 or 5.5 at least.

As if the gods had decided that quake alone hadn't caused sufficient damage for such a cosmic event, deep beneath the earth, the San Andreas and Hayward Faults began to shift. Under tremendous pressure, rock ground against rock, echoing the impact of the meteor, sending spasms racing outward in all directions. The ground shook more vigorously like a tossed blanket, uprooting trees and knocking down power lines. Sparks flew from damaged transformers, starting fires. Around him streetlamps rocked violently until their bulbs cracked, plunging him into darkness. Soon, the earthquake rattled not only the coast, but the entire peninsula as it grew in magnitude, reaching a 6.0, and then pushing on to a devastating 7.5.

Downtown, buildings constructed to handle the tectonic shifts prevalent in the area, swayed like pendulums. Glass building facades shattered, cascading shards of broken glass to the streets and sidewalks below. Older buildings collapsed altogether. Streets caved in. Fire hydrants ruptured, spraying geysers of water into the air. Fires erupted from broken gas mains.

The Golden Gate Bridge swung wildly, undulating between the towers like a plucked guitar string, but it held, though early morning motorists feared for their lives. The Bay Bridge likewise became a high-tension spring. The pavement cracked and split, as the bridge bucked and twisted along its great length. Cables ripped from moorings, but the structure remained standing.

San Francisco had suffered fire and quake damage once before in 1906 and had learned from the ensuing horrors. Some cities would have been flattened by such a tremor, but the city by the bay was made of sterner stuff. Fire departments rushed to extinguish the flames. Emergency vehicles raced to rescue trapped individuals. Police cars blocked streets and helped direct the injured to emergency medical care facilities. The damage would reach into the hundreds of millions of dollars, but the loss of life was minimal. However, the danger was not over.

Far out to sea, a wave rose. Generated by the force of the impact, the wave rushed toward the coast, climbing higher as it approached shallower water. Miles knew about earthquakes and tsunamis. He rushed north trying to reach high ground on the bluffs along the northwestern point of the peninsula, no longer jogging, but now running for his life. The sidewalk was shattered, too dangerous to follow. He cut across the park, dodging or leaping over toppled trees that rose from the mist like hurdles, scraping his legs on shrubs and flowers.

Around him, people were beginning to recover from the quake, stumbling from their homes, stunned and confused. He saw in their eyes the same fear that pushed him northwards. Perhaps, he should have warned them about the coming tsunami, but self-preservation was uppermost on his mind. He pushed forward in a blind panic, heart racing, his fear lending extra speed to his feet.

He almost made it. He was just south of Sutro Heights Park when the rumble of the approaching tsunami began to shake the ground. At first, he thought it was an aftershock from the quake, but then he looked out to sea. Even in the pre-dawn darkness, he could see a giant wall of water descending on the peninsula. With a sickening feeling, he knew would never reach safety in time. He had nowhere to go. He stopped running and watched. The wave had climbed to seventy feet when it struck the shoreline and ripped into the low-lying structures along the coast with the fury of Neptune's trident. The wave swept over him, crushing him instantly, and then dragging his lifeless body along with the tons of mud, silt, rock, and debris swept up by the onrush of water, a grinder pulverizing everything in its path.

Within minutes the entire western side of the peninsula from the Presidio in the north to Pacifica to the south was inundated. The waters, laden with bodies and debris, crashed into the hills of Forest Knolls before sweeping back out to sea, carrying with it the litter of a destroyed city.

The wave, most of it still concealed beneath the deeper water, marched through the Golden Gate Channel beneath the still shaking bridge, submerging Treasure Island, most of Alcatraz, and then swept along the wharfs of Oakland like a watery scythe. Moored ships, carried by the wave's power, careened like giant metal juggernauts through the streets of the city, ending up blocks inland. The wave swept backwards across the bay into downtown San Francisco, washing away the wharves of the Embarcadero and the Presidio before lapping at the feet of the lofty Transamerica Pyramid, 555 California Street, the Millennium Tower, and Forty Embarcadero Center.

Thousands died. Tens of thousands were left homeless, but San Francisco had survived worse disasters. By sunrise, emergency teams had scattered throughout the city. By noon, thousands of volunteers were scouring the wreckage for survivors. The city would recover.

Thirty miles out in the Pacific Ocean the earth was groaning again.

2

Doctor Robert Wingate Rutherford was familiar with panic. He understood it as part of his equations. It was a measurable number impersonally represented by a letter of the Greek alphabet. However, this time the panic reached out to touch him personally. Cold fingers gripped his heart and squeezed until icy tendrils of fear insinuated themselves throughout his body. It was a chill that sapped his strength and whispered, "Give up" in the ghostly voice of his high school gym teacher. Memories surfaced of a younger Gate Rutherford struggling to climb the knotted rope dangling from the ceiling amid the laughter of his friends. He had not given up then, nor would he now. He fought off the panic attack, dismissing what might happen, and concentrating instead on the facts.

"Girra will hit the central mid-west," he announced to his colleague, Joseph Palacio, an astrophysicist. The printout trembled in his long fingers as he spoke.

Joe swallowed hard before asking, "Where in the mid-west?"

Gate shook his head. He understood his friend's concern. Joe's family lived somewhere in Iowa. "Too many variables to tell."

"Guess," Joseph urged with a pained expression, staring into Gate's eyes with the intensity of a raptor.

"Indiana, Illinois, Missouri … I just don't know. It won't matter much. Wherever it hits, it's going to punch a hole a thousand feet deep and four miles wide."

Joe's nostrils flared, as he clenched his meaty fists. "It might miss."

Gate didn't share his friend's misplaced optimism. While his predictions were based on many variables, the mathematics was an exact science. Numbers don't lie. False hope was worse than no hope. It clouded the mind and prevented a rational exploration of the problem.

He shook his head. "Look, don't hold out any false hope, Joe. Ishom didn't miss. Girra and Nusku are coming for us like they were aimed at the Earth."

Joseph squinted at Gate with his tired brown eyes over the top of his square-framed glasses, while raising a bushy eyebrow. "Aimed?"

"Just a figure of speech. The two objects passed just distant enough from Jupiter and Mars to avoid their gravitational wells, and just high enough above the ecliptic to avoid the asteroid belt. It's bad luck, but inevitable given the solar system's violent history."

Gate grinned, but then thought better of it when he realized he was frightening his friend. Joe had a wife and a child – a family, responsibilities – whereas he was single, throwing himself fully into his work for lack of an outside life. While dying didn't particularly appeal to him, he wouldn't be missed. He decided to offer Joe a grain of hope.

"New data might prove me wrong."

Joe shook his head. "You're never wrong."

"I deal in *what ifs*. That's a fanciful way of saying, I guess."

"You guess better than most scientists do research. You're a natural born star gazer."

"I haven't used a telescope in five years," Gate reminded him.

"I haven't ridden a bicycle in ten, but I bet I still could. It's a learned thing you don't forget. With you it's number crunching."

Gate didn't argue. To him, numbers were pieces of a puzzle, each digit or bit of data fitting neatly together until the complete picture was revealed. This time, the picture looked bleak indeed. He stood, stretching his aching muscles. He had been sitting for four hours. He ran his right hand through his short sandy brown hair, leaned against his desk and arched his back, popping his vertebrae. It usually helped relieve the tension in his back.

"Jesus, Gate," Joe chided. "You keep doing that and you'll snap your spine."

Gate laughed. "My mother always told me that's why I'm so tall."

At six-one, he was four inches taller than Joe was and thin where Joe was stocky. Some called him lanky. Having once seen himself in a mirror while dancing, he tended to agree with that assessment, but he was not skinny. His slender frame belied his well-toned muscles. He might be desk bound, but he still performed his morning ritual of sit-ups and pushups to keep in shape.

"NASA moved the Disturbance Reduction System satellite into position to get a closer look at the next two objects," Joe offered.

"Good, the DRS can give us a definitive reading on the object's mass." A frown crossed Gate's face. "I'm of the opinion that the first object, Ishom, massed less than the initial observations indicated."

Joe looked at him curiously. "Why?"

"From the few radar images we got, it was massive enough to wipe out San Francisco and inundate the entire West Coast."

"It did enough damage. My God, Gate, thousands of people died, maybe tens of thousands."

Gate winced at the words tens of thousands. He had often blithely annihilated millions of people in his catastrophe scenarios, but they had been imaginary numbers, not real people. He had even once used San Francisco as a target in one of his disaster scenarios. The strike the day before had been like calling up ghosts. He grabbed his chest and took a deep breath, but a dull ache remained.

"You okay?" Joe asked.

The look of concern on his friend's face brought a smile to Gate's lips. He exhaled slowly, nodded, and said, "It just hit me hard for a second. I'll be okay."

In truth, he wasn't sure he would ever be okay again. As a catastrophist working for NASA, he had always expected an event such as this, but the reality was difficult to grasp. He sighed with relief several times over the past few years as Near Earth Orbiting masses had come disturbingly close to striking the planet, any of which could have killed thousands of people. Even then, his numbers had been certain, his faith in them true. His faith in the current numbers was just as true, and they predicted disaster.

"I suppose I had better inform the Director."

Joe glanced at his watch. "It's two-thirty. You've been working eighteen hours straight. You must be exhausted. Besides, I'm sure the Director's pretty busy right now. Between monitoring the *Lunar One* mission and keeping track of Girra and Nusku, he has his hands full."

Gate stretched his neck and yawned. Had it been so long? "I guess it will wait until morning. There's nothing we can do about Girra anyway."

"Who came up with the names? They sound like Japanese monsters."

Gate shrugged. "*Ishom*, *Girra,* and *Nusku* were Babylonian gods of heavenly fire. Someone thought it appropriate." He paused. "They didn't realize just how appropriate." He looked at Joe and noticed the dark circles under his friend's eyes. "You've been here as long as I have. It's time we both got some sleep."

Joe rubbed his eyes. "Yeah, I guess so. Melissa must be worried."

Gate smiled. Melissa, Joe's wife, never worried about her husband. He was as devoted as husbands come. He had been a guest in Joe's house many times and considered Melissa one of the finest women he had ever met. His smile faded when he remembered that her family lived in southern Indiana, not a hundred miles from Joe's folks. Even if he determined that Indiana was the target of the meteor strike, he couldn't warn her. In every disaster, public panic exacerbated the problem. Blind, uncontrolled evacuation from a potential disaster proved almost as deadly as the event itself.

The secrecy surrounding his current project was astronomical, the potential for panic enormous. The first object, Ishom, had eluded the orbiting telescopes, sneaking in unobserved. Almost before the tremors had stopped in San Francisco, astronomers were searching for any companions. They found two. If the data was correct, the two objects approaching the planet were each over three-hundred meters in diameter. Each would strike the planet at fourteen kilometers per second, leaving an impact crater seven kilometers wide and half a kilometer deep. He shook his head to clear it. He would never be able to sleep if his mind insisted on dwelling on facts and figures. To Gate, more puzzling than the lower-than-expected mass, was the fact that the three objects were spaced almost exactly twenty-four hours apart. That seemed to defy the odds.

As he and Joe left the building, he noticed lights on in several offices. Others were burning the midnight oil tracking Girra hoping for a few degrees alteration in its course that would send it sailing harmlessly past Earth and into the sun. He didn't hold out much hope. The numbers didn't lie, and they all seemed to be against them. The objects had entered the solar system from north of the ecliptic plane, so it was unlikely it had originated in the Oort Cloud. They had avoided the enormous gravity well of Jupiter that gobbled up many of the system's stray asteroids and missed Mars by a hundred thousand kilometers, passing just near enough to bend its path directly toward Earth. Girra would pass by the moon close enough to cast a shadow but would not strike it. It had been a Perfect Storm of chance. If he believed in a vengeful God, he would call it divine providence. He was sure many would, once news of Girra and Nusku became public. He thanked the stars that he wasn't the one that had to reveal its presence.

He glanced up at the night sky above Houston. A few wispy clouds streaked the waning crescent moon. He placed his thumb over the dark disk, and peered at the area just to the right and above the moon, but saw nothing. Unlike a comet with a highly visible tail, Girra was too dark and still too far away to be discernible to the naked eye, but soon an amateur astronomer would spot it, and the secret would be out. All their secrecy would mean nothing then.

"See you in the morning."

Gate dropped his hand to his side and looked at Joe, as he climbed into his Mini Cooper. He had tried to ride in Joe's car once. That's all it took. Half an hour of sitting scrunched into the tiny vehicle had been enough. "Yeah, I'll be here at six. I have to watch Girra come down. There's something strange about it."

Climbing into his Acura, the heavy guitar riffs of Led Zeppelin's *Rock and Roll* blasting from KLTE hit him like a hammer blow after the near silence of his office. He was in no mood for anything with energy that might interfere with the sleep he needed so badly. He punched the dial to KTSU, one of Houston's jazz stations. The soothing strains of John Coltrane that the radio offered up were less of an assault to his overloaded senses. The mellow jazz was like a glass of warm milk. He only hoped he could make it home before he fell asleep. Luckily, he met few cars on the two-mile drive to his apartment. He expected most normal people were in bed at two-thirty a.m. on a Thursday morning. By the time he parked his car and opened the front door, his eyelids were drooping. Before he could undress, his cell phone rang. The opening strains of Holst's *The Planets Suite* he had chosen as his ring tone weren't as sweet at such an early hour. He knew it couldn't be good news.

"Gate, this is Director Caruthers. I need you back here ASAP. We've received disturbing data on Girra from the DRS."

He let the news soak in for several seconds before responding. "What kind of data?"

"I'd rather not discuss it over the phone. We're moving Hubble to get an optical image." He paused a moment before adding, "I've already ordered *Lunar One* to investigate."

Changing the Orion spacecraft's lunar orbit mission involved substantial risks. The Director was worried. "I'll be there in fifteen minutes." He hung up the phone before Caruthers could relay any more bad news.

He glanced longingly at the coffee maker. A jolt of caffeine would help keep him awake, but he didn't have the time. He hoped the coffee urn at Mission Control was full.

* * * *

Thursday, August 9   3:00 a.m. (CDT)   Mission Control, Houston, TX –

Security at Mission Control was tighter than Gate had ever seen it. He was forced to present his ID twice to Building 30-M security guards before being allowed in. Director Carl Caruthers stood amid a sea of shirt-sleeved technicians, an oak tree in a forest of saplings. His six-foot-two frame loomed over his subordinates, as he quickly scanned tablets and hand-scribbled notes presented him by department heads. He wore his glasses atop his balding head, squinting to sign his name to reports. When he needed to look at one of the screens on the wall, he flipped the glasses back down.

Caruthers' haggard appearance was atypical of him. He usually dressed in a suit and tie. Now, a two-day growth of beard darkened his jaw. His rumpled shirt, with sleeves rolled up, looked slept in. Gate suffered a momentary twinge of sympathy for the director, but then remembered that Caruthers had spoiled his chance for sleep as well. Caruthers saw him enter and he walked over to greet him. He lifted his headset microphone from his mouth.

"I know I look like shit," he said. "So do you."

"What's the latest on Girra?"

Caruthers pointed to one of the three main screens on the wall. The fuzzy image from Hubble was visible only by the occluded stars in the background. It took several moments for Gate to focus his sleep-deprived eyes on the hole of blackness. "As you can see, Girra is so dark as to be almost indiscernible."

Gate walked closer to the screen for a better look at the teardrop-shaped object. It could be a seed, he thought, *seeds of destruction, if Ishom was any indication.* "It's damned near invisible. No wonder no one saw Ishom."

"It has an albedo of .009."

"But that's …"

"Impossible? I would have thought so, but that's what the readings indicate." He paused. Gate studied the director's face and realized that he was hiding something.

"Why did you bring me back in? I submitted my report."

Caruthers nodded. "Yeah, I read it. Good job. Typical doomsday stuff. Shades of San Francisco. I sent for you because of our new data."

This roused Gate's curiosity. "What new data?"

"According to the DRS, Girra is massing much less than we originally estimated. Either it's less dense than a normal meteor that size, or it's hollow."

Gate was speechless for a moment, as he absorbed the Director's almost unbelievable suggestion. His musings about the object's composition had been just that – musings. Now the Director was putting truth to his words. He walked back across the room and took a seat at the empty Public Affairs desk, the only unoccupied console in the otherwise busy room. As yet, the public was still unaware of the doom headed their way.

"Hollow, as in an alien spacecraft?"

Caruthers shook his head. "No, I don't think so. It still masses a hell of a lot more than a spacecraft that size would. You reported that Ishom caused less destruction than anticipated. Could this be the reason?"

Gate sighed and stood to stretch his muscles. It was going to be a long night. "Yes, it would make sense. I'll get on those new figures right away." He picked up his laptop and pointed to the glass enclosed observation gallery where distinguished visitors sat to watch the missions. Now, it was empty. "I'll work in there where it's quieter." He glanced again at the screens. One showed an interior view of *Lunar One*. Though they had just been ordered to abandon the mission for which they had trained for over a year, the crew was acting as if nothing world shattering was happening. He envied their poise, and then wondered if it was for the camera. *No,* he thought, *those astronauts are trained for emergencies. They're confident.*

He wished he had a little of their confidence. He could use it.

3

**Thursday, August 9,   12:45 a.m. (CDT)   *Lunar One*,
Lunar orbit –**

Commander Erwin Langston extended his finger over the
keypad that would fire the thrusters moving the Orion spacecraft
out of the lunar orbit they had maintained for four days and into a
slingshot rendezvous with Girra. There had been no time to run
comprehensive simulations on the new program. He would have to
trust FiDO and the superfast computer aboard the *Lunar One* to do
the job. They wouldn't see the object until they completed their
orbital pass around the moon. By then, Girra would be close
enough to be visible. If all went as planned, they would emerge a
mere four hundred meters from the object designated *Girra*.

His fellow astronauts, Todd Ingersall, Deborah Crenshaw, and
Page Mahall, watched his finger descend slowly until it hovered
just above the enter key. They all knew the importance of their
newly assigned mission. They had seen images of the destruction
in San Francisco. Now, two more potential threats had
materialized. Langston took a deep breath and touched the keypad.
The engine roared into life, pressing him back in his seat, the first
gravity any of them had felt for nine days.

"Trajectory in the green," he announced. He watched the fuel
gauge numbers drop. They were using up precious fuel they would
need for an Earth re-insertion orbit. "Engine shutdown in three
seconds." He began counting backwards. "3, 2, 1 …"

The engine quieted after firing only for fifty-one seconds, but it had imparted sufficient thrust to kick them out of orbit. The unaccustomed weight left him.

"Exploratory Mission One is now aborted," he announced with undisguised bitterness in his voice. He had trained two years for the lunar mission. "We are commencing EM-2, exploration of Girra."

"What are the chances of Girra being a natural object?"

The question came from Ingersoll, the ship's medical officer. At twenty-four, the medium-height, blond, Hawaiian ex-surfer was the youngest member of the crew. *Lunar One* was his first mission into space. Langston, a veteran of eight flights, including the initial testing of the Orion Multi-Purpose Crewed Exploratory Vehicle, understood his concern.

"FiDO couldn't have programmed a better trajectory for this thing. What do you think the odds are of three objects being so evenly spaced?"

By Ingersoll's downcast expression, he had already made the calculations.

Mahall was more upbeat. Ringlets of red hair escaped the helmet liner she wore to keep her long red hair from escaping. They danced above her forehead as if alive. Her blue jumpsuit bore the photo of her three-year-old daughter. "This could be man's first encounter with an alien species."

As the communication's officer, she had made numerous attempts at contact on every frequency *Lunar One* was capable of utilizing with zero results. Langston was of the opinion that if the objects contained aliens, they didn't want to communicate.

"If ET has come calling, he isn't interested in ringing the doorbell first," he reminded her. "The first one caused massive destruction when it hit. A few seconds earlier and it would have hit smack dab in the center of San Francisco. That's no way to make friends."

"Is it an attack?" Ingersoll asked. His question was being repeated all over the Earth by world leaders and people in the street.

"I don't know what else you would call it," Crenshaw interjected. Unlike Mahall, she advocated destroying Girra, even if they had to ram it with the Orion. "They're lobbing missiles at us."

"Who is?" Ingersoll demanded. "Where are they from?"

Crenshaw, a petite, fiery, raven-haired Australian geologist, frowned and pointed out the window past the extended portside solar panel and the blackness beyond. The gallium and arsenide semiconductors across the twin panels' nineteen-foot surfaces provided 12,000 watts of power for the ship's systems. "Out yonder somewhere. They're watching and waiting to see how we respond. Then they'll step up their attack."

Crenshaw's prediction sat icy cold in the pit of Langston's stomach. "Speculation gets us nowhere. We'll know more in a few hours." He glanced at the countdown clock. "One hour and forty-one minutes to be exact."

He watched the gray, craggy surface of the moon recede through the command capsule window. He had watched it for four days, making thousands of photos, gravimetric readings, spectrometer readings, and seismic readings, all the while wishing that his would be the first boots to touch the surface since Gene Cernan of Apollo 17 left his in the dust on December 13, 1972. It didn't look like it was going to happen. It was even more disappointing that the lunar lander that would eventually touchdown on the moon's surface after forty-six years was in the service module. NASA had wanted a full mission run through, a trial run for the real landing scheduled for 2019. The lander was so close; he could feel it pulling at him like a small moon. He turned his attention back to his crew.

"Let's have lunch," he suggested. "We might be too busy later." He didn't know if he could eat, but he had to keep them busy somehow. The Flight Surgeon in Houston would call him to task if they missed a meal.

"My turn to cook," Crenshaw said, as she released her safety harness and floated from her seat. She pushed off and sailed flawlessly across the sixteen-foot diameter cabin to the food locker, deftly grabbing a wall with one hand to stop her forward motion. She removed four entrees and loaded them into the convection oven. She added water to a foil pouch of tea and placed it in the oven with the entrees. Next, she attached a tray to each of their seats. While the food was warming, she brought silverware, juice pouches, desserts, crackers, and flour tortillas and placed them on the trays. Except for the fact that any stray crumbs or droplets of liquid could drift away, they dined as they would on Earth with proper utensils, except for the pair of scissors necessary to snip open their pouches of food.

While the food heated, Langston took the opportunity to moon gaze. As a child, he sat on the patio and stared up at the golden orb overhead that had seemed close enough to reach out and touch, but so distant as to be a magical land. He knew his destiny lay with the moon when he learned that his birth date, September 13, 1959, had been the day the Russians had landed their unmanned Lunar 2 probe on the moon's surface. At ten-years-old, he sat beside his father on July 20, 1969, and watched Neil Armstrong take his famous first step, followed by Buzz Aldrin. It had been the most glorious evening in his life, a magical moment.

He had watched all six NASA lunar landings with gleeful interest, imagining himself as one of the crew. He geared his entire scholastic endeavor toward becoming a pilot and then joining NASA. With hard work, determination, and too many sacrifices, he achieved his goal. He was circling the moon. He often wondered how Michael Collins felt, alone in orbit above the moon while his companions Armstrong and Aldrin cavorted on the surface. Now, he knew.

Twenty minutes later, a chime announced that their meals were ready. The freeze-dried, pre-packaged meals were varied, if a little bland. Ingersall especially, who enjoyed spicy food, protested that the curried chicken was designed for old people, making Langston, who thought the curry just spicy enough, feel older than his fifty-nine years. He snipped the tip of the plastic nipple from his apple juice pouch and inserted a straw. The cool juice whetted his appetite. He devoured his beef stroganoff in spite of his trepidation about the unscheduled mission changes. He used a flour tortilla to soak up the excess sauce, and then ended his NASA repast with a package of crackers and Gouda cheese for dessert. During the meal and the conversation, the rendezvous with Girra was still on his mind.

They would close with the object from behind, match speeds, and follow it back to Earth. His orders were clear. At no time were they to veer from their trajectory. Their job was to observe and report. He wasn't sure what they might add to the data provided by the satellites and orbiting telescopes, but he intended to make the rendezvous.

In one aspect, he was like the ebullient Aussie, Crenshaw. If he thought ramming any one of the objects would save a single human life on the planet, he would do it, but NASA and the Joint Chiefs had made his orders abundantly clear. He would do nothing to deter the objects or to alter their flight path. They were not yet convinced the objects were a deliberate attack. They held that any show of aggression might provoke a hostile response. He held no such doubt. Like Crenshaw, he was certain the objects were an attack.

The Orion spacecraft's approach from the far side of the moon was perfect. His worries about encountering a smaller debris field vanished when he saw the massive object. Girra's ebony exterior rendered it almost invisible against the black backdrop of space. *No wonder no one saw the first one*, he thought. It was barely visible on radar. Only through the telescope could he get an idea of its true size. Even then, it was almost invisible.

"My God," Ingersall groaned. "It's enormous."

"Three-hundred-seventy-five meters in length by two-hundred meters in diameter," Crenshaw called out from the telescope image. "That's as long as an aircraft carrier. It's almost a perfect teardrop."

"God's tears," Mahall said. Her emerald green eyes almost sparkled with admiration of the objects' symmetry.

"I doubt God is responsible for this," Crenshaw retorted, "Unless he is tired of humanity's bullshit."

"We have abandoned him," Mahall began. "If we …"

"Save the theological discussions for Sunday," Langston said. "We've got a job to do."

He didn't know if there was a God, a creator of the universe, but having experienced the wonder and beauty of space close up and personal, he didn't immediately dismiss the possibility. To him, the object looked like a seed floating in space, and it gave him cause to wonder. He had studied the Theory of Panspermia, which was the possibility that life exists throughout the universe, spread from world to world by one of three methods. The first was Lithopanspermia, where rock from meteoric impacts spreads biological matter from one solar system to another. The second, Ballistic Panspermia, was the spread of biological matter between worlds of the same solar system by the same method. The last was Directed Panspermia, the intentional spreading of the seeds of life throughout the galaxy by an advanced civilization. He was certain that Mahall would substitute God for advanced civilization, but staring at Girra floating outside the ship's porthole, he shuddered. He didn't think God was behind the objects.

The *Lunar One* module matched speed with *Girra* at a distance of 389 meters. Langston wanted to move closer, but his orders were explicit. Through the telescope, the object was plainly visible. Its composition was too regular to be anything other than artificial. Girra traveled with the narrow end of the teardrop, or seed, pointed toward Earth. It had no fins, wings, or other guidance systems that he could detect.

"The exterior appears crystalline, like obsidian or black glass," he observed.

The surface absorbed light. He couldn't discern much detail, but he observed no joints or seams, no door or windows. It appeared solid. If Girra were a man-made object, its construction far surpassed anything humans could achieve.

"I have a second object on the radar," Mahall called out, breaking Langston's concentration. "The image comes and goes. It could be a ghost image."

Langston tore his eyes from the telescope. They couldn't take a chance that it was only a radar reflection of Girra. "Where is it?"

"It's just floating there in space eight hundred kilometers from the surface. It appears to be orbiting the Earth at the same speed as the moon." She glanced at Langston with fear in her face. "Our present course takes us right into its path."

"How big is it?" he asked.

"It's just over fifty meters in diameter. I can't determine its mass. It's identical in shape to Girra, just smaller."

"How long before impact?" He could move the ship, but spending more fuel would jeopardize their homeward journey. Any course change would have to be exact.

"Eight minutes."

"Jesus!" Crenshaw snorted. "We'll never get out of its way in time. They're trying to kill us."

"No," Mahall replied. "It's just there. It's not doing anything."

"Whatever it is or whatever it's doing," Langston said, stopping their argument, "it places us in a bad position."

Langston quickly ran the numbers through the navigation computer. The answer brought back that familiar cold feeling. He could fire the thrusters for six seconds only. Any longer and they wouldn't have sufficient fuel to insert the craft into Earth orbit. They would follow Girra into the atmosphere and become a glowing light in the night sky; a falling star upon which someone's wish would never come true. The short burn limited their course of action. He didn't have time to consult CAPCOM at Houston. There was only one direction they could go.

"We're closing with Girra." He glanced at Mahall. "Advise Houston of the situation. Pray that it's enough."

All three stared at him in various stages of disbelief and panic, but no one said anything. *Good crew*, he thought. He knew instinctively that the new object wouldn't collide with Girra. If they could just get close enough to it … He fired the starboard thrusters. The craft shuddered, as the tiny jets fought to move the enormous weight of *Lunar One*. He fired one brief burst of the nose thruster to reduce the ship's velocity, hoping to add a few more seconds before the impact. He stared at the approaching object on radar. The image was hazy and indistinct. *Whatever it's made of*, he mused, *it's stealth technology*.

"Sixty seconds to impact," Mahall announced.

"Everybody strap in," he warned.

They had no time to suit up. If the ship's hull was punctured in an area they couldn't quickly reach with a repair patch, they would all die. Mahall closed her eyes and began muttering a quiet prayer. This time, Langston wasn't annoyed by her beliefs. *Say one for all of us*. Crenshaw stared out the window looking as if she wanted to do anything, even throw rocks at the object if she had to, to vent her anger. Of the three, Ingersall surprised him. The young physician was making certain the exterior video camera was operating and transmitting to NASA mission control. His cool demeanor in the face of danger calmed Langston's racing heart. He had done all he could do. Any mistakes he had made or decisions he should have made earlier were moot. Now, mathematics and physics controlled their fates.

"Five seconds." Mahall's voice was tense but betrayed no panic. Her training focused her attention to her job.

Girra loomed larger off their port side. From a distance of less than sixty meters, the object became an ebony mirror that ate light as if devouring space itself. For one split second, Langston thought the darkness would swallow up *Lunar One* as well. He had no time to ponder the object. The ship suddenly shuddered and slewed to starboard, as the object struck the starboard solar panel. The control panel lights flickered and died. Then, a second, harder contact almost ejected him from his seat. He clung to his seat harness with both hands. The ship bucked violently, as a loud shriek of tearing metal erupted from just aft of the service module. The low air pressure alarm began to wail, adding to the tension. As the ship tried to shake apart, Langston braced for the explosive decompression that would kill them. It didn't come.

"Someone locate that leak and seal it," he shouted. "Mahall, find me some power."

The craft was spinning. He risked more fuel to correct their trajectory and stop the rotation. He didn't mind spending fuel. They had fuel to spare now. He knew they were never going to reach Earth in a crippled ship.

4

Thursday, August 9   3:10 a.m. (CDT)   Mission Control, Houston, TX –

"I've lost contact with *Lunar One*."

The statement from the CAPCOM brought silence to the room. Every head turned toward capsule communicator's desk. The CAPCOM for this mission was astronaut Tray Davis who had trained closely with the *Lunar One* crew. He would have piloted the craft if Commander Langston had been unable to make the trip. His demeanor was professional, but the pallor of his face betrayed his concern. A sense of dread gripped Gate and wouldn't release him. Lack of sleep and fatigue enhanced the horror that scattered his thoughts. He knew every technician in the room was as stunned by the news as he was.

"Commander Langston fired the engine to avoid a second object, and then went silent," Davis said.

"What second object?" Gate asked. "The images didn't reveal a second object."

His question went unanswered. Around the room, twenty men and women were concentrating on re-establishing communications with the crew of *Lunar One*.

The energy, environment, and consumables operations manager, EECOM, quickly confirmed CAPCOM's analysis of the situation. "*Lunar One* indicated a rapid loss of atmosphere and a loss of power before they broke transmission."

Gate glanced over at Director Caruthers for clarification. The worried director brushed his hand across his balding head and removed his headset before collapsing heavily into his seat. His upper lip trembled slightly. For the last forty hours, the NASA director had been living on coffee, donuts, and catnaps. "That does it," Caruthers muttered quietly. "We've lost *Lunar One*."

On the screen at the front of the room, the last video transmission was replaying, showing a barely visible object approaching the Orion spacecraft. The image of Girra *Delta* grew larger, as *Lunar One* fired its engines and moved toward it. Then, the image broke up into a jumble of pixels and disappeared. Gate's first close-up look at Girra filled him with dismay. Its shape was too regular to be natural. His greatest fear was realized.

"Try to resume contact," Caruthers called out into the silence of the room. "We need to know if anyone is alive and if we can bring them home."

"They expended most of their fuel," the flight dynamics officer reminded him. "They don't have fuel enough remaining for an Earth insertion orbit."

"What about fuel from the lander?" Caruthers asked.

"They have no way to pump it into the command capsule."

Tray Davis spoke up. "They might be able to manage a stable lunar orbit. If they lost fuel and oxygen, Commander Langston would know they could never reach Earth. He would try for a lunar orbit and wait for rescue. I would."

"What would that accomplish?"

"There's a resupply ship at ISS. If we could refuel and launch a rescue mission, it could reach the moon in fifty-eight hours."

Gate felt a surge of hope. The Space X resupply shuttle *Pegasus* had been docked at the International Space Station for three days, delivering cargo and transferring new crewmembers. If it could reach *Lunar One* in time, and if they hadn't lost all their oxygen, they had a chance. He clung to that thought.

"If *Lunar One* has enough oxygen left to survive that long," Caruthers replied.

Davis nodded. "Yes, sir, I realize that, but it is a chance. It's their only chance."

Caruthers paused. He didn't want to be the first director since the Columbia disaster to lose a crew. "If they jettison the new

Orbiter satellite, they could carry extra fuel and oxygen for the return journey."

The payload officer rose from his seat and waved his hand to get the Director's attention.

"This isn't high school, Williams," Caruthers said. "If you have something to contribute, speak up."

Slightly embarrassed by the attention, Williams said, "Sir, that navigation satellite cost 1.5 billion dollars."

"Damn the cost," Caruthers snapped, making Williams jump. "We're talking people here. Someone find me a better solution, but in the meantime, contact ISS and advise them to prep *Pegasus* for launch. Remind them that time is of the essence. The current crew will have to make bunk space for the replacement crew for a week or so until we can send up another bird."

Gate listened with interest, trying to force his exhausted mind to focus on the rapid-fire conversation between Caruthers and the mission control crew. Finally, as the discussion became a rapid-fire volley of technical details concerning the rescue mission, he detached and pondered what he had just witnessed. Girra wasn't natural. Of that, he was certain. He had yearned for definitive data on the objects. Now, he had it, but perhaps at the cost of four astronauts' lives.

Gate sat at an empty desk entering the new data in his projections. Around him, men battled to re-establish communications with the stricken ship. Ideas for rescue sprouted and died, as worried men posed desperate solutions. Each proposal was dutifully picked apart and dismissed. Tempers flared, but no blows were struck. The technicians were tired, harried, and pressed for answers, but they were friends. They were a team.

They were still at it a half hour later when Gate finished his projections. The results were numbers of doom. He double-checked them to be certain. Finally, he could put it off no longer. He had to inform the director.

"I've run the new figures. They're not good."

Caruthers frowned. "What's the damage?"

"From the new data, it is evident that the objects are less dense than we thought. They're moving slower than we originally estimated as well. That could be from ..."

Caruthers cut him off. He wasn't interested in speculation. "Where will they hit?"

Gate scanned his screen. "Girra will impact at coordinates 40^0 45'13" N and 86^0 21'38" W."

"Where do those coordinate place it?"

As he spoke, one of the technicians displayed a satellite image of the United States on one of the screens. Cursors appeared, moving across the image until they bracketed a large blob of light, a city.

"Logansport, Indiana," the technician called out.

Caruthers cleared his throat. "And the other one?"

Gate checked his laptop. "Nusku will hit at 38^0 10'30" N by 115^0 48'20" W." He looked up at Caruthers, "That's just north of Las Vegas, Nevada."

Caruthers nodded and turned to the flight director. "You had better contact the FAA and advise them to redirect flights from O'Hare and Midway Airports in Chicago and McCarran in Vegas. Better yet, have them ground all flights for the next twelve hours." His voice cracked slightly, as he asked, "How many people in Logansport?"

"Eighteen thousand," the technician replied.

Caruthers' face soured, as he turned back to face Gate. "My God, Gate, first San Francisco, and now Indiana and Nevada. We have no response to this. The damned meteor shield we've begged the government for over the past ten years is still just a piece of paper sitting on someone's fucking desk." He slammed his fist on the console. "Goddamn politics. I wish every one of those sons of bitches in Washington could see this thing hit the ground. Maybe then they'd get off their collective asses."

He reached into his pocket, removed a nicotine patch, and slapped it on his right arm just above the one that was already in place. "Hell of a time to give up smoking," he growled.

Gate checked the clock on the big wall. "We have less than four hours before Girra hits. Not enough time for an evacuation of Logansport."

"Thank God, it isn't hitting Chicago."

"I don't think those in the impact zone will take any consolation from that."

"No, you're right. God help them. We can't."

An idea had been forming in the back of Gate's mind during the conversation. The Girra strike presented an opportunity to become a hands-on astronomer once more. "I need to go to Indiana. I want to be first on the scene to examine it."

Caruthers stared at Gate as if he had lost his mind. "You're a catastrophist, not a meteor man. You work with numbers."

"I'm an astronomer first," he countered. "I need to see this thing up close."

Caruthers nodded. "I guess I understand. Your figures condemned an entire city to die, and you feel guilty. It's just math, Gate. It's not your fault, but I'll have one of our jets get you as close as you think safe. By no stretch of the imagination are you to put yourself in harm's way. I need you back here."

Gate smiled. "I'm in no hurry to die. If these are friendly aliens, I want to be there to greet them."

"Do you think this is a friendly visit?"

Gate shook his head slowly. "No, I think we're at war."

Girra

5

Thursday, August 9, 4:24 a.m. (PDT) Fort Belvoir, Washington –

General Theodore Frederick Simms stood hands clasped behind his back in front of a console whose readings he didn't understand. The large projection screen overhead showed two lines – a red one representing the missile, and a blue one representing Girra. The trajectory data was displayed beside each of the blips, but the rapidly changing numbers meant nothing to him. As the head of the Missile Defense Agency, the thirty-five billion dollar agency charged with protecting the United States from a nuclear missile strike, he wasn't required to know the jargon or the scientific principles behind the job. His job was to keep the country safe.

After Iran obtained their first nuclear weapon in 2016, his group had come to the forefront in Congressional funding. Fear opened purse strings, even for clandestine projects such as his. The Minuteman II missile presently winging its way toward Girra wasn't ground based. It was stationed on a weather satellite, codenamed *Janus*, deployed two years earlier. Technically, neither the decommissioned missile nor the weather satellite existed. *Janus* contained not weather tracking instruments, but a single Minuteman II missile with a W56 1.2 megaton warhead. Part of the OMD, or Orbiting Midcourse Defense, *Janus* was designed to intercept incoming nuclear missiles. This time, it served a different purpose.

The first object that struck San Francisco had gone undetected until it was too late, and San Francisco paid the price. Now, Logansport, Indiana, was in the stellar crosshairs. He had a chance to make amends and to show his superiors just what OMD could do. Some of the scientists insisted that the nuclear yield was insufficient to destroy such a massive object as Girra. Their graphs and charts pointed out a list of numbers denoting mass, velocity, nuclear yield, and vectors. The numbers were meaningless to him, but he understood their belief in them. However, a few of them proposed a glancing blow that might deflect the object just enough to force it to miss the Earth. Simms was not a man to simply twiddle his thumbs and wait. He went with option number two. The missile would intercept Girra four thousand miles outside Earth's atmosphere.

An unsettling odor of fear wafted about the room. Simms had smelled fear in Iraq. He knew the bitter taste it left on the tongue; the sour odor it imparted to a man's sweat. His troops, this time scientists who had never touched a rifle or faced an enemy, were afraid. Frightened men made mistakes. He needed to rally them.

He cleared his throat loudly. Heads turned in his direction. "Men, we are the front line of defense for our great nation. You have trained long and hard. You are the best your country has to offer, or you would not be sitting at those desks. Our enemy is not the Russians, the North Koreans, the Chinese, or the Iranians. It is not ISIS or Boko Haram. It is an inert chunk of rock headed toward the nation's heartland. In your capable hands rests the safety of our country. I have faith in you. Do your jobs and we will emerge victorious."

They didn't cheer or applaud his speech, but he could see in their eyes that he had dispelled their fear. They moved with more confidence, sat straighter in their seats. If they failed, it would not be from lack of trying.

"Impact in three minutes," one of the technicians called out.

Simms nodded, clasping his hands tighter to stop their trembling. They trembled not from fear, but from excitement. He had every confidence they would get results.

The red dot representing the missile slowly approached the larger blue blob of Girra. He held his breath as the two dots merged. Nothing happened. The screen didn't light up like a video game. There was no sound of an explosion. No TILT sign appeared. He waited impatiently for a report.

"We have detonation, Sir," someone called out.

A few cheers erupted. Simms relaxed, placing his hands on the console in front of him, as the tension released from his body. After several seconds of silence, he demanded, "Well? Did we do it?"

One of the technicians lowered his head, refusing to look into the general's eyes. "No change in Girra's course, sir. It's still headed for Earth."

Simms slumped against the console. He had failed. His agency had failed. "Nothing?" he asked. His voice was plaintive, begging for some morsel of good news.

"No, sir. Zero deflection. It's almost as if the energy was absorbed by the object."

He sat down hard in his seat. After a few moments, he looked up. The blue dot on the screen continued toward Earth.

"Time to impact?" he asked.

"Fifty-four minutes, twenty-seven seconds."

"Notify Washington," he said. Under his breath, he whispered, "God help Indiana."

Ignoring the looks of disdain in the technicians, he pulled out a silver cigarette case and stuck an Egyptian cigarette in his mouth. He had learned to enjoy them while stationed as a military liaison before the Arab Spring uprising. He lit the cigarette and inhaled deeply. He had a feeling that where the Joint Chiefs would be sending him for his failure, he might not be smoking many more Egyptian cigarettes.

* * * *

Thursday, August 9   8:30 a.m. (EDT)   Logansport, Indiana –

Kevin Andrews rolled the two-wheeler loaded with cases of *Pepsi* products from his delivery truck into the open rear door of the Logan's Run Golf Course clubhouse. Twelve miles east of downtown Logansport, Indiana, the golf course was his first stop of the morning. He liked to begin his run at his farthest stop and worked his way back to the warehouse. He was eager to finish up and drop by McDonalds for a late breakfast of a sausage biscuit, hash browns, and a cup of hot coffee.

He enjoyed the clubhouse stop because of the fine looking middle-aged women in their short skirts usually putting on the green just outside the door. It allowed his voyeuristic tendencies full rein. He thought older women were hot, maybe because of his Aunt Agatha, who had allowed him to fondle her naked breasts when he was ten. Mature women knew more about sex than the twenty-somethings that he usually dated could dream of. Even at such an early hour, the putting green was crowded with women eager to beat the heat of the day.

Sid Meyers, the food and beverage manager at Logan's Run, took his job seriously. He insisted on counting each case and inspecting it for damage before signing the delivery receipt. Kevin waited patiently, staring out the door at a blonde on her hands and knees lining up a shot.

"That one's real wet." Kevin jerked his head around at Meyers' comment, chuckling when he saw Meyers pointing to a damp case of soda with his ink pen. He thought Meyers was talking about the blonde. *Get your mind out of the gutter, Kevin.* "Take it back."

Kevin shrugged. "I can get another one from the truck to replace it. Just take a sec."

"Okay," Meyers said.

Then Meyer's low jaw went slack and a look of puzzled fear spread across his face. The room grew brighter until Meyers stood in Kevin's shadow.

"What the hell?" Kevin asked, as he spun toward the door. A second sun appeared a few degrees above the one he knew so well, growing so bright it hurt his eyes. The new sun was quickly growing larger as well. The women playing golf also noticed the strange phenomenon. They stopped their game and watched the sky. Their bodies seemed to draw in their shadows, shortening as the object approached overhead. Meyers remained rooted to the spot, but Kevin's curiosity was aroused. He walked outside, shaded his eyes with his hand, and looked up at the frighteningly beautiful object.

As the fireball loomed larger, his knees grew weak. He knew that whatever it was, it wasn't good. His skin began to tingle and his face grew warm. The object passed overhead less than two thousand feet above the clubhouse. The shockwave of its passing struck him a few seconds later with the roar of a thousand jet engines slamming his ears. A hot wind followed the object from the east, bending the trees and sending the women tumbling head-over-heel across the putting green. He couldn't hear their screams, though he knew they must be screaming. He knew he was.

He clung to a tree to keep from being blown away and followed the object with his frightened gaze. The fireball struck downtown Logansport, near Market Street and South Third Street. A blinding flash of light, brighter than a hundred suns, illuminated the city for one brief second. Then, the entire city disappeared beneath a mushroom cloud of dirt and smoke. Seconds later, the ground bucked wildly beneath his feet, knocking him to his knees. The tremor was the weak, outer edges of the 6.9 magnitude earthquake shaking the still standing outskirts of Logansport to pieces. Cases of soda cascaded from his truck and burst open, spilling their contents across the parking lot. He watched in horror, as a cloud of dust and debris rushed toward him, flinging people aside and upending golf cars carts. The blistering wind picked him up from the ground and slammed him into the tree beside him. He fell dazed and in agony amid the azaleas planted at its base. When he tried to move, he knew his ribs were broken.

Less than a minute later, chunks of ejecta, large rocks superheated by the blast, rained down on the golf course, creating washtub-sized divots in the manicured fairways. The chaotic scene reminded him of an artillery barrage. Through pain-glazed eyes, he watched one rock grow larger as it fell toward him. His last conscious thought was that his soda deliveries were going to be late.

* * * *

Ted Millhouse also saw from his automobile, the fiery object descending toward the city on I-35, as he headed southeast toward the city of Walton, Indiana. As a regional sales rep for a tri-state farm-implement company, the area around Walton was fertile sales territory. He grew up on a farm, and his connection to the land allowed him to build a rapport with his clients. He knew immediately that he was witnessing something phenomenal, something he could use to break the ice with potential customers.

He slowed, as he watched the blinding light crossing the sky toward the west through his driver's side mirror. When the roar of what he assumed to be a meteor began to shake his car, his hot coffee spilled into his lap. As he slammed on the brakes, the car skidded off the road and into the grass median, almost clipping a minivan in the left lane. The car slid to a stop facing northwest toward the meteor. He leapt from the car to brush the scalding hot coffee from his lap with his hand. As he looked up, the object struck. A brilliant flash of light turned morning into the brightest noon he had ever witnessed. His shadow became an ebony paint smear on his automobile. The intense glare almost blinded him. He closed his eyes, but the intense light penetrated the flesh of his eyelids. He had seen nuclear mushroom clouds in movies and on the Discovery Channel, and this reminded him of one. Was the country at war? Was he already doomed by radiation?

"My God," he whispered to himself, as the ground began shaking. He fell back against his car and watched the tsunami of dust and debris rush toward him. The wind swept over him in an instant, flinging him over his car, down an embankment, and into a concrete culvert. The pain as the bones in his right leg shattered hit him seconds before his head slammed into the concrete, knocking him senseless.

He didn't know how long he lay there, but the rumbling was over and the air was still when he regained his senses. He looked down and saw the shattered bones of his right leg protruding through his pants. Panicking, he tried to move his leg. The pain that shot up his leg was excruciating, threatening to make him pass out again. The severity of his situation gripped him like an icy fist. He might be dying, and any emergency services that might have survived the explosion would be directed towards Logansport. He was on his own. He struggled to crawl from the culvert, using his one good leg and his arms to propel himself up the steep slope. He clenched his teeth tightly and ignored the pain. After an agonizing eternity, he reached the level of the road and wept at what he saw.

The horizon to the northwest, where Logansport had been, was a dark mass of roiling clouds, punctuated by flashes of lightning and flame. Clouds formed concentric rings above the devastated city, slowly tattered by the prevailing westerly winds. Whatever had happened, meteor or nuclear bomb, it had wrought destruction on a massive scale.

His mind fought a losing battle to maintain its grasp on reality, as the pain threatened to shut down his body. He could expect no help from others. He didn't know the scope of the destruction, but doubted anyone would worry about an individual on a highway when tens of thousands were dead and many more injured.

Ted rolled over on his back and stared up at the sky. It was at that moment that he saw a second fireball streaking westward high above. A single tear rolled down his cheek. "It's the end of the world," he whispered.

6

Thursday, August 9   3:22 a.m. (CDT)   *Lunar One*, Near Moon orbit –

The leak inside the service module proved a minor one and easily patched, but a piece of metal dislodged by the collision had pierced one of the reserve oxygen tanks, bleeding its precious contents into space. The collision jostled the object they had hit from its position and sent it streaking toward the moon's surface. Its impact on the moon's far side left a light-colored scar in the dark gray dust where it struck.

The Orion spacecraft had fared a little better. They had managed to restore partial power, but not communications. Houston didn't know if they were dead or alive. Presenting a bigger problem was the amount of fuel remaining. He had burned too much of it in a futile attempt to avoid the object. The remainder was insufficient to insert them into a safe Earth orbit. At their present trajectory, they would miss Earth by approximately six thousand miles. Langston could see only two possible solutions, neither of them optimum. He was mission commander, but he would leave the decision up to his crew.

"As I see it," he began, "we have two choices." The others stared at him with attentive dread, knowing that either choice would be severe but eager for any good news. "One," he continued, "We can maintain our course toward Earth and hope they can intercept us in time. Judging by Ishom's impact, I think they're going to be somewhat busy with Girra. I don't know how that might interfere with a launch, but I suspect the chance of a successful rendezvous will be small." He waited as they digested the information. "Our second choice is more risky. We can assume a lunar orbit and wait for rescue. Then, I'll take the lander to the surface, and investigate that alien artifact."

He was met with stony silence, as his three comrades pondered his choices. Crenshaw was the first to speak.

"I vote for the moon. Earth needs any information we can provide."

"We have no way of communicating with Earth," Mahall rightly pointed out.

"What about the lander?" Ingersall suggested. "It has a radio."

"It doesn't have the range to reach Earth," she replied. "It was designed to route communications through the service module."

"Can you repair the radio?" Ingersall asked.

She hesitated before answering. Langston knew her well enough to know that she wouldn't sugar coat her reply. "I don't know. The outboard antenna was damaged by the collision, and the power surge blew a lot of relays. We might replace the antenna, but it would require an EVA. I've never made one."

"I have," Langston said. "As commander, it's my job anyway."

"If we had a pump …" Ingersall began.

"We don't," Langston reminded him. "We can't transfer fuel from the lander, but we can use it. If we decide on the moon, I'm going down to the surface." He looked at each of them slowly. "I need one of you to go with me."

Crenshaw volunteered without hesitation. ""I'll go. I want to see that thing up close."

Ingersall cast a forlorn look at the three of them. "I guess the safety of Earth is more important. We're expendable. I vote for the moon."

"I'm not expendable," Mahall protested. "I have a daughter. I want to live."

Langston ignored her outburst. "You and Ingersall will remain on the *Lunar One*. If help arrives in time, you'll leave Crenshaw and me behind if necessary. I intend this to be a two-way trip, but the lander wasn't intended for use on this mission. I don't know if it's flight ready. It was just along for the ride, but we have it, and I'm going to use it. If I die out here, I'm going to die on the lunar surface. We have to make a decision quickly. Every minute we continue toward Earth makes it more difficult to achieve lunar orbit."

"Okay," Mahall said, nodding briskly as if to convince herself. "We try for a lunar insertion."

"Then it's decided. We'll fire the engines in two minutes. Everyone strap into their seats. It's going to be a rough ride."

Langston held his breath, as he fired the engine for the last time. His hasty calculations called for a twenty-two second burn to achieve a stable orbit, using the moon's gravity to pull them in. The engine roared to life, pressing him into his seat. To his dismay, it sputtered and died less than twenty seconds later. They had no more fuel. He fought the controls to keep the unstable craft steady, as he watched the numbers on the navigation computer. It was going to be close. He hoped he hadn't doomed them all to a slow, lingering death.

He sighed with relief as Crenshaw reported half an hour later, "High lunar orbit established at nineteen point six kilometers above the surface. It's not optimum, but it will hold for ..." She paused to double check her figures, and then frowned. "Sixty-one hours."

"No one can reach us in sixty-one hours," Ingersall moaned. "There's no ship on the pad. We'll crash."

Crenshaw chuckled. "Don't worry, Todd. We'll probably all suffocate before then."

"That's over two and a half days, Ingersall," Langston pointed out. "A lot can happen in two and a half days. Don't forget, *Pegasus* is at the ISS." He unbuckled his harness and floated from his seat. "I'm going below to prep the lander."

He thanked the NASA engineers for loading the lander as it if were a real mission instead of using a mock up to simulate the payload. With full oxygen reserves, he and Crenshaw could remain on the surface more than forty-eight hours, but he didn't want to rob the Orion of any of its already depleted oxygen supply. He would take enough for only forty hours. If they hadn't learned anything useful by then, they would return to *Lunar One*.

The lightweight lunar lander stored in the service module looked nothing like the massive Apollo landers of the 1970's.

While they were squat and ungainly, the *Armstrong* more closely resembled a spherical deep-sea diving bell perched atop a cylinder. The cylinder's living quarters supported a forty-eight hour lunar mission, while the two-passenger return sphere contained nothing but a rocket and two seats. The *Armstrong's* new design had been rigorously tested in the NASA labs, but Langston understood the dangers. An engine failure either during landing or on takeoff would spell disaster.

As he labored at removing the securing braces, his mind wandered to what was happening back on Earth. Had Girra struck? If so, how many people had died? Was Crenshaw correct in her alien attack assessment? It seemed farfetched, but he could furnish no more viable explanation. If an examination of the alien object that struck the lunar surface could yield any useful information, he was willing to take whatever risk necessary to secure it. The possibility of restoring communications and reporting to Houston was much higher than that of a successful rescue.

Four hours later, he completed his task. He was tired and sore from the unaccustomed exercise, but the time alone had allowed him to collect his scattered thoughts. He was older and supposedly wiser than his crew, but damned if he felt wiser. Dropping to the surface in an untested craft was a damned fool way of playing the hero. Did he suggest the landing in hopes of learning something, or was it simply a last-ditch effort to reach the moon? He made a second exterior survey of the *Armstrong's* surface for damage from the collision, but found nothing. He had one last task to perform – the exterior antenna.

He took a short twenty-minute rest break before donning his spacesuit with Crenshaw's help. After placing her face against his faceplate and smiling, she sealed the service module hatch behind him and depressurized the compartment. Removing the Simplified Aid for EVA Rescue, or *SAFER,* from its cabinet, he attached the unit to the back of his suit. The twin controls extended around his sides, allowing him to fire any of the twenty-four fixed-position nitrogen jet thrusters for free maneuverability. He opened the cargo bay door.

"Exiting the ship," he said into his microphone.

"Roger, Commander," Mahall answered.

His first step out into space brought on an intense feeling of vertigo. The moon swept below him so closely that he could almost reach down, and scoop up a handful of lunar dust. It seemed to draw him down to its surface, which, given time, it would. He waited a moment or two for the vertigo to pass, and then he fired the thrusters. When he saw the damaged solar panel, he marveled that the entire ship hadn't been destroyed. Deep gouges along the hull, if just a few inches deeper, would have instantly vented the ship's atmosphere into space in an explosive decompression. They had been lucky.

He spotted the stump of the sheared-away communications array. "The antenna is gone," he reported. "I'll attempt to install the secondary system."

The backup antenna had limited capacity, allowing only audio communications, but it would suffice. First, he removed the broken mast by loosening the four bolts securing it to the hull. He worked slowly and carefully. Working in zero gravity was tricky, requiring coordinated movements and patience. Any mistakes in space could be fatal. His crew depended on him. The first thee bolts came away easily, but the fourth had cold-welded to the frame assembly. After an hour, his patience was wearing thin. Like a shade tree mechanic, he resorted to kicking it with the toe of his boot until it loosened. He pushed the broken mast and watched it float away. Then, he opened the outside storage compartment and retrieved the new antenna. He was sweating in spite of the suit's air conditioning, and the moisture was fogging his visor. He forced himself to take a few minutes to calm down. Finally, the replacement antenna was in place.

"Finished," he reported. "Any luck?"

"I'll be another couple of hours restoring fused circuit boards," Mahall responded, "but I think it will work."

"Keep at it."

He took a few minutes to gaze at the moon's surface. Soon, he would set foot on the surface. Would he leave it? Only time would tell.

7

Thursday, August 10, 11:30 a.m. Bagdad, Iraq –

Captain Aiden Walker watched two men enter the house on Abu Nawas Street near the Arbataash 4th Tarmuz Bridge directly across the Tigris River from the U.S. Embassy. Both were known agents of ISIS, who had effectively cobbled an independent Muslim state from parts of Syria, Iraq, and Lebanon. Only a thin strip along the Tigris River from Bagdad to the Persian Gulf remained in Iraqi control, and that was slipping away quickly. The men wore Western business suits and carried briefcases, but he knew the two were not discussing a business deal. They were on his watch list and were the reason for his presence.

He turned to his rooftop companion. "How many does that make?"

His friend, Sergeant Bill Costas, glanced over at him. Costas, like Walker, had slept less than five hours during the past forty-eight hours. Both men were exhausted. He blinked his eyes rapidly after staring through the binoculars. "That's seven."

Walker stood and adjusted the plain wooden *egal* headband holding the black *ghatra* over his head. The white linen *dishdasha* and black *abaya* he wore made him hot and uncomfortable in the noonday sun, but his native attire, his dark complexion, and his passable knowledge of Arabic allowed him to move freely about the city which was rapidly becoming unfriendly to Westerners. A loudspeaker in the minaret of a nearby mosque announced the *muezzin's* midday call to prayer, the *Zuhr*. He fought the urge to respond. As an African-American born in Dearborn, Michigan, he understood the perspective of the nations of the Middle East from a minority's viewpoint, but he could not condone the violence associated with radical Islam. Islam was a religion of peace and understanding usurped by zealots. His own conversion to Islam had been through research and reading the Koran. To him, Islam was the religion that eased his troubled mind. But not today.

The *muezzin's* words haunted him. "Allah u Akbar." *Allah is great.* "Ash-hadu an-la ilaha illa Allah." *I bear witness that Mohammed is Allah's prophet.*

The faithful would be answering the *salat,* the call to prayer. He could not.

"I think it's time to make our move," he said.

Costas nodded and removed a remote control from a pocket beneath his *dishdasha.* He telescoped the antenna and pressed the start button. From the roof of a low building half a kilometer away, a drone rose into the air. He allowed the circular, battery-powered, four-rotor craft to hover at two hundred feet in altitude until he focused the camera slung beneath its underbelly. He panned the camera until the four-inch screen on the remote showed their position.

"Wave at the camera," he said, raising his hand in the air, smiling, and waving.

The thirty-pound drone carried ten pounds of Semtex studded with hundreds of twenty-millimeter ball bearings. It was a lethal combination. He directed the drone toward the building below them. Any observers would be busy heeding the *muezzin's* call. Once the drone reached the river, Costas dropped it to within ten feet of the surface to avoid detection. In the unsteady wind currents along the river, it was a challenge. He played the remote like an X-Box controller, avoiding boats moored on the bank, posts protruding from the water, and curious waterfowl.

Walker checked in with command on his cell phone. He punched in the number and waited until a familiar voice answered, "Post Office."

"This is the mailman on route six. Package is on its way."

"Deliver the package, Mailman, and return home."

"Say again, Post Office." The change in plans concerned him. He and Costas were due to rendezvous with the rest of his team and travel to Tikrit for their next mission.

"Deliver package per instructions, postage due. You've been assigned a new route. We're bringing home all mailmen. Return to Main Branch immediately upon delivery."

He looked over at Costas, who was busy operating the drone. Costas had overheard the conversation. He glanced back at Walker and shrugged.

"Affirmative, Post Office. Package in the mail slot now. Will collect postage due. Returning home."

Postage due was the okay for detonation. Fifty feet from the target, Costas stopped the drone and lined it up with a window. "Here's a package for you," he directed toward the house's inhabitants. "I hope you bastards are looking out the window."

He thumbed the power lever forward. The drone put on a burst of speed and crashed through the window. Once inside, he pressed the detonator button. The mud thatched roof of the building lifted and buckled. Flames shot from the windows and cracks in the roof. The front door sailed through the air like an errant surfboard and smashed the roof of a black Mercedes parked fifty feet from the house. The stunned driver leapt from the car and stared helplessly at the destruction. The roof collapsed into the building, raising a billowing cloud of smoke and dust. Chunks of masonry showered the waters of the Tigris River. Finally, a charred cinder block wall fell inward, fanning the flames. As the thunder of the explosion died away, the final words of the call to prayer ended. "La ilaha illa Allah." *There is no God but Allah.*

"Scratch seven terrorists and one safe house," Costas said. He placed the remote back under his *dishdasha*, rose, and stretched his stiff muscles. "If we're returning to base, does that mean I can get rid of this bed sheet? I think it's got fleas."

Walker smiled at his companion. "You can get dipped and drunk tonight."

"Good deal."

As the pair left their rooftop perch, Walker wondered why all special teams were being recalled to base. Something big must be happening somewhere.

* * * *

Less than an hour, Walker sat in the office of Alan Dire, the Postmaster his boss. Like Walker, Dire wore casual clothing instead of a uniform. Walker still wore the white *dishdasha* and black *abaya* he had worn on his mission, but he had stopped by his apartment on the embassy grounds long enough to shower and shave. Dire wore khaki slacks, a white short-sleeved shirt, and sandals. Walker had never seen him wear a coat and tie except at official embassy functions. Most of the five hundred or so remaining embassy staff weren't aware of his official title, Major, U.S. Army Special Operations. Most thought he was a civilian contractor. Dire's fourth floor corner office of the U.S. Embassy had a magnificent view of the Tigris River flowing below.

Contrasted with Walker's dark skin and six-foot frame, Dire's complexion was so pale as to be pasty, and he barely topped five-feet-six-inches in his sandals. His habitual scowl disguised his gentle disposition, though many men had paid the price of dismissing him as easy going. Articulate when he wished to be, Dire could summon language so colorful as to make a well-salted sailor blush.

"I watched your little exhibition across the river," he began. "Excellent job. You singlehandedly eliminated two-thirds of ISIS' chiefs of staff."

"I had Costas with me, sir," Walker replied.

"Yes, Costas," he said, rolling his eyes. "Is he still a royal pain in the ass?"

"Yes, sir. He can be a bit problematic at times, but a bottle of scotch and a hooker calms him down every time."

Dire frowned. "I suppose he's in the *al-Khaleej* district enjoying a little R and R."

After the fall of the police and army during the Iraq war, local residents took it upon themselves to chase prostitutes from neighborhoods. As the economy improved, they slowly moved back. *Al-Khaleej* now harbored several thriving brothels. Dire didn't disapprove of Costas' need for female companionship, just seeking it in neighborhoods outside the Green Zone.

"It seems to be his favorite haunt," Walker admitted.

"I hear they had to hire extra prostitutes just for him." Having dispensed of the less formal niceties, Dire leaned back in his seat and narrowed his eyes. "I suppose you want to know why I called you back in."

"We were going to Tikrit. Has that changed?"

"Yes, something new has come up, something in the States."

"What's happening back home that would require my team? Homeland Security has the personnel and the equipment to deal with anything."

"Not this," Dire replied.

Now, Walker was intrigued. "So, tell me what's going on."

"An invasion." Dire paused to let his words sink in.

Seeing that Dire was not going to expand on his statement, Walker asked, "Invasion? Who?"

"Not who, what." Seeing Walker's blank expression, he asked, "Have you not been watching the news?"

"I've been a little busy."

"San Francisco almost got wiped out by an object from space yesterday. Hell, Logansport, Indiana was wiped out by the second one this morning. A third one is on the way."

Walker suspected Dire wasn't talking about meteors. "What are they?"

"Something alien. Each one is a thousand feet in length and so black it's almost invisible in space. Very stealth. The objects did some damage, but the Pentagon thinks there might be something inside the objects, something even more dangerous. The Missile Defense Agency activated *Janus* to fire a nuclear missile at the second one, Girra. It didn't even scratch it."

Because of his top-level security clearance, Walker was aware of the MDA's Orbiting Missile Defense and the *Janus* satellite. Most people weren't. If the military was willing to risk revealing that it had a nuclear weapons platform orbiting the planet, someone at the top was scared.

"So, what is my team supposed to do?"

"The third object, designated Nusku, is headed for Nevada. You realize what's in Nevada."

Walker nodded. "Groom Lake. We've been monitoring the test flights of the *SR-80 Lance*."

"The Brass doesn't think the destination is a coincidence."

Walker agreed. The experimental high altitude rocket-propelled jets were the only aircraft capable of mounting an effective defense against an attack from space. "Too bad they aren't in full production now."

"Congress is often too slow to act. That's why we have you."

Walker studied Dire's face, trying to decide just what he and his men were in for before asking, "Just what did you have in mind?"

"For now, I want you in Nevada. If the situation warrants it, I need you and your men ready for action. I'll arrange transportation."

"Why us?"

"You're the best we've got. I think we're going to need our best for this situation."

"And if nothing happens? If they're just rocks from space?"

"Then consider it a vacation. Go to Vegas, see a show, lose some money in the slot machines – forget all about of this conversation."

As he sat there nodding as Dire spoke, Walker suspected he wouldn't have time to see the sights. "Can I inform Sergeant Costas of our mission?"

Dire smiled. "You can tell that big lug whatever you want. Tell him you're making a booze-and-broads run. He'll like that."

One question bothered him particularly of the many that crowded his head. "Why America?"

"If the U.S. is under attack by aliens, our enemies here on Earth might take the opportunity to shift a few boundaries, settle a few old scores. Maybe the aliens are counting on our species' own stupidity and distrust to help them along."

"When do we leave?"

"You're heading to the airport as soon as you leave my office. It's going to be a balls-to-the-wall trip."

Walker nodded, and then smiled. "I never liked flying first class anyway."

"You stay frosty over there, son. I don't want to lose you. You're too valuable an asset."

"My mama didn't raise a fool, major."

Dire gestured at Walker's *dishdasha*. "Try to find something a trifle less distracting to wear. I don't want some nervous bastard taking pot shots at you."

"I'll find something appropriate." He rose. He had a lot to do in a short time. "Anything else?"

"Yeah, give Costas a big wet kiss on the lips for me."

"I'll fight aliens, sir, but I draw the line at kissing Costas."

As he walked out of Dire's office, he glanced out the window at the Tigris River and wondered if he would ever see it again.

8

Thursday, Aug. 9   2:20 p.m. (CDT)   *Mare Moscoviense, Moon –*

He was on the moon! Commander Langston couldn't help the sense of wonder that coursed through his veins, as he took his first few steps on the lunar surface. He had never expected to touch the surface of the moon during his long NASA career. He had no Neil Armstrong immortal words to impart to worldwide listeners glued to their televisions and radios. He had no audience other than Crenshaw bouncing along behind him in the low lunar gravity humming *Waltzing Matilda* in her soft contralto voice into her radio microphone. Nevertheless, it was a momentous occasion being the first person to step foot on the moon after almost half a century.

"Thank you, God," he whispered. *Finally, I made it.*

The Z-4 spacesuit he wore had seemed merely uncomfortable in zero gravity. On the lunar surface, it required all his strength to move about. The eighty-five kilo suit added to his eighty-four kilos, might just weight over twenty-eight kilos in the moon's five-sixths gravity, but his mass was still over one-hundred-sixty kilos. Inertia remained constant. Each step had to be carefully considered to avoid a potentially deadly fall. He tried to quell the feelings of exultation and concentrate on his mission.

The alien teardrop had crashed in a small crater in *Mare Moscoviense* located between latitudes 20^0 and 30^0 north of the lunar equator on the moon's far side a kilometer from their landing site. It lay out of sight just over a crater's rim. They had no lunar buggy, so they trudged through the ten-centimeter deep regolith that clutched at their boots with each step. He had always imagined that he would have been ecstatic to explore the lunar landscape, to chip off rock samples, to feel the moon's texture even if with gloved hands. However, he ignored the exotic rock formations and the glassy-edged ejecta from meteorite impacts, though he longed to pick up a moon rock and stuff it into his pocket as a memento.

The sun was high overhead, casting deep shadows that made each step treacherous. He wished he could see Earth from where he stood, but it was on the opposite side of the moon from him. The sound of his breathing and the whisper of his air-conditioning unit echoed in his helmet, but around him was only the silence of a vacuum.

"How do we cross that?" Crenshaw asked.

Before them, looking like a long, sinuous shadow on the ground, a deep *rille*, a crack in the lunar surface, spread across the *mare* as far as they could see. To go around it would take too long, leaving them little air for the return trip. He walked up to the edge and stared into its stygian depths. The shadow cut across the near wall like a knife's edge, swallowing everything below it in deep, impenetrable darkness. The bottom could have gone on forever. He had no way of plumbing its depths. He eyed the three-meter span with trepidation, but they couldn't turn back. *How indeed?* He asked himself.

"We jump," he said. He could think of no other way across. It was foolish and risky, but he wouldn't let a mere ditch stop him.

"I'll go first," Crenshaw said.

Before he could stop her, she raced across the surface in long bounds and leaped. His heart skipped a beat, but she sailed over the yawning chasm and landed nimbly on the far side, ending her leap with a pirouette made slightly awkward by her suit.

"It's easy, Commander," she called back to him.

Here goes. He took two preliminary bounds and leaped. It was like jumping over a black line in the dirt, except he knew the line fell away to immeasurable depths. He landed on the far side before he realized that he had held his breath. Like Crenshaw, he was unable to hide the grin on his face.

"It's like flying," he said.

The remainder of the journey was easy in comparison. They climbed the gradually sloping side of a ninety-meter deep crater until they stood at the rim. The crater was six hundred meters in diameter, fully illuminated by the sun except for the shadow of the crater wall. The jagged far edge rose another twenty meters higher. Only the low lunar gravity kept the inward leaning fingers of rock thrusting from the surface from crumbling into the crater.

"There it is," Crenshaw called over the radio.

He followed her pointing finger down until he discerned an unusually shaped shadow spilling across the lunar surface. The forward edge of the object had buried itself meters deep in the loose regolith just beneath the far edge of the crater, leaving the rear protruding into the star-studded sky. The teardrop had not been damaged by the crash. Its ebony surface bore no marks from the impact. They descended the slope carefully. Even in one-sixth lunar gravity, a ninety-meter fall could be deadly.

Mahall's first assessment of the object proved to be correct. The alien artifact was neither smooth nor solid. Its crystalline lattice structure gave it the appearance of a carved jewel. Large portions of the object were so delicate and open that he could have stepped through it. As they drew near, its true size became more apparent. It measured at least fifty meters in diameter. Only a third of it was visible. The remaining portion lay embedded in the regolith and the basalt beneath it.

"I see no windows or hatches," Langston noted. "I don't think it is manned."

"By little green men?" Crenshaw added with a twinkle in her voice.

Langston reached out his gloved hand and rested it on the cradle's surface. A slight vibration startled him. "It's alive."

Crenshaw took a step backwards. "Alive?"

"Well, I feel movement, power flow, something."

"Perhaps it's automated," Crenshaw suggested, "relaying commands to the Girra objects."

"Or relaying telemetry back to its source," Langston added. "If we could disable it, we might cut off communication between the Girra objects and its creators."

"Disable it? How? We have no explosives, no cutting tools. I don't know if a torch would even scratch this substance. Crashing into the moon didn't seem to do much damage."

"There must be a way."

"There's nothing we can do," Crenshaw insisted.

Langston wasn't convinced. The object might provide the key to the alien objects on Earth. Whatever their purpose, he didn't think it was a friendly visit.

"Let's take some photos and make some measurements, and then return to the lander. Maybe Mahall has managed to re-establish communications with Earth."

As Crenshaw took digital photos, he closed his eyes and rested his hand once more on the ebony surface. It seemed as if the alien object was whispering to him in a voice he could not understand. Was it talking to Girra or Ishom? What was it saying? Could he talk to it, make it understand him? He closed his eyes and sent his thoughts into the object. After a few moments, he realized it was a wasted gesture. They could do nothing. They were casual observers, unable to contact Earth even if they did discover something useful. Had his desire to land on the moon's surface been an attempt to learn more about the aliens, or simply a fulfillment of a lifelong dream?

His mind began to fill with something … images too blurry to interpret, as if viewed through spectrums not visible to humans. His heart began to race, as if his oxygen level was dropping. A fear gripped him, clutching his chest like a giant hand, like the fear he had to fight on his first EVA when he saw the Earth spinning below his feet drawing him down. He wanted to run, run anywhere, but his boots were frozen to the ground. The panic grew in intensity, until he thought his heart would explode. His fear became anger, a rage that threatened to overwhelm him. He clenched his fists and bit his lip to fight it. He realized the rage wasn't coming from him. It was coming from the aliens, from the dark void of the teardrop. He wanted to destroy it. Destroy it before it destroyed him.

"Finished."

He glanced up as Crenshaw spoke. She had completed her photographs and was walking back to his position. The rage and fear vanished as if he had imagined it. His lip bled, so he had felt it. How long had he been mesmerized? He shook his head to clear it.

"Let's grab a bite to eat and decide what to do next."

As he walked away, he could still hear the quiet whispers gnawing at the edges of his senses.

NUSKU

9

Friday, August 10,   5:25 a.m. (PDT)   Worthington Mountains, Nevada –

Howi Pacheco had awakened well before dawn, brewed his coffee, cooked breakfast, and packed his burro, Annie. He had been an early riser for all of his sixty-two years. His father, a Paiute Elder, had instilled in him the virtues of honor, hard work, and self-reliance. Howi had not risen to the level of his Tribal Elder father, but he believed in hard work, and he was self-reliant. For forty-one years, he had scoured the deserts of central Nevada in search of silver and gold. He had prospected the Humboldt National Forest from Timber Mountain to Skull Mountain. The fact that it was BLM land didn't bother him. They had taken the land from his ancestors. He suffered no remorse in borrowing it for a short time. He had yet to find the mother lode and had long ago abandoned all hopes of becoming rich. However, he had managed to pan enough flakes and dig up enough nuggets to get by.

Now, he was on his way to the old Friberg mine near the Worthington Mountains. The gold mine had operated until 1948. He was certain gold could still be found in the area. To him the journey was an adventure. He loved the desert as only someone born to it could. The searing summer heat and the bone-chilling winters were just a part of the cycle of life. He loved the stands of pinion, Ponderosa pine, junipers, and bristlecone pines in the mountains and the cholla and sagebrush in the valleys. He was brother to the Bighorn sheep, the cougars, and the eagles. He was at home in the sparse landscape. The silence, broken only by the soft whispers of the wind, lulled him to sleep at night.

He had visited a big city once, Las Vegas. The neon skyline had frightened him, made him feel like an intruder in a golden palace. The people walked like ghosts, unaware of where they were or of the people around them. He had eaten popcorn, watched a John Wayne movie, and left without sampling any of Vegas' more alluring vices.

The sun was just marking the sky east of the Worthington Mountains, creating bright lines than traced the slopes like veins of silver. The valley was still in deep twilight, but he and Annie were both sure-footed and eager to be moving.

"Looks like a rich strike, eh, Annie," he said to his burro, pointing to the illusion of silver veins in the mountains. Annie brayed and he chuckled at his joke.

He stopped long enough to pull the pint of *Old Crow* from his back pocket. Whiskey was one of the few things he missed from the cities. The limited space in his and Annie's packs meant he could never carry enough to last. He eyed the bottle judging its low contents.

"Only a few swigs left, Annie," he said. Annie said nothing. He took a long swig, allowing the harsh liquor to trickle down his throat slowly, relishing the burn. "That's good stuff," he said. He replaced the cap then shoved the remainder back in his pocket. "I'll save it for later."

Annie brayed and jerked at her reins. "What's wrong, Annie?" It took him a few moments to realize the sky was getting lighter. He looked to the east. The sun was now well above the peaks. *No*, he thought. *That can't be the sun. It's too far north.* The fireball grew larger and brighter, washing the desert floor a golden hue. He covered his eyes to reduce the glare, but continued staring at the strange object. He followed its path, as it passed his position to his north. His face tingled from the heat. Then the sonic boom struck him like a thunderclap.

Annie, frightened by the loud noise, pulled free from his grip and bolted. He ran to stop her, but at that moment, the horizon to the north erupted in a brilliant fireball that almost blinded him. Above the fireball, a dark cloud rose high into the sky. He had never witnessed such an event. He knew it to be a *puha*, one of the power spirits that inhabited all things. Fear gripped him like a cold vise, freezing his legs. He couldn't move, but continued to stare at the cloud transfixed by its awesome beauty. Seconds later, he saw the wall of dust sweeping toward him. He had no time to flee, even if he wasn't rooted to the spot. The wall of wind and dust knocked him off his feet and sent him tumbling over the broken ground. Dust flayed his exposed skin like sandpaper. The roar accompanying the wind deafened him.

Then, the earth began to tremble. It bounced him around like the popcorn in the popper he had seen in Las Vegas. Rocks as large as his fist bounced high into the air. It shook so violently, he thought his insides were going to explode. He felt as if *Bone Crusher* had attacked him. Finally, the shaking subsided, but the earth continued to groan in agony. The sky to the north still roiled with dark clouds. Lightning flashed in the midst of the darkness. The sun rose over the mountains, but its light brought no warmth or comfort. It paled to the light he had just seen.

He looked around. Annie lay on her side a dozen yards away, dead. He tried to crawl to her, but his legs wouldn't cooperate. He looked down, saw the odd angle of his right ankle, and knew it was broken. He also noticed that his skin was blistered and bleeding. Blood trickled into his eyes from a gash in his forehead. Oddly, the pain was muted, as if it would come later.

He knew he was going to die. He couldn't walk. Annie was dead. It was a two-day walk to any help. He didn't fear death. He had lived a long life and death would come as a welcomed friend. Not until he reached into his back pocket and discovered the broken bottle of *Old Crow* did he become angry. He looked up at the sky.

"*Wikinumi,*" he yelled to the Paiute god. "You play your pranks on me like Coyote."

Exhausted by his ordeal, he lay back and began to recite the first words of a medicine song his mother had taught him. "Now all my singing dreams are gone, but none knows where they have fled nor by what trails they have left me."

* * * *

Colonel David Starnes, commander of Creech Air Force Base in southern Nevada, had been aware of Nusku's approach from space. After the destruction caused by its companion objects, Ishom and Girra, he had placed the base on high alert. The object was too far away to observe except by unreliable radar imagery, but the impact registered on the seismographs as a magnitude 6.5. Windows rattled in his office. The glare of the blast lit up the northern horizon for several minutes. He didn't know if it was by design or just good luck that Nusku landed in the sparsely inhabited deserts of Nevada, but it had missed his base.

Home of the 432nd and 732nd Operations Groups, Creech was the center of operations for the military's pilotless aircraft. Within minutes, he had a fleet of drones flying toward the object. The unmanned drones relayed images of the crater to video screens in the operations room. He watched the screen bleary-eyed from staring at the smoke-filled images. As he paced the room, he chewed on the unlit Dominican *Escudo Cubano Rothschild* protruding from the corner of his mouth. The fat, dark cigar was one of his few weaknesses, but he couldn't smoke around the delicate drone aircraft controls or the equally delicate operators. He always felt as if he was walking into a video arcade when he entered the dark, air-conditioned building and saw the pimply faced kids sitting at the consoles. At sixty-two years of age, they could have been his grandchildren.

"Can you clean up that image?" he asked one young lieutenant.

"No, sir," he replied. "There's too much smoke and particulate matter."

"Particulate matter?"

"Dust from the blast, sir," the lieutenant explained.

"Can we get a team in there?"

"It's much too hot, nearly three hundred degrees around the crater's edge. The heat won't dissipate for ten or twelve hours."

Starnes growled to relieve his frustration. He had the most advanced drones the military had to offer at his disposal; and yet he was helpless.

"Switch to Infrared."

The image changed, becoming a green field with a bright red circle surrounded by a lighter red circle, like a bull's eye. How appropriate, he thought. The colors flared and faded. As the image field widened to encompass the surrounding area, small red dots representing burning trees and brush appeared.

"Why is the image pulsing?"

"I'm not sure, sir. The object could be out gassing, or it's moving."

"Moving?"

The lieutenant looked up at him with a confused expression. "The crater could be unstable, sir. It's difficult to tell from the images. I'm no expert on meteor craters."

Starnes leaned on the console and stared at the screen. "Whatever is down there, I don't think it's friendly."

"Friendly, sir," the lieutenant asked. "What do you mean? It's a meteor, isn't it?"

"Three meteors landing exactly twenty-four hours apart? That's pretty good timing for happenstance. Have you ever watched *War of the Worlds*?"

"With Tom Cruise?"

Starnes sighed. *These young people have no clue. I feel like a schoolteacher.* "No, the 1953 movie with Gene Barry. The Martians landed in groups of three."

The lieutenant looked even more confused. "Martians? Sir, these objects didn't come from Mars."

Starnes removed his cigar, pointed it at him, and said, "No, lieutenant, but just where the hell did they come from."

GIRRA

10

Friday, August 10   8:30 p.m. (EDT)   Logansport, IN –

Twelve hours after Girra struck, Gate got his first look at the destruction. The blast obliterated everything within a radius of five miles and leveled buildings several miles beyond that. Fifteen thousand residents – men, women, and children – evaporated in a flash, while twice that number died within hours of the initial impact from burns and injuries. The crater that had once been Logansport, Indiana, was shrouded by a blanket of steam, as the waters of the Wabash and Eel Rivers plunged over the edge of the precipice into its unknown depths. The ground around the crater was still too hot for any human to venture more than a quarter of a mile into the impact zone, but aerial drones revealed the tragic aftermath of landfall.

The rubble of shattered trees, buildings, and scorched earth swept from the impact site by the hurricane force winds of the blast formed a wall of debris almost a mile from ground zero. The western downrange edge of the ellipse was over eighty feet high. The wall was slightly lower on the eastern, northern, and southern borders. The microphones on the drones picked up the rumble of cascading earth and the hiss of steam. The Wabash and the Eel Rivers, shifted from their original courses by the newly formed earthen dike, found new paths, drowning dead neighborhoods in muddy fresh water lakes. The geography of the area had been forever altered.

Gate had seen the blurry images captured by low-flying unmanned aircraft, but now he stared at the total destruction below him from the right-side rear passenger seat of the OH-58 Kiowa helicopter. Director Caruthers had carried through on his promise to transport him to the landing site before impact. He witnessed Girra strike Logansport from a distance of thirty miles. He was still close enough to feel the earth tremble at the impact, and to be almost blinded by the brilliant fireball of incineration, but nothing had prepared him for this. Now, as he surveyed the devastating sea of ruin close up, his facts and figures, his catastrophe projections, and his carefully crafted computer simulations, meant nothing. This was real. This was what death from the stars looked like, and he was sick to his stomach. The heavy heat thermals rising from the scoured landscape didn't help the situation. They jolted the observation helicopter sideways and bounced it up and down like a coin-operated carnival ride.

"This is as close as I can get," the nervous pilot reported. "It's already 120 degrees outside, and we're still half a mile away."

Colonel Terrell Powers nodded. He had accompanied Gate into the blast zone for a military inspection. He loosened his tie and undid the top button of his sweat-stained uniform blouse. "What kind of readings are you getting?"

The beach ball-shaped MMS, the Mast Mounted Sight perched atop the rotor, used its television, thermal imaging, and laser range finder to peer into the murky depths of the crater. Of the three, only the range finder was producing any tangible results.

"The crater is between nine hundred feet to fifteen hundred feet deep," Gate answered. "The readings are unstable, as if the bottom is moving."

Powers whistled appreciatively. "Is the object intact?"

"There's something big down there, but I have no idea of its condition or size. One thing is certain; it's no common meteorite."

Powers nodded. "That's what they told me at the briefing before the flight, but I didn't believe them. I guess I do now." He wiped his forehead on his sleeve. "It's damn hot. It might be days before we can get near it. Make one more pass and …"

The pilot interrupted him, "Colonel, there's something moving in the smoke." He pointed to the starboard side of the chopper. Through the roiling cloud of smoke and steam, a darker object rose from the crater. "What the hell is that?"

"Get us closer," Powers ordered.

Gate pressed his face against the glass, as the pilot veered toward the crater. The helicopter danced sideways and stood on its nose for a terrifying few seconds, as a sudden thermal struck it from below. The pilot fought the controls until the chopper leveled, and then banked away.

"We can't get any closer and live," he said, visibly shaken by the near disaster.

An ebony structure as wide as a railroad car and shaped like a kitchen knife erupted from the crater and flew past them so closely that its backwash spun the chopper in the air. Gate clung tightly to his seat harness to keep being tossed around like dice in a croupier's cup. The pointed end of the object struck the ground at the edge of the crater with a tremendous thud, raising a cloud of dust. Very quickly, more objects joined the first. Each was segmented like an insect leg. Only vaguely visible at first, something else rose from the smoke, something much larger attached to the black appendages.

Gate was struck speechless as a massive head appeared. It was black like the legs, as wide as a football field and over a hundred feet thick. The head was flattened with overlapping plates of the black material covering the entire head, protecting it like armor plating. Instead of eyes, two oblong strips the color of fried egg yolks sat high on the face between boney protuberances of the ebony material. One unblinking eye stared at the helicopter.

"My God," the colonel gasped. "Girra is alive!"

As Gate watched mesmerized, the creature, a black oblong measuring almost nine hundred feet in length, pulled itself free of the crater. House-sized clumps of earth cascaded from its curved flanks. Standing on six pair of legs, it shook itself like a wet dog. Chunks of rock flew from it like missiles. Gate held on as the pilot frantically dodged the stony projectiles. Then Girra strode from the crater's edge and turned in a circle, as if getting its bearings.

From head to short, stubby tail, the creature resembled a cockroach with its overlapping plates. The trailing edge of each plate was upturned and serrated, rising to a height of twenty feet along the back of the creature. Six pairs of spiky legs, three forward and three near the rear, propelled the creature nimbly away from the crater.

"It's a monster," the colonel said.

Gate agreed with the colonel's unscientific assessment. The creature raised goose bumps on his arm. He stared fascinated, as Girra began moving to the northwest, not lumbering as its size might suggest, but gliding sinuously on its twelve amazingly coordinated legs. It scampered over the eighty-foot earthen dike created by the impact, its bottom clearing the dike by twenty feet. The pilot dared a closer inspection of the creature, swooping in to within a hundred feet. A series of bumps or blisters scarred the length of the creature's sloping sides, protected by the upturned plates. Each blister was over ten feet long and six feet high. Gate couldn't guess at their purpose.

Girra trod through demolished buildings and bridges, as easily as brushing aside tall grass. Each spiked leg left deep craters in the asphalt of the highway and exploded any building it impaled. It was fascinating to watch, but Gate knew it had not come to Earth to observe. Its purpose was a sinister one, as deadly as its arrival had been.

He suddenly remembered Ishom off the coast of California. If it contained another of the creatures…

"Colonel, you had better contact the Pentagon and inform them of what we've witnessed. San Francisco is in great danger."

As Colonel Powers looked at Gate, the color drained from his face. "I'll contact them, but I'm not sure they will believe me."

"I want to follow that thing. In the meantime, I'll download everything we have to NASA."

"It'll be dark in twenty minutes, and that monster is as black as shadow," the pilot reminded him. "How can I follow it at night with no moon?"

"Try," he said.

He was taking no chances. Whoever, or whatever had sent Girra and the other objects to Earth, he suspected it was not a friendly visit.

Girra quickly revealed its true intent. Ten miles from the crater, the circular cluster of tubular structures on the creature's face which he had mistaken for some type of feelers suddenly came to life as a nest of writhing tentacles, each one tipped by a clump of smaller tentacles. The hundred-and-fifty-foot long, armor-plated tentacles whipped down and into buildings, deftly retrieving items, holding them up for the creature to examine, and then flinging them aside. They moved swiftly, and the gathering darkness made following their ebony shapes difficult.

When a cavernous vertical opening appeared in the space between the cluster of tentacles, Gate was appalled to discover that it was a mouth lined with rows of serrated teeth the size of automobile hoods. Then, to his horror, he identified some of the objects the tentacles grasped as human beings. The tentacles dropped its struggling captives into the yawning chasm, where they were torn to shreds by the razor-sharp teeth before disappearing down its enormous gullet.

"My God! It's eating people," he shouted in disgust.

As he spoke, a pair of F-15 Eagles swooped down from the sky in attack formation.

"Go get 'em, boys," Powers yelled, pumping his fist into the air. "It's time to show this thing just who the hell it's messing with."

Gate heard one of the pilots say, "Fox One," over the radio to announce missile launch. Eight silver streaks detached from beneath the jets' wings, as their payload of AIM-75 Sparrow missiles raced for their target, deadly twelve-foot-long rocket-propelled lances tipped with eighty-eight pounds of deadly high explosives. The missiles struck just above the slit of the now closed mouth. The explosions produced fireballs and clouds of smoke, but did no visible damage to the creature. In fact, the dark material comprising Girra's armor absorbed the energy of the explosions. Pulses of light trailed from the impact sites around the head down its sides, fading to darkness many yards away. The jets banked sharply to the left and came around for a second pass.

This time the F-15s fired their AIM-9L/M Sidewinder missiles. The ten-foot-long missiles delivered almost twenty-one pounds of WDU-17/B annular blast-frag explosives to their targets, producing a circle of expanding dense steel rods like shotgun pellets. The metal rods were capable of disintegrating an aircraft, but the results against Girra were as disappointing as the earlier attempt. The creature continued its path of destruction. A third pass with the inboard M61A1 20 mm Gatling guns proved just how dense the creature's skin or armor plating was. Gate watched with disbelief as the bullets bounced off without causing any damage, producing only short pulses of light along Girra's armor.

"Its skin or whatever is covering it seems to be composed of some type of crystalline substance, denser than diamond, dispersing the energy of the explosions. It must be similar to the pod or landing craft that transported it here. It survived the rigors of space and an impact with the planet. Conventional explosives aren't going to scratch it."

Powers stared at him. "We've got bigger bombs in our arsenal. We'll bring the bastard down."

The F-15 Eagle attacks had not gone unnoticed. As the jets made a second Gatling gun pass over the creature, they came within range of the tentacles. Several of the tentacles surrounding the mouth darted into the air, plucking the jets from the air with the speed of a lizard's tongue, and slammed them to the earth at the creature's feet. The crews had no time to eject. Gate fought down a sinking feeling, as he watched the aircraft burst into massive fireballs that lit up the dusk, showering flaming debris and aviation fuel over houses and automobiles not already trampled by the creature's passing. Then, the tentacles resumed their grisly task of scooping up human beings from the crowd of fleeing people and shoveling them into the gaping mouth.

The deaths of the brave Eagle crews and the horrific fate of the hapless civilians sickened Gate. This was no war. It was a massacre. "I've seen enough. Let's go."

"No," Powers said. "We have to follow it. I want to see the bastard taken down."

Gate nodded helplessly. He was along for the ride. As they headed north parallel to Girra's path, the pilot hugged the ground to avoid an incoming flight of F-22 Raptors. Gate prayed the stealth fighters had better luck than the F-15 Eagles, but deep inside he feared God wasn't listening.

He was right. As the Raptors zeroed in on their target, Girra delivered yet another stunning surprise. The mysterious blisters dotting its surface began to open and pour forth hundreds of flying creatures. Each of the eight-legged monsters was nine feet in length and darted about or hovered motionlessly on two pairs of leathery wings. The new flying creatures attacked the Raptors, in some cases colliding with them midair to bring them down. Though not as bulletproof as Girra, the highly mobile creatures proved difficult to kill. A dozen aircraft were destroyed during the first few minutes of combat. Those pilots who managed to eject safely were quickly snatched up by the flying creatures and delivered to Girra's waiting mouth. One pilot, unaware of the fate of the F-15s, approached too close to Girra's head and came under attack by the highly mobile tentacles. He ejected safely, but one of the writhing tentacles snatched him from the air and delivered him to the mouth. Scores of the flying creatures were killed, but their numbers didn't seem to diminish. Finally, lack of fuel forced the surviving Raptors to retreat.

Gate was no biologist. He didn't know if the flying creatures were young Girra or alien life forms in a symbiotic relationship with Girra. For all he knew they could be some kind of cosmic lice. After the Raptors left, the creatures swarmed from Girra and swept across the surrounding countryside, seizing cattle, pigs, pets, and humans and conveyed them to Girra, after first delivering a sting designed to either kill or subdue.

Witnessing one such attack, Colonel Powers commented, "They're like wasps." The name stuck.

The helicopter pilot wanted to leave the area before the Wasps noticed them, and Gate was in complete agreement, but Colonel Powers insisted on following the creature. As a compromise, they remained as far from Girra and its host of flying brood as possible while still maintaining contact. Girra trampled small towns into dust, destroyed highways and railways, while the Wasps depopulated the surrounding area. Gate imagined he was bearing witness to the end of mankind.

"We're going to need to refuel," the pilot informed them an hour later. "There's a small airport just north of Wicmac."

Gate checked the map. Wicmac was a small city of twenty-five-hundred along the banks of the Tippecanoe River, made famous during the Presidential election of 1840, when 'Tippecanoe and Tyler Too' became William Henry Harrison's campaign slogan. Arens Field lay just two miles north of the city.

"It seems to be the closest airport," he agreed.

"We won't have much time," the pilot said. "The creature will be there in less than thirty minutes."

"Then it's a quick in and out operation," Powers said.

As the chopper flew low over the city, Gate was shocked to see streetlights burning and people lining the streets.

"Wasn't the area evacuated?" he asked the colonel.

"The order was given. The radios and televisions have been broadcasting the news for three hours."

"The fools are having a party," the pilot added.

"We have to warn them," Gate said.

"We have to refuel first. We're running on fumes."

"You refuel while I go talk to the city leaders."

Powers grabbed Gate's arm in a tight grip. "Our mission is to observe Girra. We don't have time to play Paul Revere. They've been warned."

Gate shook his arm free. "They don't realize the danger. We can't just let them die."

"We may not have much choice," the pilot said. "Look, it's too late."

Barely visible against the moon, a cloud moved swiftly toward the city – Wasps. The cloud descended on the population, who too late recognized the threat. The creatures quickly overwhelmed anyone caught in the open, stinging them into submission and transporting them back to Girra in a steady line. Others began tearing into doors and windows of businesses and homes seeking anyone hiding from them.

"Uh, oh, we've been spotted," the pilot warned.

Gate glanced out the window. Several of the Wasps broke off from the main group and they were headed directly toward the helicopter. His head butted the glass with a painful thud, as the pilot veered sharply to avoid a head on collision with one of the creatures. Colonel Powers pulled his .45 from its holster and gripped it tightly in both hands. Gate, though no crack shot, wished he had a weapon as well.

The Kiowa helicopter was unarmed, on a reconnaissance mission. Their only chance was in outmaneuvering the nimble flying creatures. Gate had faith in the pilot's abilities, but knew the Kiowa was no match for the more maneuverable Wasps. The pilot dropped to treetop level, twisting and turning to keep the Wasps from clinging to the chopper. Gate held his breath, as tree limbs scrapped against the window. Powers began firing through the glass, but the .45 slugs did little if any damage.

"Get us on the ground," Powers ordered.

The pilot dodged one of the creatures and banked sharply to the left, heading for an intersection downtown large enough to accommodate the chopper. He was too late. Before they could touch down, one of the creatures flew into the tail rotor. The whirling blade chopped the creature to pieces, but the impact sheared the rotor from the shaft. The helicopter began spinning wildly. The pilot fought the controls valiantly, but Gate knew they were going to crash.

"Hold on!" the pilot yelled.

The chopper rolled sharply onto its left side just before it plunged to the ground. It struck the pavement and skidded thirty feet before slamming into a large oak tree. The impact jerked Gate forward and sideways in his harness, bruising his ribs and leaving him dangling helplessly in his seat. Powers released his harness and climbed past Gate without even checking on his condition. The colonel heaved open the door and stood on the fuselage, firing his automatic at the creatures surrounding them. Gate's last image of the colonel was of a Wasp's long, thin stinger piercing Power's chest. The colonel's expression was one of utter surprise. He glanced down at the stinger, still dripping its venom, fired one more shot at it, and then disappeared from view as the creature jerked him into the air.

Panic coursed through Gate's veins. He fumbled with the harness to free himself with trembling hands. Finally, the catch released, and he dropped to the bottom of the canted chopper. He crawled forward to check on the motionless pilot. The bent metal post of a street sign protruded through the shattered canopy into the pilot's abdomen, pinning him to his seat. Gate checked the pilot's pulse, but he was dead.

The helicopter shuddered as one of the Wasps landed on it. Gate looked up at the creature's abdomen. Overlapping plates of the same dark substance covering Girra protected it. The segmented wings appeared leathery, but Gate suspected they were composed of some harder substance. He watched the abdomen expand and contract as it breathed and realized that the ebony plates pulled slightly apart with each breath, leaving gaps of exposed flesh. They weren't invulnerable, just difficult to kill. He pulled his body as far under the pilot's feet as he could and assumed a fetal position, hoping to conceal his body. After a few minutes, the Wasp left.

Still shaken by the crash, he crawled from the wreckage through the shattered Plexiglas canopy. His chest and back ached, but he had no broken bones or serious injuries. Staring down the deserted streets, he realized an eerie silence had descended over the town. A few dismembered corpses lay in the streets, but most of the town's inhabitants were gone, victims of the Wasps' swift and merciless attack. He was alone.

He leaned against the helicopter fuselage and arched his back. With a loud snap, his vertebrae realigned. He twisted his upper torso and sighed as the pain eased. There was nothing he could do about his bruised ribs. Holding his left side, he marched down the main street searching for survivors. The Wasps had smashed many store and home front doors and plate glass windows. Broken glass littered the sidewalks, forcing him to tread carefully. One woman lay half inside a bookstore window display, impaled on the glass.

Passing a gun shop, the urgent need to arm himself overcame him. As he stepped inside through the shattered door, he was startled to see a Wasp just inside the store. His heart almost stopped before he realized the Wasp was dead. The store owner had managed to kill it with a high-powered rifle round, but not before the creature had savaged him with its razor-sharp mandibles, almost cutting his body in half.

Gate picked up the blood-covered rifle at the man's feet. The Ruger fired a .308 caliber Winchester round. At close range, with an experienced shooter pulling the trigger, it had brought down the Wasp, but the last time he had fired any weapon was when he was sixteen years old. If he had any hope of protecting himself, he needed a weapon requiring less expertise. He spotted a Mossberg 500 shotgun in the case behind the counter and smiled. He had fired shotguns at targets in summer camp as a teenager. The Mossberg 12-gauge delivered a stronger kick than the 20-gauge he had fired then, but he thought he might be able to hit a Wasp with it. It required less accuracy and still delivered quite a punch at close range.

He quickly located a box of 12-gauge double-ought shells and loaded the Mossberg's six-round magazine. He stuffed an extra magazine and the remaining shells into his pants pockets and cautiously exited the store. An occasional scream in the distance reminded him that the Wasps weren't gone, just ranging farther out in search of prey. Down the deserted street, he reached through the front of a broken bottled water dispenser standing outside a small market and grabbed a bottle of spring water. He downed most of it to quench his thirst, took a second bottle, and shoved it down the waist of his pants for later. He finished the first bottle, as he walked down the street searching for survivors. He found no one. The Wasps had completely depopulated the town. What would they do in a city the size of Chicago?

In the distance, he heard the dull thuds of Girra's legs as it marched northwest. If he wanted to get back into action, he had contact someone to rescue him. He tried a telephone in a shop, but the line was dead. He had dropped his cell phone back in the helicopter. He retraced his steps, crawled inside the chopper, and found his phone wedged beneath the seat. He climbed down from the helicopter and held up his phone. To his dismay, there was no signal. As he continued to search for a signal, a noise in an alleyway startled him. He raised the shotgun and moved quietly toward the alley. He felt silly stalking one of the creatures, but was angry enough not to care. At first, he saw nothing. Then, the top of a metal dumpster moved.

"Come out of there," he yelled, then realized that if it was one of the Wasps it certainly wouldn't understand English.

The top lifted and a small boy peered over the rim. "Are they gone?" he asked in a frightened voice.

Gate relaxed and lowered the shotgun. "Yes, I think so. Climb down."

The boy, about ten, crawled out, dropped to the ground, and walked over to stand in front of Gate. He stared up at Gate's tall height, and then his gaze moved to the shotgun Gate held in his hands. "Did you kill any?"

Gate laughed. "No, they were gone before I found the shotgun. Are you alone?"

The boy looked around, noticed a dead body, and cringed. "I don't know. I was with Joey and his father. We got separated. I don't see them anywhere."

"Where are your parents?"

"We live on a farm south of here. They stayed home."

Gate tried not to let his expression falter, but he had seen the devastation to the surrounding farms as they flew over them. It was doubtful the boy's parents were alive. He wanted to pursue Girra, but he couldn't leave the boy alone. He needed to find a vehicle and transport the boy to safety. He could follow Girra later, tracking it by its path of destruction.

"Come on. I'll take you home."

The look of fear on the boy's face was all the warning Gate had. He turned and looked up just as a Wasp's head appeared over the edge of a roof less than six feet above his head. The creature stared down at them through a narrow visor-like band across its forehead that Gate assumed served as its primary sensory organ. He stared at the creature for several moments, studying it as it did him, but when the creature's wings began fluttering, he raised the shotgun and fired three quick blasts at the creature's head. To his surprise, the shotgun pellets penetrated the soft flesh beneath the creature's neck. It keened shrilly and collapsed on the roof, a yellow ichor dripping from the gaping wound.

The boy stared in shock. Gate shook him to get his attention. "We have to leave. That sound might bring others."

Before leaving, he took several photos of the dead creature with his cell phone. On impulse, he poured the water from the plastic bottle and collected some of the creature's blood for later examination by a biologist. He spotted a Honda 450 motorcycle parked at the curb outside a pizza shop with the keys still in the ignition. Since most of the roads were destroyed, the dirt bike would allow him to travel cross-country in pursuit of Girra, but first, he had to search for the boy's parents. He slid the shotgun through the leather strap on the seat and cranked the bike.

"Hop on."

The boy's eyes lit up at the prospect of riding a motorcycle.

They crossed fields and farm roads, passing demolished farmhouses and barns. Finally, they came to another flattened structure.

"That's my house," the boy called out, nearly in tears.

"Stay here," Gate warned him. He stopped the bike at the end of the long driveway. He slid off the bike and approached the house slowly, holding the shotgun with both hands.

The house was smashed almost beyond recognition. A metal bedpost protruded from the wreckage, and a broken cuckoo clock lay in the dirt in front of the house. Just as he turned to leave, the door of a tornado cellar opened, and a man climbed out. He stared at Gate with apprehension, but when he saw the boy running down the lane, he cried out and raced toward him.

"Billy!"

A woman, Billy's mother followed him. Gate watched the happy reunion until the man asked, "What happened?"

Gate couldn't find the words to explain fully. "We're under attack. Wicmac has been destroyed, and everybody in it is dead. Your son was very lucky, as were you."

The old man looked around at the ruins of his farm and nodded.

"What will you do now?" Gate asked.

The farmer removed his cap and scratched his head. "Do? Why, I guess we'll rebuild."

Gate admired his resilience. "I mean now."

The farmer nodded his head toward the east, away from the destruction. "Head to my cousin's house, if it's still standing."

"It should be safe. Can I help you?"

"That bike don't look none too safe to me. We'll walk. It's just a few miles across the fields as the crow flies."

Gate hesitated, but he knew there was nothing more he could do for them. "I have to go north."

"You following that thing?"

Gate nodded.

"God help you," the old man said and turned away to tend to his family.

Gate was no hero, nor was he a coward. He was well aware of the danger he faced. He had come very close to death already tonight. He was a catastrophist. He worked with numbers and data. Now, he had witnessed firsthand the results of his calculations. *Perhaps*, he thought, *it's also an act of penitence. This creature sprang from my numbers. I have a responsibility to find a means to stop it.*

Determined, he squeezed the throttle, leaving the farm and the dead town behind him.

ISHOM

11

Friday, August 10, 5:20 p.m. (PDT)   San Francisco, CA
–

Captain Harold Trantham sipped his coffee as the bright white, forty-five foot Coast Guard Response Boat cut through the waters of the Pacific Ocean in the Golden Gate Straits. He grabbed the forward rail with one hand as the boat veered suddenly to avoid something. The sea was calm, but the water was filled with debris from the tsunami. Pieces of demolished houses, automobiles, snapped trees, and people had followed the receding wave back out to sea. Trantham and his three-man crew were searching for survivors.

It had been almost thirty-six hours since the meteor had crashed into the ocean, causing the earthquake and tsunami. So far, they had pulled over fifty bodies from the water, but only a handful of survivors, the last one earlier in the day. His doubt was growing that they would find many more. Between the sharks, the frigid water, and the strong current, no one could survive a day and a half in the bay.

The twin sixteen-hundred-horsepower diesel engines pushed the boat at speeds up to forty-two knots, but now, they were just cruising at fifteen knots through a sea of flotsam, patrolling the waters near the Golden Gate Bridge. He leaned against the .50 caliber machinegun mounted on the foredeck. In his five years as a Coast Guard captain, he had never fired the weapon except for practice, and he hoped he never would. He had joined the Coast Guard to save lives, not fight smugglers or terrorists. Today, he wished he was somewhere else. He was not saving lives. He was a corpse finder.

The coffee helped keep him fresh, but it had been a long day, unseasonably cool. The churning of the deeper cold water by the meteor impact and the sun-warmed surface currents had produced a thick mist. In some areas, it was merely a thin layer hugging the surface. In others, it billowed into strangely sculpted shapes like cloud topiaries of mythical creatures. The sun hovered just above the horizon, painting the water and the mist blood red as it set, taking any heat it had provided with it. In the distance, the center span of the Golden Gate Bridge visible through the mist glinted in the last rays of the dying sun. If not for the grisly reason for their being there, the sunset would have been beautiful. Instead, it reminded him of a sea of blood. Night was quickly falling. Locating bodies in the dark and in the mist would be difficult, especially when so much debris littered the water. It was time to head back in.

As he turned to call out to the helmsman, he noticed a flash of light in the far distance. He decided it had probably come from one of the two Navy cruisers patrolling near the Farallon Islands where the meteor had landed. He didn't think they were there searching for survivors, as they had announced. The islands were uninhabited. They had come for another reason, and that reason worried him. He had heard about the second meteor that had obliterated a city in Indiana and the one that had crashed in the deserts of Nevada. It all seemed too much for coincidence. What was the military hiding from them?

"I'm picking up a mass of debris on radar about two clicks out forty degrees to starboard," the pilot called out.

Trantham sighed and spilled the dregs of his coffee over the side. As much as he was ready to call it a day, they had to investigate as long as there was even a slight chance of survivors.

"Take us there," he said.

He scanned the area indicated with his binoculars but saw nothing but swirling mist. "Are you sure about that reading?"

"It's still on radar." A moment later, the pilot said, "Captain, it's moving toward us at thirty knots."

"Moving?" At thirty knots, it had to be a ship.

He raised his glasses again. Still nothing. He decided that the radar was on the blink, when he caught a slight movement in the distance, a bow wave like the one his boat was raising, but he could see nothing behind the wave that might cause it. Then, he adjusted his binoculars for a wider view. The wave extended across a front over three hundred feet wide. Barely visible behind the wave, he noticed a dark object coming toward them. It was too big for a submarine and had too low a profile for any other kind of vessel he could imagine. As it got nearer, he noticed the spikes rising from the black object, like the masts of a dozen ships. A sudden chill gripped him. The presence of the cruisers became more ominous.

"Get us out of here and contact those Navy cruisers. They might want to see this."

* * * *

Large areas of San Francisco were still without water or power. A few scattered fires still raged in outlying neighborhoods, but most were under control. Emergency shelters had been designated for tens of thousands of survivors displaced by the quake and the tsunami. Despite the severity of the disaster and the enormity of the logistics involved, thirty-six hours later San Francisco was coping.

Leslie DeSalle bandaged another leg, this time a six-year-old girl orphaned by the flood. Leslie was long past feeling anything. Her pool of empathy had dried up hours ago. Now, she cleaned wounds, wrapped bandages, and stitched lacerations like an automaton. The other RNs around her were like her, overworked, overwhelmed, and exhausted. Help was supposed to be pouring in from other cities, but so far, she had seen only a trickle. Of course, the earthquake and tsunami had devastated the entire Bay area, stretching emergency services paper-thin.

She didn't know if her home in Noe Valley still stood. She had been on duty at Saint Luke's Hospital when the quake struck. Saint Francis memorial and Sutter West Bay hospitals downtown had suffered severe damage during the tsunami. Many of their patients had been transferred to Saint Luke's, which resembled a wartime field hospital with bodies lying in hallways, parking garage, and in every waiting room. A triage unit had been set up in the emergency room parking lot, deciding which patients needed medical treatment first. Most of the patients were surprisingly quiet and cooperative, dazed by events beyond their capacity to understand them. A few, especially the children, cried or moaned constantly, creating an undercurrent of background noise that, after several hours, rang like tinnitus in her ears, setting her nerves on edge. She wanted to clap her hands over her ears and run screaming from the ER.

Cheryl Hunt, the RN supervisor, approached her, noticed Leslie's pale complexion, and said, "Take a break, Leslie. You're about to fall over."

Leslie noticed that Cheryl's condition appeared no better. She was an eternal optimist, but the usual sparkle in her eyes had dimmed and her taut face betrayed her anxiety. Leslie nodded. "Thanks, I need some fresh air."

"Go to the roof," Cheryl suggested. "It's too crowded everywhere else."

A few minutes later, she stood on the roof of the twelve-story building. Her hands trembled as she tried to light her cigarette. Instead of fresh, the air was damp and cloying with the sharp smell of smoke from burning buildings. Even over that, the astringent odor of disinfectant clung to her clothes and her hair.

Only a few moving lights broke the twilight falling over the city, mostly emergency vehicles moving through the rubble of the streets. Like Saint Luke's, some buildings had backup generators, creating pools of light like beacons to the survivors. Helicopters patrolled the air above the city searching for survivors, or ferried the injured to hospitals in Oakland and Alameda. She exhaled a cloud of smoke. The nicotine cloud hung before her face, unmoved by any breeze. The occasional crash of masonry as some building collapsed punctuated the sound of jackhammers and backhoes searching the debris for survivors.

The roar of jets overhead startled her. She glanced up to see six jets streaking north just above the city skyline. Suddenly, flashes of light erupted from them and raced toward the water – missiles.

"What the hell?" she muttered. Dropping her cigarette, she leaned on the roof ledge and stared in confusion.

The missiles streaked downward to the mist-covered waterline and exploded. For a brief moment, she saw something dark in the water, barely visible through the mist. Then, as flares began to descend slowly on parachutes from the jets, the object became clearer. At first, it closely resembled a long, black barge. She thought nothing of this. Many ships and barges had come loose from their moorings during the tsunami, but why would the Air Force fire missiles at a barge? As the object neared the shore and rose from the water on six pair of pointed, articulated legs each as wide as a boulevard, it looked like a giant black crab. Fear clamped down on her chest and sent a cold chill rushing through her body. It was something nightmarish, unearthly. She knew immediately that she was seeing something deadly, something connected to the strange meteorite.

The creature rose until it towered over the drowned Embarcadero. The jets continued firing missiles at the creature as it neared the wharves. A Navy cruiser soon joined in, but the explosions did no more than create patterns of light that raced along the creature's ebony back and sides reminding her of an octopus or squid. It crawled from the bay near Union Street, waterfalls of water cascading from its shiny surface. Twin oblong glowing patches on each side of its horrendous face were unblinking eyes scanning the cityscape. It strode into the city like a battering ram, crushing buildings in its wake. It stood taller than Telegraph Hill with the Coit Tower topping it like some kind of phallic symbol.

The creature stepped over or crushed homes and buildings along Broadway and waded into the Financial District with a dozen long strides. When long tentacles attached to the creature's face began destroying buildings, the cephalopod resemblance became even more apt. Terror struck her to her core. He knees grew weak and unable to hold her erect. She fell to a sitting position on the rooftop shaking in rage and fear.

She watched in horror as the creature attacked the fifty-two-story 555 California Street building, home of Bank of America and many of the city's financial corporations. It rammed the building with the front of its hard shell or carapace. Windows not shattered by the earthquake spilled glass onto the ground. She thought of the people trapped inside the building, of the people in the streets below, and wept. She forgot her patients downstairs, dismissed her worries about her home. She was witnessing an event of Biblical proportions, an apocalypse. Her gaze fell upon the cross atop nine-hundred-foot Mount Davidson canted to an angle by the earthquake. She had never been much of a Christian. She had gone to church on religious holidays and for weddings, but never on a regular basis. She had never prayed. She crawled to her knees and folded her hands.

"Help us, Lord, in our hour of need."

She didn't know what else to say. Words failed her. She could have prayed for herself or for the people in the path of the creature, but she knew they were all doomed. God wouldn't answer her prayers. Who was she, a nurse who sinned and didn't attend mass? Perhaps others more in God's favor, priests or nuns, might have better luck, but not her.

The tremendous hammer blows of the creature pushed steel and concrete beyond its endurance. It stood on the three rear pairs of legs, using the front three pair to rake the building like steel claws. Brick and masonry crumbled beneath its savage attack, exposing naked steel beams. With a sound like ice cracking, one side of the building's upper floors slid to the street in a cloud of concrete dust. The hospital roof upon which she sat shuddered and swayed with the incredible impact. Tentacles explored the open cavity, withdrawing with people struggling in their grasp. Other tentacles battered the open wound of the building, yanking aside steel girders, warping them until the weight of the building grew too much for them. The entire structure collapsed in slow motion, the top ten floors becoming a projectile that crashed into nearby buildings. When nothing was left of the skyscraper but a pile of smoking rubble, Ishom moved on to the Transamerica Pyramid.

Her city died around her. The crashing of buildings became its screams, the shuddering of the ground its death throes. She closed her eyes to drive out the hideous scenes of destruction and the explosions and closed her ears to the screams of the dying. She sat for a long time frozen by the horror, unable to run, as the noise grew louder. She knew the creature was getting closer. The hospital began to shudder. The roof swayed and undulated beneath her. Windows shattered on floors below her. Screams rose toward the roof, drowned out by the din of destruction. She dared not look up into the face of evil. A great wind swept over her, as if something large had passed overhead. Then the roof collapsed beneath her.

* * * *

Isaac Studivant sat in his Hotwire office on the sixteenth floor of 333 Market Street in the shadow of the Transamerica Pyramid. His only source of light was the emergency lighting in the hallway and the battery-powered lantern sitting on his desk. Because of the earthquake and tsunami, the power was off throughout most of the city. Earlier in the day, he had carefully threaded his way through the mounds of fallen debris and piles of rubble, the plethora of emergency crews, and the throngs of curious onlookers to try to salvage what he could in his office. He parked on the street since the underground parking garage was flooded. The elevators weren't working, so the long climb up the darkened stairwell had been a chore even for a thirty-year-old who considered himself to be in good shape.

His office, like most of the businesses in the building, was in disarray after the earthquake. His window overlooking Beale Street was gone, along with most of the wall. A warm breeze smelling of rotting fish wafted through the office, blowing his long brown hair over his eyes. The papers he had left on his desk when he left were missing, perhaps joining the confetti from other buildings on the street below. His Tiffany lamps lay smashed on the floor. His artwork had fallen from the walls. A cut-crystal brandy decanter had ripped through his favorite painting, a seascape by local artist Frederick Holtz. The decanter, too, lay smashed and empty on the tile floor. He regretted that even more than the loss of the painting. He could use a drink.

His phone wasn't working, which was just as well. No one was using Hotwire to book rooms in the city. He considered going back home, but his house in Mission Delores had suffered enough damage during the quake to render it uninhabitable. A yellow sign posted by the city warned him to keep out. He had barely escaped the structure with his life. For two days, he had been sleeping in the back of his Acura. He had hoped to sleep on his office sofa, but it had vanished with the missing wall.

He dismissed the first detonations he heard as more of the numerous gas explosions that had been occurring throughout the city from broken gas mains. Fires raged in many neighborhoods. As he stared out his window, he noticed the jets flying low over the Bay. He recognized the streaks of fire from their wings as missiles. Curious, he got up and ambled to the damaged wall. Barely visible even by the dozen parachute flares drifting down over it was a large, black object approaching the piers of the Embarcadero. Farther out in the Bay, somewhere near the darkened Bay Bridge, a Navy ship launched cruise missiles at the object. He had difficulty grasping the significance of the action unfolding before him, but somewhere deep inside he knew it didn't bode well. When the massive ebony object rose from the sea, towering over the dockside warehouses near North Beach, he knew he had a problem.

The gargantuan creature, for creature it had to be, strode ashore on twelve massive legs like an alien spider. It stood for a moment, taller than Telegraph Hill, unheeding of the explosions around it, as if searching for prey. Colorful lights raced down its flanks with each explosion. If fear had not paralyzed him, he might have found the display beautiful. When the creature began wading through buildings as if they weren't there and moved in the direction of the Financial District, he knew it was time to leave.

He took the stairs at a breakneck pace, not stopping until he was on the street. By that time, the creature had smashed through the neighborhoods east of Telegraph Hill and destroyed the eastern outskirts of Chinatown. The military didn't stop its assault in spite of the civilian population. Jets continued pouring machinegun fire and raining missiles onto the creature's back. Houses exploded from misfired missiles. People on the street, already affected by the earthquake and tsunami, stared at the creature dumbfounded, as if unable to comprehend its presence.

Isaac saw a lone policewoman pointing her revolver in the creature's direction. Her hands shook so badly that Isaac doubted she could hit it if it were right on top of her.

"Run, fool," he yelled at the officer.

She stared at him for a moment, and then nodded. She re-holstered her revolver and walked back to her squad car, which was blocking Isaac's Acura. As she sat down and called in her report, Isaac debated waiting until she moved or abandoning his car and running on foot. He quickly dismissed any thoughts of running when he saw the length of the creature's monstrous strides. It had already reached Maritime Park. It attacked the twenty-five story One Maritime Plaza building with its front legs, pawing at the structure like a dog begging at the door to go outside. Within minutes, the building lay in ruins at the creature's feet.

"Let's get out of here," he suggested to the officer, as he opened the passenger-side door of the squad car and slid in beside her.

"What is it?" she asked. Her face was a mask of terror. Her hands trembled on the steering wheel. He wasn't sure that she was capable of driving.

He glanced at her badge. "A creature from the pits of hell, Officer Daley," he replied.

She nodded and cranked the car.

By the time they reached the end of the block, racing the wrong way down Market Street, the monster had waded into the massed high-rise towers of the Northern Financial Center. Without stopping, it smashed into buildings with its massive body, turning them into piles of rubble. As buildings fell, they crashed into surrounding buildings, toppling them like dominoes. It raised its upper body on its rear set of legs and used its front legs to pierce the sides of the 555 California building. The pointed legs raked down the sides, pulling down walls and steel beams. Weakened floors collapsed onto the floors below. Suddenly, the entire building pancaked upon itself, leaving a five-story-high pile of smoking rubble. Clouds of concrete dust raced down the corridors of streets between buildings. The scene reminded him of the collapse of the twin Towers in New York. He wondered if people had been in the building, searching the wreckage as he had been.

As if drawn by instinct, the creature focused on the tallest building in the city, the Transamerica Pyramid. By now, he had associated the strange, alien monster with the meteor that had barely missed the city, Ishom. Its massive hulk rose above the police car like an ominous dark cloud. Isaac waited for one of the legs to smash into the patrol car, ending their escape. Ishom smashed into the side of the Pyramid like a battering ram. The top of the tower swayed, as a shower of debris fell into the streets. Daley swerved the car wildly to miss chunks of masonry and falling debris. Isaac held his breath, expecting to be smashed into a pancake at any moment.

He watched in awe, as one of the creature's legs speared a delivery truck, hoisted it into the air, and flung it aside. The truck crashed into the tenth floor of a nearby building, balancing precariously half in and half out of the building. The black tentacles slithered serpentine into the openings created by the creature, withdrawing various objects and a few people wriggling it its grasp. Until now, the creature had seemed almost an automaton, a faceless berserker machine, but when a vertical slit opened in the creature's head, revealing rows of razor-sharp teeth, it became even more terrible to behold. The tentacles dropped its struggling human cargo into the mouth. As the mouth closed and the teeth began moving, he turned away sickened to his stomach.

He had watched horror movies and enjoyed the thrill, laughing at the most horrid scenes. He knew the terror wasn't real. Now, the horror seemed surreal, as if it was too much for the human mind to absorb. The deaths from the earthquake and the tsunami had not touched him personally. He had been more concerned for his own home and his business. Seeing fellow human beings become nothing more than morsels of food for a gigantic alien monster caused a visceral reaction, a fear handed down from ancient ancestors in his DNA. He wanted to flee, gibbering into the night. He fought this instinct and tried to think logically. If Ishom was intent on destroying the Financial District first, they had to head south or east to the Bay.

"Head south," he told Officer Daley."

To her credit, she didn't question his decision. She turned south at Beale Street. Fire trucks and police cars lined the streets, rescuing people still trapped days later beneath tons of rubble from the earthquake. He noticed their attention focused on the devastation behind him rather than the rescue, but they didn't halt their work. As he glanced through the side mirror, the top fifteen floors of the Transamerica Pyramid fell to one side, crushing 333 Market Street as it collapsed. As it had with other buildings, the creature reared its front half on the side of the building and used its massive legs to rip into the building, tearing away walls and ripping out structure support beams as easily as one might gut an animal.

As if a three-hundred-foot long monster were not enough, to his horror, the creature disgorged a horde of flying creatures from holes in its sides. They swarmed over the city, almost invisible in the twilight. He watched as one of the nine-foot-long creatures swooped down and snatched a firefighter from a ladder, gripping him in its legs. The hundreds of the flying monsters crashed through windows and prowled streets and alleys in search of prey.

He was so intent on keeping track of the creatures that he slammed into the dash when Daley stopped the car suddenly to avoid a truck blocking the street.

"Back up," he yelled, as he rubbed his bruised shoulder. He fastened his seat belt to avoid further injury.

Before she could put the car in reverse, one of the flying creatures landed on the roof. It bucked under the weight. She pulled her weapon and emptied it through the roof and into the creature. The creature stopped moving. She glanced at Isaac with relief, and then uttered a muted gurgle, as a long, wasp-like stinger ripped through the metal roof and impaled her through the chest. Her lips trembled as she stared at him, imploring him to help, but he was too stunned to react. She was dead before the stinger withdrew. The driver's door flew from the car, ripped off by the creature. It plucked Officer Daley cop into its embrace and flew away with her.

Isaac abandoned the car, but grabbed the pump shotgun hanging from the rack behind him. He wasn't sure if he could fire it, but the weight of it in his hands made him feel safer. He ran for an open doorway, looking for escape from the flying creatures. He knew he had to head south to stay out of the black monsters path, but the presence of the flying creatures made that impossible. Just as he reached the building's revolving door, one of the creatures landed on the sidewalk a dozen feet from him. He stared at it, as he pumped a shell into the chamber and fired. To his dismay, the pellets simply bounced off the creature's hard black shell. As it reared to attack, it exposed its abdomen and throat. In a blind rage, he fired two more blasts without bothering to take aim. One of the shots pierced the skin between plates of ebony armor. The creature gushed a foul-smelling yellow liquid onto the sidewalk and backed away. Emboldened by his minor victory, he walked toward the wounded creature, firing creature until the gun was empty. It emitted a high-pitched shrill and collapsed on the sidewalk.

Above him, two military helicopters braved the narrow canyon of skyscrapers. Their machineguns ripped into the flock of flying creatures. Several fell dead from the sky. The gunner continued to pump out bullets, many of which struck the surrounding buildings and streets. When chips of asphalt began flying around him, Isaac realized that the gunner couldn't see him or else considered him collateral damage. He covered his head with his arms and fell to his knees until the helicopter passed overhead.

He tossed his useless weapon aside and began running away from the mass of flying creatures and the helicopters. Three of the flying creatures attacked one of the helicopters, throwing their bodies into the rotors. One of the blades sheared away, impaling the asphalt just yards from Isaac. The chopper spun wildly out of control and crashed into the side of a building. It burst into flames. Burning fuel dripped onto the sidewalk and created a stream of fire. Isaac covered his eyes and leapt through the flames. The heat singed his arms but didn't engulf him, as he feared. Now, he had only one direction to run – East. He didn't stop until he reached the Embarcadero Ferry.

Too exhausted to go any farther, he collapsed on the street and watched as the black behemoth methodically destroyed every building it encountered. Around him, scores of people sat or stood, becoming spectators to the destruction of San Francisco. They were either unaware of or too stunned to run from the flying creatures filling the night sky. He remained where he was just long enough to catch his breath, and then continued to the pier. His only escape lay to the sea. He hoped to find some boat moored along the docks, but found nothing. Boats not destroyed by the tsunami were busy ferrying the wounded and homeless across the Bay to Oakland.

A harried ferry employee fought away people struggling to get aboard an already overcrowded ferry. Some had wads of cash thrust out toward him, seeking to buy their passage with their life savings. He ignored them, as he shoved the crowd back from the ferry.

"We're too full," he yelled over the din. "We can't take any more passengers or we'll sink."

The frightened crowd wouldn't listen to him. Even as the ferry pulled away from the dock, people leapt to reach it. Some made it, but many more fell into the water, swept under the ferry by the undertow of the engines. The ferry foolishly had all its lights blazing. Isaac didn't know light attracted the flying creatures, but it certainly illuminated the people crowding the decks. He decided to leave the dock before the creatures came.

He found an overturned yacht carried ashore by the tsunami and crawled inside through the open hatch. Through a porthole, he watched the ferry leave. Before it had managed two hundred yards from shore, the flying creatures found it. He listened to the screams, as the creatures swooped down on the ferry like seagulls following the wake of a fishing boat. Silhouetted by the lights, he watched the creatures tear into the crowd, ripping and slicing bodies with their mandibles, and impaling them with their stingers. The carnage took less than half an hour. The ferry, its lights still blazing, drifted silently on the dark, blood-soaked waters.

He waited for the creatures to find him, but they never came. Exhausted, he curled up in a ball on the canted bulkhead, closed his eyes, and tried to sleep. Throughout the night, the sound of crashing buildings and explosions jarred him awake from his fitful, nightmare-filled naps. By dawn, the sounds of destruction had receded farther south, as Ishom marched down the peninsula in its march of destruction. He crawled from his refuge and stared toward downtown San Francisco. It no longer existed. The city had once boasted a beautiful array of both modern and classical-façade high-rise buildings. Now, only piles of smoking rubble remained. He had seen ancient *tels* on a trip to Israel, mounds of earth that looked like small mountains but contained the ruins of ancient cities built layer upon layer on the bones of older cities. San Francisco resembled a *tel*.

The silence was almost as frightening as the sounds of destruction had been. The stench of concrete dust, smoke, and rotting flesh permeated the still dawn air, an odor that would haunt him for the rest of his life. He looked to the south and saw more smoke rising. The creature was working its way along the peninsula and toward Oakland. He hoped they had time to evacuate the city. Ishom seemed in no hurry in its grisly, almost as if it realized that nothing the puny human military did could harm it.

Isaac realized that he had nowhere to go. His home was destroyed, and his office no longer existed. Even his car was gone. He was a homeless person, a refugee in a city of thousands. He didn't know if he could access his money. Certainly, none of the local ATMs still functioned, and he had less than a hundred dollars in his wallet. Instead of anxiety he thought he should be experiencing, he felt free. He had survived. He felt the urge to sit on the beach and feel the sun on his body, but not the beaches on the Bay side. With the sun at his back, he faced the Pacific coast and began walking west.

NUSKU

12

Friday, August 10, 5:50 p.m. (PDT) Creech AFB, Indian Springs, Nevada –

At almost the same moment Colonel David Starnes received word that Girra was emerging from the crater in Indiana, Nusku crawled from its crater north of the base. He fought his revulsion at the first glimpse of the jet-black monster stalking the landscape on its dozen angular legs. His gut told him that he was looking at a new enemy, not a visitor from the stars. When the creature began moving south toward Las Vegas, he didn't wait for orders from the Pentagon.

He turned to his aid. "Launch ten MQ-9s."

The Predator B drones were armed with an array of weapons, including GBU-12 laser guided bombs, AGM-114 Hellfire II missiles, and AIM-9 Sidewinder missiles. He was certain he could stop the creature in its tracks. He chewed on the stub of his cigar and drummed his fingers on the console in front of him, as the drones winged their way to their target. He cracked a wide grin when they struck the creature. When the smoke cleared, he saw to his dismay that the weapons had little effect. He needed something bigger.

"Arm a second wave with AGM-130 missiles armed with BLU-109s. Launch everything we've got."

His aid stared at him. "Bunker Busters?"

"Why not? They can penetrate six feet of concrete. If they can't bring that creature down, nothing can. I'm not going to screw around this time."

Starnes had faith in the Bunker Busters that had proved so effective in the Iraq War. If he had access to the much more powerful BLU-113s with twenty feet of penetration, he would have been even happier. He waited impatiently as the twenty-six Predators were rearmed and launched. As they winged their way to their targets, his eyes burned from staring at the screen at the front of the room. Kids hardly older than his teen-aged son manned the controls of the deadly unmanned aircraft. To them, it was a video game. To him, it was a new way to fight a war.

Suddenly, the air around the creature swarmed with hundreds of flying creatures emerging from holes in Nusku's sides.

"What the hell?"

His aid answered. "They're called Wasps, Sir. At least that's what they named them when they appeared from Girra."

"Wasps?"

His aid shrugged. "Because they fly and they have stingers."

This time, as the drones swept toward their target, the flying creatures intercepted them, flying directly into the paths of the Predators. He watched six disappear from the screen. He was quickly losing his weapons.

"Fire all missiles now."

The AGM-130 missiles arced toward the creature too swiftly for the Wasps to intercept. They struck but produced no damage.

"God damn it!" he yelled. "Send in the Bunker Busters."

The GPS guided BLU-109s struck within inches of their designated targets. After the smoke of the explosions cleared, Nusku was still standing, in fact continuing on its way as if nothing had happened. Colonel Starnes was stunned.

"What the hell is that thing?" he demanded from anyone in the room. They all stared at him. His face hardened. "Let's see if it can withstand a nuke."

"Sir," his aid reminded him, "We need Presidential authorization for a nuclear strike."

Starnes waved his hand in irritation. "Yes, yes, I know. While we're sitting with our thumbs up our ass, that thing is getting closer to Las Vegas. You heard what the first one is doing in Indiana, didn't you? Go. Contact NORAD. They can get approval from the President. Let's blast that fucker to bits."

He turned back to the screen. The swarm of Wasps hovering around the creature formed a dense protective shield. No more drones were going to get through.

"Recall the drones," he snapped. Each six-million dollar drone cost over three-thousand dollars per flight hour. If he couldn't save the country, he could at least save money.

* * * *

Friday, August 10,   2:15 a.m. (CDT)   *Mare Moscoviense,* Moon –

Twelve hours had passed since landing on the moon. Their second journey to and from the teardrop had been exhausting and as frustrating as the first. This time, Langston had not touched the object, yet it still drew his mind as if a magnet. He ordered Crenshaw to eat and rest, though they were both eager to renew their examination of the crashed alien object. His reasoning was that tired people made mistakes, and they couldn't afford one. Too much was at stake. Neither of them had eaten much. Crenshaw managed a couple of hours sleep, but bad dreams, nightmares, troubled Langston's fitful rest. The horrific images evaporated whenever he tried to focus on them, but they left impressions that frightened him.

He knew something terrible was happening on Earth, though they had no communications since the crash. Ishom, Girra, and Nusku were not simple meteors, of that he was certain. They posed a much larger threat than impact destruction. Dark notions of death and destruction flooded his mind as viewed from a non-human source. The thoughts surrounding the images were strange, convoluted. There was a pattern to the destruction that he could not see. The imagery was too alien, too diffuse. Either this was all true, or he was crazy and imagining everything. The latter seemed more appealing.

When he had touched the teardrop, even with his gloved hand, he had sensed a presence inside the structure. It had flowed into him like a shock of static electricity. The teardrop was more than a simple conveyance. It was some kind of way station, a

86

clearinghouse for data between the objects and their alien owners. He believed it was the key to the problem. He resisted the idea of confronting once again the structure for a third time, but it drew him like a beacon.

First, he contacted *Lunar One* still orbiting the moon, some nineteen kilometers above them.

"*Armstrong* to *Lunar One*."

Mahall answered quickly, eager to hear his voice. "This is *Lunar One*."

"What's your situation?" he asked.

"We've dropped another kilometer in the last six hours. Our last orbit will occur in thirty-six hours."

The numbers were a blow to his stomach. That was two hours fewer than their original estimate. Sixty-six hours was pushing it. No one could reach them in time.

"To what do you attribute the change of orbital status?"

"That ... thing," she almost yelled into the microphone. He could feel her distress and impotence to do anything across the space between them. "That alien thing is drawing us down."

"That's impossible," he replied, though he wasn't certain it was.

"Each orbit over that thing, I can feel the ship shudder, as if it's reaching out to grab us."

"Calm down, Mahall. You're imagining things. Check your oxygen pressure."

"We reduced oxygen levels to conserve what little remains, but I'm not suffering from oxygen deprivation. That thing is drawing us down."

Langston was dismayed by the apparent change in Mahall's attitude. At first, she had viewed the alien objects almost reverently, a chance to communicate with an alien species. Now, she showed apprehension.

"How is Ingersall?"

"He's helping me with the comm repairs. We had to replace all the wiring between the antenna and the computer. We had to strip wiring from the service module, but we're almost done. Maybe two hours."

He didn't remind her that had been her estimate seventeen hours earlier. "Increase oxygen levels and keep me informed of any more changes. Langston out."

He didn't say, but they all knew, that if their orbit was dropping, they would have more than enough oxygen to last until impact, despite the ruptured tank. There was no reason to conserve it.

"Mahall out."

"Is she crazy? That thing can't be pulling the ship down. It's impossible."

Langston turned to Crenshaw. "No, she's not crazy. She's frightened, and she's exhausted. I am too. Whatever the reason, we have less time than we thought."

"Maybe she's starting to think God isn't out there where those things came from." She paused. "But the decaying orbit is caused by something," she suggested, and then glanced away as if embarrassed. "I ... felt something out there when we were near the teardrop."

His senses tingled. "Oh?"

"It's not benign. It's alive somehow."

That she had mirrored his thoughts so well disturbed him more than the idea that he had been imagining everything.

"Let's stick to the facts, shall we? Get suited up. It's time to make more observations."

She swallowed hard and nodded, though her face revealed her concern.

During the trek to the alien object, Langston reviewed what they knew, and it was very little. They had no tools powerful enough to penetrate the surface, no instruments capable of providing a scan of the interior or intercepting any signals that the object might be emitting. He had experienced no increase in gravity near the object, so its mass was not affecting *Lunar One*'s orbit, but he feared Mahall might be right.

This time, they had brought more equipment from the lander with which to take measurements of the object. They dragged their possessions along behind them in a four-wheeled lunar buggy like a couple of homeless people. They had also brought shielding laboriously removed from the lander cradle to construct a bridge across the chasm.

The teardrop was a shadow puppet cast by an invisible hand. It lay across the surface of the moon like an ancient artifact, a totem of a forgotten race, or a fragment of an abandoned temple. Its presence filled him with dread, as if it would reach out and yank his soul from his body, if he truly had a soul. He had doubts. Maybe Mahall felt it too. With her deeply religious background, such a confrontation with evil would frighten her, challenge her beliefs.

The teardrop swallowed the meager light of the faraway sun as if a rift in space. *Not that far away,* he thought. *The sun is actually closer at this moment than if I were on Earth.* The objects edges were blurred and indistinct, creating an optical illusion that seemed to make it undulate like a heat mirage. He tore his eyes from the object to help Crenshaw set up a video recorder, a wide-spectrum electro-magnetic detector, and a sound detector. Sound could not travel through a vacuum, but sensors in the soil would pick up any vibrations coming from it.

After setting up the equipment, he circled the object, studying its outlines. The *bas relief* designs carved into its surface could have been either art or structural. If art, they resembled nothing he had ever seen. If structural, he could see no purpose for them. His gaze followed the convoluted lines until he became dizzy. He held his hand above the ebony surface. A spark jumped between the object and his glove. For an instant, he saw a great lumbering multi-legged creature crossing a vast rocky plain beneath a dark purple sky mottled with crimson clouds. Then, it was gone.

"Are you okay?" Crenshaw asked.

He nodded, but then realized she couldn't see him nod in the bulky spacesuit. "Yes."

Crenshaw held an electronic notepad in her hand, glancing down at it and then up at the teardrop. "The temperature of the object hasn't changed, even though the ambient temperature is over a hundred-degrees centigrade. It seems to be absorbing the sunlight without heating."

This piqued Langston's interest. "How is that possible?"

"I have no idea."

Langston stared at the object. Were the shadows deeper along the sides? He squinted for a closer look. The ground vibrated and the teardrop moved.

"Did you feel that?" he asked.

"Yes. It dropped another two meters. The buried end is raising a mound of soil."

The thought produced a shudder in Langston. There was no appreciable seismic activity on the moon. It was as if the teardrop was deliberately trying to free itself. If it did, what would happen?

"It's trying to pull free," he said.

"Or maybe its position is simply shifting in the lunar soil."

Crenshaw's suggestion made more sense than his far-fetched idea, but he knew he was right. "I think it's shifting to re-establish contact with the Girra objects."

"This is all just speculation," she replied. "We have no proof of any of this."

"You felt it, just as I did. It's trying to communicate with us, or we're intercepting some of its messages. I'm positive it's communicating with the three objects it accompanied to Earth, controlling them. If we could stop it somehow ..."

He left the thought unfinished. They had no way to interfere with gravitons or to damage the object. They were casual observers to the destruction of their home planet.

"As you said, we're just speculating," he admitted.

As he saw it, they were long on theories but short on facts. He was certain that he was right about its function as a relay station, but with no way to prove it or even test his theory, there was little they could do but observe.

The ground trembled again, causing a rockslide. Boulders the size of small cars careened down the steep slope, slamming into the teardrop.

"It's getting dangerous around here," Crenshaw said.

"We'll leave the instruments. Maybe they will discover something."

As they hurried back up the crater's rim, Langston glanced back over his shoulder at the towering peaks balanced so delicately above the teardrop. If the object was trying to dig itself out...

"How much does the Orion mass?" he asked.

"About twenty-five tons. Why? Are you calculating the effect the object might have on *Lunar One*?"

"No, I'm wondering what effect *Lunar One* might have on it."

Crenshaw turned to face him. He couldn't make out her expression through her darkened faceplate, but there was no disguising the dread in her voice. "You're not thinking what I think you're thinking."

"*Lunar One* has less than thirty-six hours to live. I see little chance for rescue by that time."

"But you're suggesting we all become martyrs even if we have no clue if we might make a difference."

"I don't want any martyrs. We'll return to *Lunar One* and wait as long as we can for rescue. Then, you, Mahall, and Ingersall will take the lander, all the remaining oxygen, establish a stable orbit, and wait for rescue. I'll plot a course that will plunge the Orion into the crater as close to the teardrop as I can. It should produce a large enough explosion to cause a massive landslide and cover the teardrop with thousands of tons of rock."

"If you think it will work, we should do it now. The teardrop might break free before then. I'll come with you. That will give Mahall and Ingersall more oxygen and more time."

Langston braced himself, as he skidded down the outside slope of the crater, leaving a cloud of dust that hung suspended in the air but did not blow away. "No. No one dies until all hope of rescue is gone. Then, it will be me. I'm the captain, and the captain always goes down with his ship."

"I know you were in the Navy, but you were a pilot, not a ship's captain."

"I am now, and this is an order, Crenshaw."

"Yes, Sir."

She snapped a crisp salute with her gloved hand, but he could hear the anger in her voice. He understood her willingness to sacrifice herself against an enemy of Earth, but crashing the Orion was a one-man job – his job. The others had no guarantee of rescue. In the end, his might be the kindest death.

GIRRA

13

Saturday, August 11, 12:35 a.m. (CDT)   Hammond, Indiana –

General Elliot McCabe lowered his night vision goggles and wiped his perspiring forehead. He had seen enough. For four hours, wave after wave of jet fighters and attack helicopters had mounted an unprecedented assault on the Girra creature and its host of flying creatures. The winged creatures had thrown themselves into jet engines and into the rotors of helicopters to bring them down. Scores had died, but more of the creatures took their places, pouring from the blisters dotting Girra's serrated segments. McCabe wondered if the creature was hollow, a kind of mobile aircraft carrier. The jet aircraft had been forced to land to refuel and rearm, but Girra's march continued unabated.

Now, it was his turn.

An entire armored division waited just outside Hammond, Indiana for Girra. If Girra could not be stopped that night, almost ten million people in the metropolitan Chicago area would be at risk. The city was under evacuation, but he knew that only a few hundred thousand would ever make it out in time. The expressways were jammed with automobiles and traffic was at a standstill. The elevated trains were being swamped at each station by mobs of frightened passengers. The airports had been reopened, but re-routing planes into the area took time, time they did not have.

A ring of steel open at the end facing the approaching creature surrounded the city of Hammond, Indiana. The steel was the Third Armored Division, comprised of four battalions of 150 M1 Abrams tanks capable of firing conventional rounds and Excalibur rockets, 60 Bradley fighting vehicles, and 3,000 men armed with machineguns, mortars, and shoulder launched Serpent rockets. In addition, 115 M114 and M198-155 mm howitzers augmented the armor. McCabe believed it more than enough firepower to meet Girra's challenge. Once Girra was destroyed, the military could concentrate on Nusku in the Nevada desert and Ishom in San Francisco. He shook his head in wonder at whoever had named these creatures.

"Sounds like a Saturday morning Japanese anime cartoon show," he commented aloud.

"What, sir?" his aid, Major Frank Wojohowitz asked.

"Nothing, Frank, just musing."

McCabe had not witnessed first-hand, but had heard of the creature's cannibalistic feeding frenzy. When not involved in battle, the flying units tracked down and delivered hapless civilians to supply the creature's incessant feeding. Most of the aircraft had been lost in attempts to keep the creatures engaged to keep them from attacking citizens. While one part of him understood the concept of a weaponized monster that fed on the enemy, it was *his* people dying, *his* people feeding the creature. It had to be stopped.

"Tell the artillery batteries to commence firing when the creature is within range."

While Wojohowitz dutifully relayed his order, McCabe did a rapid mental calculation of the amount of explosives he was about to deliver to the creature. The Abrams fired 105 mm shells, each delivering 4.8 pounds of high explosive *amatol* to their target. In an hour, they could rain down almost 30,000 pounds of explosives. The 155mm howitzers were heavier, delivering 15 pounds of TNT to the target. In an hour, they could fire 69,000 pounds of high explosives. That was almost fifty tons of destructive force, not counting the smaller firepower of the mortars, Serpent rockets, and LAWS rockets. He was confident that nothing on Earth, from the heavens, or from hell itself could stand up under that kind of withering firepower.

"Almost within range, sir," Wojohowitz reported.

McCabe nodded. His throat tightened as it always did before a big battle. It wasn't fear. He had seen action in Kuwait, Iraq, and Afghanistan. It was apprehension. So much could go wrong. The Bradley armored vehicles were positioned to keep the flying creatures occupied, but what if the creature had not yet shown its full power? The fate of Chicago, perhaps the country, depended on the next hour's fight.

Through his binoculars, he saw the swarm of flying creatures, Wasps someone had aptly named them, moving ahead of Girra. There were hundreds of them, like an alien air force. The stillness of the night erupted with the thunder of the 155 mm howitzers firing from a distance of five miles. Even at that distance, their shells could penetrate almost two inches of concrete. He had confidence in his men, his equipment, and in God. Let the battle commence.

The Wasps moved swiftly and were among the defenders before the first shells struck Girra. The staccato bursts of nearby machineguns and anti-aircraft weapons interspersed with the screams of the dying. Lines of tracers arced through the air, crossed by the fiery tails of LAWS and Serpent rockets. Many scores of the Wasps died, but not enough. They fell into the masses of soldiers like demons, rending flesh and stabbing with their stingers. Men screamed, as Wasps wrenched them from the ground and conveyed toward a horrible death.

The flashes of huge explosions illuminated Girra's massive bulk, as it lumbered toward them. The slow moving target seemed oblivious to the barrage of artillery and tank fire. Flares dropped around it, illuminating it for the artillery spotters. Its ebony body absorbed the light of the flares, reflecting nothing. It was as if the creature were a moving shadow, a Girra-sized hole into nothingness, visible only as a jagged silhouette against the setting moon and flashes of explosions.

"Nothing affects it," Wojohowitz said. "It's like we're throwing water balloons at it."

"It has to have a weakness," McCabe replied, but he, too, was exasperated by the lack of success. He had watched men and armor wither under such bombardments, while feeling sorry for the enemy on the receiving end. He hated this enemy as no man could hate another human being. It was like hating a hurricane or a tornado, and he was as helpless as he would in raising a fist against a force of nature.

The slow but relentless movement of the creature brought it into the midst of the first squadrons of tanks. He watched one of his Abrams explode as an artillery shell struck it. Either he had to move the tanks back or …

"Order the artillery to cease fire."

Wojohowitz stared at his superior officer aghast. "But, sir, they're our most effective weapon."

He glared at Wojohowitz. "They're doing nothing. Let the tanks worry it for a while. They're more mobile. We have to see what the creature is capable of."

"You're sacrificing your tanks?"

McCabe watched another tank explode. "It's either the tanks or Chicago. Which would you sacrifice? Hammond is lost. We have to buy Chicago more time. Now, order the artillery to cease fire and move them back closer to the city."

Wojohowitz swallowed hard. "Yes, sir."

McCabe knew how his aide felt. It was his men he was sacrificing, not hunks of metal. He knew them, had trained with him. They trusted him, and he was betraying them. Even if they could forgive him, he could never forgive himself.

* * * *

Saturday, August 11 1:30 a.m. (CDT) Chicago, Illinois –

Hammond, Indiana, was no more. Gate had watched the great battle between alien and man's machines from a distance of three miles. The thundering roar of artillery and tanks accompanied the brilliant flashes of light raining down tons of explosive firepower on the Girra, all to no avail. Its seemingly indestructible ebony armor resisted even the largest explosions. Its slow pace remained unfaltering. As he had witnessed in Wicmac, the Wasps swept down among the defenders like avenging angels, killing and rending flesh, transporting immobilized victims to Girra. Girra's great bulk trampled man and machine before they could be withdrawn to a safe distance. It had been a valiant effort but one doomed to failure.

He had followed in the creature's wake, seeing firsthand the dead and dying, the stunned survivors, and the wanton destruction. It was as if a hundred F5 tornadoes had ravaged the landscape. Buildings were crushed and forests twisted and splintered. Roads and bridges smashed, power lines downed, railroad tracks bent and curled under the creature's enormous weight. If the aliens' intentions were to crush Earth's cities flat, lay waste to the countryside, and route its inhabitants, they were succeeding. He held out little hope for Chicago.

Just north of Hammond, he traded his motorcycle for an abandoned four-wheel-drive Jeep. He stopped long enough to siphon gasoline from another vehicle and place a call to Director Caruthers in Houston from his now working cell phone. As he expected, the news wasn't good.

"Ishom contained one of the creatures. So did Nusku. San Francisco has been completely destroyed. Nusku is closing in on Las Vegas," Caruthers said without preamble. "The military managed to evacuate most of Vegas' population."

"San Francisco?"

"Ishom attacked after sunset. No one was prepared. I'm afraid the loss of life was very heavy. After destroying San Francisco, the creature marched down the peninsula and then turned north to Oakland. They managed to evacuate a large part of its population in time. We don't know where the creature will head next."

Gate had feared as much. The attacks had been well coordinated. He was certain the aliens had a master plan of some kind. If only, he could figure it out.

"Have we heard anything from *Lunar One*?"

Caruthers was silent for a moment. "Nothing at all. We're trying to pick them up on a telescope. Gate, maybe you had better get out of there. I can arrange transportation. Come back to Houston where you can do more good."

"I appreciate your concern, but I've got to see this through. As soon as I've learned all I can, I'll return to Houston."

"Well, stay safe, if you can."

He hung up before he accepted Caruthers' offer. He was tired and hungry, his ribs ached, and he had seen death up close and personal for the first time in his life. It wouldn't take much coaxing to sway him, but he had to see the thing through. He chose a farm road that had survived Girra's march north. He met few people fleeing south. Most abandoning the Chicago area were moving north or west. Those who could commandeered anything that could float and sailed out onto Lake Michigan to wait out Girra's rampage. As he drove north, the distant sound of explosions reached him, jets making more futile attacks on Girra and its host of Wasps. The waste of lives sickened him. The military had the bit between its teeth and refused to abandon the attack in spite of the lack of progress thus far. Traditional weaponry wouldn't stop the creature.

Nukes might. He knew the use of nuclear weapons would be a last resort, possibly causing as much damage as the creature itself, but the military was rapidly running out of options. Ishom, Girra, and Nusku could slowly and methodically destroy every large city in America, wrecking the country's infrastructure and economy. While the behemoths were highly effective, he doubted the aliens would restrict an attack to only three of the creatures. More alien craft were probably already on their way to Earth, each containing one of the creatures or something worse. The military had to deal a crushing blow soon, something to give the aliens pause to rethink their strategy.

Girra continued its wake of destruction north closely following I-90/94, eliminating the Interstate as a route of evacuation. In the southern suburbs of metro-Chicago, the creature trampled homes and businesses, while the Wasps, unseen in the darkness until too late, plagued the mobs of people along the roads still trying to evacuate. Thousands went to feed the creature's hunger. China Town, nested in the crook of I-55 and I-90/94, quickly became a blazing inferno. Fires sprang up everywhere the creature passed, spreading north and west on the southerly winds. The conflagration soon became the largest fire since the great O'Leary's cow disaster of 1871. The wall of flame moved more swiftly than the fleeing humans. The Wasps darted just ahead of the flames, plucking people from the edges of the conflagration like birds snatching insects ahead of a forest fire.

From a relatively safe position atop a switching tower in the railroad marshalling yard along the Chicago River, Gate watched Girra enter the Loop area, heart of America's banking and retail centers. In the pre-dawn darkness, backlit by the flames of the burning city, the ebony creature's berserker rampage resembled a scene from hell. Through the shroud of smoke draped over the city, he witnessed destruction on a scale not seen since the bombings of Dresden and Berlin in WWII. Girra simply trampled smaller buildings beneath its massive spike-like legs, as if dancing an alien jig. Schools, museums, churches, banks – all suddenly ceased to exist. At the fourteen-hundred-foot-tall Willis Tower, the creature presented a new tactic. It used its tremendous mass to its advantage, butting the base of the structure like a battering ram until the tower began to collapse. The upper thirty floors toppled over onto the adjoining buildings, crushing them beneath its weight. Then Girra deployed its writhing nest of tentacles, using them to lever chunks of masonry from the standing rubble, methodically dismantling the building. Its attack was thorough, destroying each building before moving on to the next.

The creature shrugged off the fighter jets and helicopters harrying it as if they were annoying mosquitoes. All the while, the Wasps dipped into buildings and amid the piles of rubble, snatching up terrified survivors. More horrible than this scene of destruction, Gate watched helplessly as Girra's forward legs derailed an El-train, one of the last trying to evacuate the city. The train and its dozen cars full of people plunged off the collapsing elevated tracks. The cars piled atop of one another and burst into flames. The creature's tentacles reached into the shattered cars, plucking people from the flames and delivering them to its yawning mouth. Thankfully, he couldn't hear their screams amid the clamor of destruction.

When Girra had completed its methodic destruction of the Loop area, it concentrated on the parade of Magnificent Mile skyscrapers along Michigan Avenue. The Tribune Tower went first, followed by the Wrigley Building, Trump Tower, and the John Hancock Center. As before, the tentacles came into play, telescoping to their full length and rooting through the debris like snakes pursuing rats. Clouds of concrete dust billowed through the streets, choking the life from any survivors the creature missed.

He watched riveted for three hours. That was how long it took Girra to devastate the city completely, reducing Chicago and its environs to untidy rows of smoking rubbish that had once been neighborhoods. Then, leaving only the rubble-strewn corpse of a city behind, the creature turned west, following I-290 out of the city. Gate watched it disappear into the distance, the heavy rumble of its passing slowly fading, only to be replaced by the steady collapsing of unstable buildings and the explosions of fire-ravaged buildings left in its wake. He had learned nothing useful that might help defeat the creatures, but he had learned one thing. Their enemy was determined and significantly more advanced than humans were. The aliens could sit back, seed the planet with deadly ebony seeds, and watch Earth's devastation with glee, risking nothing but brutish, unthinking monsters. Unless someone came up with an effective defense, or a potent offense, Earth was doomed.

With fingers numb from the constant clenching of his fists in rage and anger, he punched in Caruthers' number on his cell phone. The Director answered immediately.

"Gate, where the hell are you?" he shouted into the phone.

"Chicago."

"Chi … are you crazy?"

"Not any more. I've seen enough. Can you arrange transportation back to Houston?"

"Certainly, but you might want to go to Nevada instead."

Curious that Caruthers would suggest another trip, he asked, "Why?"

"They're going to nuke Nusku. You might want to watch."

The prospect of seeing one of the alien creatures destroyed by one of man's deadliest weapons appealed to him in a dark way. His morbid scientific curiosity was satisfied. Now, he wanted to see the aliens suffer in whatever manner humankind could employ. He needed to see the aliens suffer to ease his own anguish and regain his sanity.

"Yes," he hissed. "I would very much like that."

"I'll have a helicopter sent to your location. Where are you?"

Gate glanced at the nearby muddy waters of the Chicago River. Debris and bodies floated downstream toward Lake Michigan. The smell of burning oil and dead bodies rankled his nostrils. He didn't want to remain in the area.

"I'll meet it at Soldier Field."

"Okay."

He hung up. There was nothing more to say. He was sure Caruthers had seen scenes of the annihilation of Chicago on television and probably had a better view than he had. What pitiful words he could summon could never relay the massive destruction, the loss of life, or the futility of resistance. He worked with numbers. When even numbers failed, of what consequence were mere words. An artist might put to canvas what he was feeling, but to do so would require copious amounts of dark colors to match his mood.

He barely glanced at the wreckage and desolation on each side of him, as he picked a careful path through the rubble of West Roosevelt Road. He picked alleyways through deserted South Loop neighborhoods to avoid automobile clogged South State Street and South Michigan Avenue. Most residents abandoned their vehicles and fled on foot. Clouds of dust hung in the air, mixing with the dense smoke. Ash and dust blanketed every surface, painting the town a dull shade of gray. The stench was horrendous – exposed sewers, escaping gas, the stench of death. As he drove, he was surprised to see a handful of survivors emerging from the rubble, filthy, stunned, and frightened. He stopped to pick them up and shepherd them to Soldier Field along the western shore of Lake Michigan. The stadium had been spared the rampant destruction, an island of stability in a sea of waste. He would not leave anyone behind.

NUSKU

14

Saturday, August 11   1:15 a.m. (PDT)   Creech AFB, Indian Springs, Nevada –

Twenty hours later after boarding a plane in Bagdad, Walker and his team touched down at Creech Air Force Base, Indian Springs, Nevada, one of the largest military remote aircraft facilities in the US. A whirlwind of plane changes in Ramstein, Germany, Dobbins Air Force Base in Marietta, Georgia, Offutt Air Force Base in Bellevue, Nebraska had left him exhausted. The brief naps he managed to achieve in the noisy transports did little to remedy his lack of sleep and added to his uncertainty. He had learned from the pilot of the creatures inside the three objects, as he had diverted the plane from Andrews Air Force Base in Maryland for Dobbins in Georgia. What little he could learn of the three visitors from space from the newspaper he picked up in Georgia didn't quell his growing unease. He was beginning to believe that he and his team were expendable. He had faced the possibility of death many times, but always there had been a way out, an escape clause. This time, it didn't appear as if he would see home again.

While the others had been sleeping during the Nebraska to Nevada leg of the journey, he had said his evening prayers, *Isha.* The preparation had focused his disjointed thoughts, the words of the Koran had calmed him, the feeling of unity with Allah had succored his wounded spirit, but he was given no answers. He was adrift in a situation for which his training had not prepared him. He and his team were about to go into combat with a monster, a creature from another world.

It would have been comical if not true. He had seen news coverage of Ishom's rampage. San Francisco and Oakland were smoking ruins. Hundreds of thousands had died in the carnage in both cities. Millions more were now refugees fleeing in every direction. The creature was now moving toward Los Angeles. In the heart of America, Girra's swath of destruction through Indiana ran from Logansport north to Evans. It would soon be in Chicago. Entire divisions had sacrificed themselves in a futile attempt to stop the creature. Nusku had landed far away from any large cities in the middle of the Great Basin, but its inexorable advance on Las Vegas was so far unimpeded. Creech would be under attack by morning.

Colonel Starnes met him as he stepped off the ramp of the Hercules C-130 transport. Starnes stood in the pool of light cast by one of the two jeeps' headlights. Starnes was a tall, thin man sporting a bushy white moustache above thin-set lips. A fat black cigar protruded from his mouth with two inches of white ash clinging precariously to the tip. His gray eyes were cold but commanding. He had the stoic appearance of a man who possessed little humor and brooked little divergence from all things military. Just the sort of man Walker detested. He removed the cigar and pointed it at Walker.

"Captain Walker," he said. "I have a warehouse at your disposal. Your weapon is waiting for you. To be honest, I would much prefer it somewhere else."

Walker appreciated the colonel's honesty. No one wanted a nuclear warhead lying around, not even a low-yield W54 taken from an AIM-26 Falcon missile. "We'll try to put it where it will do the most good."

Starnes jammed the cigar back in his mouth, inhaled, and blew a cloud of smoke. "Our original plan has been scrapped."

Walker didn't like the sound of that. "Why?"

"The drone delivery of the nuke won't work."

He had suspected that the plan someone had conceived had been too simple and too easy. Nothing was ever easy.

Starnes counted off the problems on his fingers. "First, the blisters remain open for only a short time, creating a very limited window of opportunity. Second, we've learned that remote signals don't penetrate very far through the black material covering the creature. It seems to absorb energy. None of the drones we sent into it broadcast for more than thirty seconds. We don't know what's inside it. Third, well, there is no third. The first two obstacles are sufficient."

"So, we do nothing?"

"We have an alternative plan. You and your men have a few hours to catch some sack time and have some chow," Starnes said with his lips clenched around the cigar. "*Operation Bellyache* will commence just after dawn. We can't wait any longer than that."

Walker winced at the nomenclature, *Operation Bellyache*. "Couldn't they have come up with a better name?"

"Someone seems to have a sense of humor. I find little humor in possible annihilation."

"Well, the W54 nuke should give it a bellyache. Are they certain a 250-ton yield is sufficient?"

Starnes hesitated. "The theory is that the super dense ebony skin of the creature will contain and enhance the blast, blowing out its guts. The low yield should reduce the problem of radioactivity."

"What do you think?"

"Captain, we can't risk a larger strike. Your weapon has to work."

"That's a lot of pressure."

"I heard you work best under pressure."

Costas and his men threw their gear into the back of one of the second jeep, and then climbed in. Walker crawled in behind Colonel Starnes.

"Has anyone figured out a way to get the nuke inside the creature?"

"You're not going to like it." Starnes pulled the cigar from his mouth, tapped the end to knock off the ash, and motioned the driver to take off.

"I figured as much."

The colonel yelled to be heard over the noise of the jeep. "When the Wasps swarm, the blisters remain open for a few minutes after the last of the creatures have left. We're going to drop you onto Nusku's back." He paused a moment to search Walker's face for signs of surprise. When Walker betrayed no such surprise, he continued, "You and your men will rappel down the creature's flanks and enter through one of the open blisters."

Walker nodded. Since he had first seen an image of the creatures, he had suspected the only safe way inside the creature was through one of the blisters. From the number of Wasps each blister produced, they had to be cavernous.

"Why risk my entire team? I could go in alone."

"Commendable, but no one knows what you may find in there. You couldn't carry the weapon and fight off any Wasps you might encounter. It's better to be prepared."

"How do we reach Girra – helicopter?"

Starnes shook his head. "No, choppers can't approach the creature because of the Wasps. We think the noise attracts them. We've created paragliders that mimic the Wasps' appearance. They should allow you to penetrate the swarm unmolested."

Even with the military's enormous resources, designing a paraglider within a few hours that would fool the Wasps was an iffy proposition. "Should being the operative word."

Starnes shrugged his thin shoulders. "It's a risk. You were given a choice."

"Some choice – let more of our cities die or fly a drone inside the damned thing from close enough to smell its stinking alien-ass breath. Well, at least is considerably cooler here than Iraq."

A slight smile creased the colonel's face. "They said you were the top choice for the mission. I would like to see you come back alive."

"It's high on my list of priorities as well, Colonel."

The jeeps stopped in front of a small building with a sliding door and no windows. Portable generators flooded the building's exterior with light. Six heavily armed soldiers patrolled its perimeter. Two .50 caliber machineguns nestled behind sandbag redoubts kept away the curious. Starnes was taking no chances with the nuke.

"A truck will pick you up at in five hours for a final briefing."

Walker nodded. "At least we won't have to walk."

As the jeeps drove away, Ty Howard, one of Walker's men, slid open the door revealing the interior of the building. Five cots sat in a row the middle of the room. A port-a-potty in a corner proved to be their bathroom. Five folding chairs and a table holding a coffee urn and three chafing dishes was their mess hall.

"I see they spared no expense," Howard said.

"What a shit hole," Costas quipped, as he dropped his gear on the floor. "I've slept in better dives in Iraq."

"Don't worry about the accommodations. We won't have much time for sleep," Walker reminded them. "Chow down, and then do a complete weapons check. I want this mission to go off as smoothly as a virgin's left butt cheek."

Costas snickered. "Yeah, they could at least provide a condemned man with a last toss in the sack with a paid-for hooker."

"Tomorrow night, I'll pay for a dozen hookers, all shapes and sizes. Tonight, we prepare for the mission. Check out our delivery system."

Howard plopped down on one of the cots fully dressed. "Somebody turn out the light, will you. I've got a sweet dream to finish." He rolled over on his side and pulled a blanket over his head.

Jackson, the quiet man of the group, sat cross-legged on the floor, his disassembled M16 across his lap. He methodically cleaned and examined each part before replacing it. That accomplished, he removed each round from the half dozen clips spread out at his feet, carefully inspected them, and refilled each clip.

Walker poured a cup of coffee and examined the contents of the chafing dishes. One contained bacon and sausage. The bacon was so crispy that it was almost black. Another held unpalatable, runny scrambled eggs. The third was divided into two compartments. One held a mucilage-like mixture he assumed was sausage gravy, and the other rock-hard biscuits. He shoved a wad of bacon into one of the biscuits and found a quiet corner to sit. While munching on the biscuit and sipping coffee, he reviewed the photos of Nusku.

The creature was the size of a walking mountain, surrounded by a swarm of angry Wasps. Safely reaching the creature's broad back would be difficult enough. Rappelling down the sides and gaining access through an open blister was pushing the boundaries of luck. Once inside, he had no idea of what they might face. From the number of Wasps pouring from each blister, the cavities were sizable, but no one knew if they interconnected or led deeply enough into the creature's interior for the nuke to be effective.

If they managed to deliver the nuke and extract themselves, it still remained to reach the creature's back and soar away before the bomb detonated.

"Piece of cake," he whispered to himself.

He watched Costas walking toward him, forking up mouthfuls of runny eggs and sausage from a paper plate. Costas sat down on an upended crate across from him.

"That nuke is a piece of work. It weighs close to fifty kilos. Those fancy gliders had better be able to fly with the added weight, or else whoever carries it will drop like a rock."

"That's my job."

"The hell it is," Costas protested. "I'm the weapons expert. I'll carry it. You keep those damned giant mosquitoes off my back."

"If all goes as planned, we won't have to worry about the Wasps."

"Hell, Captain, I like your vote of confidence, but this mission is a crap shoot, and you know it."

"They all are."

Costas took a big bite of eggs, swallowed, and said, "Yeah, but sometimes we get the roll of the dice. This time …"

Walker had more practical concerns. "What's the delay time on the device?"

Costas shrugged and pointed his fork at Walker. "That nuke has a thirty-minute delay. If we dally too long making our exit…" He held his hands together and quickly spread them apart. "Kablooey."

Costas' demonstration was crude but effective.

"Then we haul ass out of there."

Costas nodded. "I'm all for that."

"Get some sleep. Tomorrow's going to be a busy day."

Costas laughed. "Sleep? Who the fuck's got time for sleep. I'm going over that nuke with a fine-toothed comb. I don't trust these army boys. They sleep in real beds at night. I bet they even wear clean underwear."

Walker rose and checked on his men. Howard was snoring softly. Jackson and Costas were busy. The fourth, Corporal Michael Evans, was smoking a cigarette by the door, which was open just a crack. Even so, a hot dry breeze entered the warehouse.

"Get some sack time, Evans."

"Just enjoying the night, Captain. You ever just sit and listen to the silence?"

"Not often."

"You should. It's highly enlightening. You can learn a lot."

"What do you hear?"

"I hear fear."

A cold hand crawled up Walker's spine at Evans' cryptic revelation. "Fear?"

"Everyone here is afraid. You can see it in the way they walk, keeping one eye toward the north. You can hear it in their short, clipped conversations. Their voices are schoolboy high. They know Nusku's out there, coming for them, and they're frightened."

"And you?"

He smiled and tossed his cigarette out the door. "Oh, I've been afraid many times, but not now."

He questioned Evan's puzzling answer. "No?"

"I'm resigned to the fact that we're not getting out of that creature alive."

Walker tried not to let his dismay show on his face. A soldier certain of his death made mistakes. "No one dies on my watch, Corporal. We'll get in, set the nuke, and get out, all in one piece."

"Do you really believe that, Captain?"

"If I didn't, I wouldn't take the mission."

Evans shook his head slowly and smiled. "I doubt that. I think you would strap that nuke to your back and let the bastard swallow you if you thought you'd win. You don't like losing. That's why I follow you, but this time we're up against aliens. We're going into the great unknown using tried and true tactics. There's no room for error. I think this creature still has a few surprises in store for us."

"Get some sleep. I'll roust you when it's time for the briefing."

Evans nodded and sauntered back inside. Walker watched him walk away. Evans was a good soldier, a veteran of fifteen missions with him. If he felt the icy fingers of fate gripping him, how did the others feel? He stifled a yawn. He wouldn't be getting any sleep, but he could at least rest. Tomorrow was going to be a busy day.

15

Saturday, August 11, 1:25 a.m. (CDT) *Mare Moscoviense*, **Moon –**

The last journey back from the teardrop had been a struggle. Lack of sleep over the past forty-eight hours and the yoke of responsibility weighed heavily on Langston's shoulders. Mahall had finally re-established contact with Earth after rewiring almost the entire Orion spacecraft. When Mahall relayed Director Caruthers through to the lander, the Director almost sobbed as he spoke.

"I have some terrible news, Commander. Each of the three alien objects did tremendous damage when they crashed in the U.S. Tens of thousands of people died. Last night, at about 7:30 Houston time, each object disgorged a gigantic alien creature hundreds of feet long. They're unlike anything we've ever seen, vicious, armored monsters. Each one is now in the process of devastating major cities. Chicago and San Francisco have been annihilated. Las Vegas, Oakland, and Los Angeles are in the crosshairs. Hundreds of thousands of people are dead, and none of our weapons have any effect on the creatures."

Crenshaw's face turned red from anger. She closed her eyes and rocked back and forth in her seat. Langston had trouble swallowing. The air seemed too thick to breathe. He didn't feel anger. He was numb. He knew the Director well enough to realize that he was leaving out more than he was revealing. He didn't want to burden them with details and events over which they had no control.

"What about the nuclear option?" he croaked through a suddenly dry throat.

"It's being considered for Nusku in the desert of Nevada. The other two ... well, it would cause as much damage as the creatures."

Maybe his decision to land on the moon had been a sound one after all.

"Sir, we have been examining the alien craft that collided with us. The collision forced it to crash on the moon. I considered the opportunity to learn something about these objects worth the risk. Now, I feel more than ever that it is the key to these creatures." He hesitated. Did he reveal only their observations, or also include his and Crenshaw's strange feelings around the object? Normally, he would keep such information private. Neither of them wanted to face a mental evaluation once they were back on Earth. He decided to hold off unless their observations could be confirmed.

"Commander, you took an awfully big risk. The lander was aboard *Lunar One* for a test run, not for a landing. I hope your decision was based on more than simply wanting to take a stroll on the moon." Langston knew the Director had chastised him for the record before asking, "Did you learn anything useful?"

"I will send a data burst with everything we have." He motioned for Crenshaw to create an encrypted file to transmit over the slower audio connection. "We believe it is in communication with the alien objects."

"You mean directing the creatures?"

He glanced at Crenshaw. She crinkled her nose at him but didn't object to his conclusion. "We're not sure of that, but we think the teardrop is relaying information between the creatures and their source."

"Have you detected anything, any signal?"

"No, but I'm sure I'm right."

To his relief, Caruthers didn't laugh at him. "Hmm, I'll have our people scan the EM spectrum for some kind of signal. I do have some good news for you."

"We could use some."

"*Pegasus* is on its way to rendezvous with *Lunar One*."

Crenshaw reached out and squeezed his hand. "That is good news," he answered. "When can we expect it to arrive?"

"In just over thirteen hours." He rushed to add, "Mahall advised me of *Lunar One*'s orbital decay and gave me the figures. I have everyone here at Mission Control working on the problem to see if we can come up with a better flight plan to shave some time from our estimate."

Caruthers tried to keep his tone positive, but Langston knew you couldn't cheat physics. So did Caruthers. *Pegasus* was traveling as fast as its engines could push it, but they would still have to match orbits with the Orion before docking. Even if they achieved success on the first attempt, they would be over an hour late.

"I appreciate the heads up, Sir. Crenshaw and I are returning to *Lunar One* shortly. I have a plan that just might work."

"Care to share some details? Maybe we can help."

Langston sighed. "Not just yet. I need to confer with my crew before making any final decisions. We need to discuss options."

After a long pause, the Director said, "The final decision is yours, of course, but don't do anything hasty. We want you all back here safe and sound."

Had the Director guessed what he was planning? Of all the possible scenarios the mission specialists in Houston were reviewing, he was certain one similar to his had been broached. They would also know of the oxygen requirements for three people as opposed to four people. It was a matter of the simple, concrete math of oxygen consumption versus the immutable physics of space travel. He needed every pound of oxygen that could be spared to create a large explosion.

"When *Lunar One* picks up the *Pegasus* on our radar, we'll know more about time constraints."

"Langston, I ..." the Director choked, and then went silent.

"We all knew the risks before we left, sir. It's been an honor."

"We'll do all we can."

"We know, sir. We appreciate the effort. We need to conserve power. *Armstrong* signing off."

He faced Crenshaw. A slight smile played on her lips. "Your idea is making more sense now. Anything we can do to stop these creatures is worth the risk."

"I concur. It's time we returned to *Lunar One* and inform them of my plan."

"I've calculated the amount of liquid oxygen in reserve. Even if we use some of it for the *Armstrong,* we should have enough to make quite an explosion. Let's blow that teardrop to hell and back."

Langston nodded, as he pressed the ignition switch to lift off the moon's surface. He was too wrought with emotions to speak. He would be back soon with a vengeance.

NUSKU

16

Saturday, August 11   5:20 a.m. (PDT)   Creech AFB, Nevada –

Gate remembered little of the flight from Chicago to Nevada. His mind was numb from the scenes of utter chaos he had witnessed over the past twelve hours; destruction on a scale even he had trouble digesting. His worst-case catastrophe scenarios paled in comparison to the real thing. Only a handful of survivors reached Soldier Field before the helicopter came for him. The pilot was reluctant to take on extra passengers, but Gate had insisted that they fly out with him. He would leave no one behind in that city of the dead.

When the jet touched down at Creech, he noticed the air of urgency at the base. He imagined men and women in every military base in the country were just as tense and just as frightened. An orderly quickly ushered him into the commander's office. The base commandant, Colonel Starnes, reminded him of Colonel Powell, brusque, efficient, and confident. He wondered if all colonels came from the same mold.

"Doctor Rutherford, I'm not sure why you're here, but if NASA went to all the trouble to transport you here, I'll assume you're some kind of VIP." He glanced at his watch. "In one hour, we're sending in a team with a small nuclear device. They will enter the creature through one of the open blisters, leave the device, and escape before it blows."

"Inside the creature?" he asked incredulous. "Why not just drop a nuke on it?"

"According to the experts, the yield needed to destroy the creature would contaminate the surrounding countryside for centuries. The radioactive fallout would reach Las Vegas and Denver. It would kill as many people as the creature."

Gate slammed his fist on the desk, startling the colonel. His own vehemence surprised him, as he said, "You don't understand, Colonel. These creatures are here to devastate the entire planet. Saving a city now just means destroying more later on. I've seen the creature in action. That black crystalline armor is impervious to heavy explosives. It acts like an energy sponge. It will take a big nuke to stop it. Blast it to hell with everything you've got."

Starnes' expression didn't change. He picked up the black cigar in the ashtray on his desk and pointed it at Gate. "While I appreciate your anger, I have guidelines I must follow. If we start lobbing nuclear missiles around, China, Russia, North Korea, or Iran might think we're going to target them next. We don't need a full-scale war on our hands."

"We're at war now, Colonel."

Colonel Starnes jammed the cigar into his mouth and leaned back in his chair. His eyes became hard and cold. "I follow orders, Doctor Rutherford. My opinions don't count for much. Do you think I like sending men into harm's way? I'm sending men inside that thing. What do you think of their odds of surviving?"

Gate could see that the colonel resented the orders he was given, but he would follow them to the letter. He regretted his outburst. He was attacking the wrong enemy.

"This team – can you add one man?"

Starnes lifted his eyebrows in surprise. "You, Doctor Rutherford? Why on Earth would you risk your life?"

Gate took a deep breath. *Why indeed?* "For an opportunity to see inside that creature. This is the only chance I'll ever get. If this works, we can end the menace. If not, we need to learn as much about them as we can. We can't penetrate their armor, but they must have another weakness. Perhaps it lies within."

Starnes shook his head. "I can't authorize a civilian …"

Gate stared hard at Starnes. "With all due respect, Colonel, there are no civilians in this war. It's a war of extermination. We live or die as a species. What does one life matter?"

Starnes stared back with those dark gray eyes. Perhaps he saw something in Gate that struck a sympathetic nerve. Perhaps he simply acknowledged Gate's desperation. "You realize your chances of returning are slim to none."

Gate repressed a shudder, as he said, "I was in Chicago, sir. After what I've witnessed, I have to do all I can to stop this creature. If I can transmit my findings, it might be worth it. I sent a sample of Wasp blood to NASA's biology lab for analysis. Maybe we can develop a biological weapon from it. If not, anything I can learn inside the creature, any samples I might obtain, could mean the difference between survival and annihilation.

To his surprise, Starnes nodded. He held out his cigar. "This is supposed to be a no-smoking area. I used to sneak outside to light up. Now, well, I allow myself small indulgences. I'd go with you if I could. I'll speak with Captain Walker. He's the team leader and will be responsible for you. You'll need his approval. I won't foist you on his team without his consent."

Gate relaxed. "I can convince him."

"Then you had better prepare yourself. They leave in twenty minutes."

Gate smiled to himself. He had gotten what he wanted, a chance to learn something about the creatures. He found he didn't fear dying as much as he had imagined. Dying was inevitable, like growing old. No one wanted to do either, but everyone died eventually. If they couldn't discover a way to stop the creatures, they would all die soon anyway.

Gate's meeting with Captain Aiden Walker didn't go as well as he had hoped. When informed of his desire to accompany the team into Nusku, Walker vehemently rejected the idea.

"No way in hell. I've worked with this team for two years. I know how they think. Moreover, I trust them and they trust me. I won't jeopardize their lives or this mission for a scientist's whim."

Gate recognized the same fatigued look in Walker's eyes that he was certain was evident in his. He needed the captain's approval and tired men had short tempers. He summoned all of his diplomatic skills in an attempt to persuade the Walker. Luckily, they were almost the same height, so he didn't have to symbolically look up to him.

"Captain Walker, we are almost certainly going to die inside that creature, if we make it that far. You have your reasons for going. I have mine. If anything I learn can help defeat these creatures, then I feel my death will be worthwhile."

"Very commendable, Doctor Rutherford, but we're going to splatter this monster's guts all over Nevada. You can pick up a handful, toss them under your microscope, and learn all you want."

"I appreciate your confidence, but if you're wrong, then we've learned nothing. If I become a liability, leave me. I'll take my chances. The colonel is setting up a special frequency for my equipment so I can transmit data."

Walker looked at him with piqued curiosity. "What equipment?"

"A digital camera, of course, plus a small LIDAR rig to map its innards."

The Light Detection and Ranging equipment had been his idea. If, as some believed, the blisters open onto a vast tunnel network within the creature it could be a clue to the creature's weakness. He had suggested that Director Caruthers used his influence to request the equipment from the company that had recently developed the miniature LIDAR system. The Director had moved mountains, performed miracles, and the equipment had been waiting for him on his arrival at Creech. He had intended for the army team to carry it on their mission, but during the flight to Creech, he had determined to use it himself. He could offer an instant interpretation of the data the sensors produced.

"LIDAR?" Walker asked. "Any remote sensors?"

Gate nodded, glad for any opening Walker offered. "Yes, I'll carry four tiny sensor drones. They're the size of hummingbirds and operate automatically, sending information to the LIDAR unit."

Walker scratched his chin. "Can you fire a weapon?"

"Yes," he answered. "I killed a Wasp in Indiana."

Walker cocked his head to one side. "I'm impressed, but still not persuaded. I noticed that you're favoring your left side. Are you injured? This is no pleasure jaunt, Doctor."

Gate could see that he was losing. He tried one last gambit. "Look, Captain, I was in Chicago. I saw what Girra did. I … I stood by helplessly and watched people die by the tens of thousands. I need to do this. My ribs are fine."

Walker stared directly into his eyes, as if reading his soul. Gate was waiting for a no, when he nodded and said, "Okay, you can come with us, but you're on your own. I can't spare a man to babysit. Keep up or find your own way out."

"That brings up an interesting question. How are we going to get inside?"

Walker smiled. Gate was certain that he was going to like the captain's answer. "We're flying in, like one of your hummingbirds, Doctor Rutherford. Come on. I'll get you geared up and introduce you to my team. Remember, you do what any one of them says with no questions or delay, or they might just shoot you."

Gate didn't know if Walker was kidding, but he nodded, trying not to smile.

"Why not wait until dark? It might be safer."

"We don't have time. Besides, those things can see in the dark better than we can. It's now or never."

Gate nodded. He was going inside one of the creatures. Now, if only he could come out again.

His pack was heavy and cumbersome and tended to drag him backwards. Besides the camera and LIDAR equipment, he carried a canteen of water, a coil of rope, a 9 mm pistol, an M16 rifle, and extra clips of ammunition for both. With his helmet, combat boots, and camouflage uniform, he looked like one of the team, though he felt oddly out of place among men who killed for a living.

His first sight of the strange hybrid paragliders they were to use dismayed him. Their four wings and coloration resembled the Wasps, but unless the Wasps were, as they hoped, acting merely on instinct, they would quickly recognize the paragliders as not one of them, and he and the captain's team would join the other hapless victims that had fed the creature. When he saw the C-23

Sherpa transport that would carry them to a height of ten thousand feet before deploying the paragliders, he reconsidered his decision. To fit inside the *Sherpa*, the wings of the gliders would be folded. Only after dropping from the cargo door would they open. Dropping like a rock while hoping the wings opened as specified was a ride he wasn't looking forward to.

Noting his look of disdain, Walker said, "You can always back out."

Gate shook his head. "No, I can do this."

"If you feel the need to puke, don't do it above me," Evans chuckled.

He nodded toward the nuclear device. So much power so close troubled him. "Is that it?"

"That's it," Costas replied. "Don't get near it if you're thinking about having children."

"It looks heavy. Will the gliders carry the added weight?"

Costas chuckled. "I'll find out in about twenty minutes. I get the honor of packing the bugger."

"Load up!" Walker shouted.

"Have you said your *Asr* prayer, Captain?"

Walker smiled at Costas. "I put in a few words for you, too, Costas."

When Walker walked away, Gate looked at Costas questioningly.

"Didn't you know?" Costas said. "Our captain is a devout Muslim. Says his prayers and everything."

"I thought you and your men were stationed in Iraq."

"Oh, we were, and we killed lots of Muslims. The captain said *Allah* told him it was okay to kill fanatics and terrorists. I don't know what Allah says about monsters, though."

"Are you Muslim?" Gate questioned.

Costas laughed. "Me? I believe in booze, broads, and bullets. I kill what they point me at. Didn't you know? I'm an MFin' badass weapon. Today, I get to kill monsters."

Gate shook his head, unsure of what he had gotten himself into.

As they boarded the C-23 *Sherpa*, Colonel Starnes sat in his jeep watching, a fresh cigar in his mouth. He remained until the C-

23 began taxing down the runway. Walker and his men looked at ease, joking and laughing among themselves, ignoring him. Gate understood red-nosed Rudolf, not being included in any of the reindeer games. Upon entering the plane, Evans had stretched out and closed his eyes. Gate envied his composure. He couldn't shake off the feeling of impending doom that gripped his soul like a cold claw. Things changed when they caught their first sight of Nusku striding through the desert twenty miles north of Alamo, a ranching community of a thousand people. The moving mountain drank in the first rays of the dawn, its blackness making it appear to be the shadow of a cloud passing overhead. Clouds of alkali dust billowed up at each lumbering step of its twelve legs.

Costas was struck with awe. "Look at that bugger," he exclaimed, as he poked the window with his finger. "It looks like a giant bedbug." He rubbed his hands together, smiling. "I can't wait to squash that thing."

Walker was more respectful. "You saw the other one in action?" he asked Gate.

Gate nodded. "It destroyed everything in its path. Luckily, this one landed in the desert far from any major city. We've had time to prepare."

Walker raised an eyebrow. "You think it landed here by accident?"

Walker's question surprised him. "There's nothing here. It could have landed in Vegas just as easily."

"The creature is less than thirty miles from Groom Lake. Do you think that's just coincidence?"

"Area 51," Gate said. "That's near here?"

Walker nodded. "Every experimental aircraft we've developed came from Groom Lake. They're working on a new high altitude fighter jet capable of leaving Earth's atmosphere, a hybrid rocket plane."

"I've never ..." he squinted at Walker. "How could you know about it?"

Walker smiled. "My team has set up flight monitoring stations in Afghanistan and Iraq. I'm no scientist, but I can read data. Believe me; it works. The *SR-80 Lance* would make a nifty defensive weapon against an alien invader."

Gate weighed Walker's estimate of the creature's destination and found it wanting. Like most military men, the captain considered military installations as prime targets, but he had missed the most obvious target. "I think you're wrong. Groom Lake might be a good military target, but there's a bigger target south of there."

"Vegas?" Walker questioned.

"Hoover Dam. It provides four billion kilowatt hours of power per year and holds twenty-eight-billion acre-feet of water that irrigates half the farms and provides drinking water to the entire Southwest. If the dam were destroyed, the entire Southwest would dry up and blow away. What better way to eradicate an enemy?"

A red light on the wall began flashing, ending their discussion.

"Get ready!" Walker called out. "Two minutes!"

Each man donned the harness securing him to his glider. Walker helped Gate into his. The gliders were smaller than the Wasps. They were little more than a carbon fiber frame draped with nylon cloth. Gate thought it was somewhat insubstantial and felt like he was about to leap from a perfectly good airplane wearing a kite.

"A quick lesson, Doctor Rutherford. Lean in the direction you want to go," Walker advised. "We'll circle the creature as we descend. Hopefully, our Wasp friends will welcome us as one of them. When you land, lift your legs and let the frame take the impact. If we get separated, drop to the ground away from the creature and hide." He checked his watch. "A flight of F-16s should be here about now. Their job is to draw the creatures away from Nusku to give us a clear shot."

"Call me Gate. Calling me doctor makes me think you believe I can treat your wounds. I can't. I'm a scientist, not a physician."

"Okay, Gate," Walker said with a snicker.

The cargo door began to drop. Gate's heart began to race as open sky appeared in front of him. Costas had the nuclear device strapped to his chest like a parachute. He carried the heavy case to the rear of the plane as if it weighed nothing. With the door open, Gate had a spectacular view of the desert ten-thousand feet below, but he didn't have time to enjoy the sight. The green light flashed and Costas leapt from the plane. Gate followed his descent as far as he could, but the burly sergeant quickly disappeared from view. One by one, the others jumped until only Gate and Walker remained. Walker nodded toward the door.

"Your turn. I'll follow you down. Remember, the wings extend automatically. Don't panic when they snap into position and jerk you upward."

Gate took a deep breath, exhaled, and leaped.

He experienced a few moments of wild panic, as the wind whipped through his clothes and slapped him in the face, but then the wings extended and he was soaring. He had parasailed a couple of times in the Cabo San Lucas, but there he had been able to see the water reassuringly close below him. It had been invigorating and fun. Dangling ten-thousand feet above the desert floor with the possibility of a Wasp attack or a nest of writhing tentacles waiting, he wasn't having any fun.

The others below him were flying in a wide circle. He leaned back and saw the silhouette of Walker's glider directly above him. Remembering what Walker had said, he edged the glider down and joined the circling group. As the ground grew closer, he began to make out more detail. What he had taken as a flat saltpan was in reality a rugged, rock-filled plain. He didn't relish the idea of crashing. He could barely make out the flight of F-16s as they arrived. At first, they were just glints of reflection in the early morning sun. Then, they shot by just beneath the gliders. The Wasps swarmed out to intercept them. As planned, the jets made a limited attack designed to draw the creatures away from Nusku, and then flew away slowly. Some moved too slowly and paid the price with their lives. Gate hoped the plan worked. He didn't trust their camouflaged gliders to pass the creatures' scrutiny. He held his breath, as the creatures flew past him, ignoring him.

As they dropped closer, Nusku looked like an obsidian outcrop set with rows of jagged peaks. Only its forward motion betrayed it as a living organism. From six-thousand feet, it looked too small to land on, though he knew it was the size of an aircraft carrier. Sooner than he wanted, it was time to land. He watched the others approach from the side, aiming for the largest segments near the creature's center section between the three pairs of legs to avoid the sharp spikes. They hit the flat black surface, skidded along for a few yards, and came to a rest. They quickly fanned out along the creature's back. Gate had a good view of the five-story mouth and the nest of tentacles directly below him. He determined that, at the first sign of movement from them, he would abandon his plans of entering the creature and fly as far away as quickly as possible. They remained motionless, so he went in.

The row of sharp-edged spikes rose beneath him. If he struck them, they would slice him to ribbons. Landing the paraglider on a moving object required some finesse. He was glad the creature moved slowly. He urged the paraglider to one side. The landing wasn't as rough as he expected, just a sudden jarring thud and a moment of fear. He remembered to lift his legs. The glider skidded a few yards before coming to rest thirty yards from the others. He had a little trouble releasing his harness with his shaking fingers, but he eventually managed. Walker landed beside him, smiling.

"We made it," he said.

"So far," Gate replied.

Walker's team began uncoiling rope. Evans secured the rope by attaching a grappling hook to one of the spikes. He jerked the line to secure it and trailed the rope back to them.

"Time to go, Gate," Walker said. "You'll come down next to last after Evans. He pointed to the metal ring attached to Gate's harness. "Your locking carabiner will secure you to the rope and allow you to drop gradually. The belaying descender will automatically brake if you fall. Play the rope slowly through the loop with one hand and hold on with the other. We'll grab you at the bottom. Got it?"

Gate nodded, though he still didn't understand the technical names for his equipment. He would let someone more experienced control everything. All he hoped was that he didn't fall. One at a time, the others dropped from the creature's back. After a few minutes, Evans nudged him in the back.

"Your turn."

Gate nodded and slipped over the edge. He was delighted to find that he didn't dangle in free space. Instead, he slid down the creature's sloping side in the shadow of the upturned serrated edge of a body segment. He examined the edge more carefully. The overlapping plates fit so tightly that they left no alien flesh exposed. The creature was completely armored. Considering the ebony material's ability to both absorb and transfer energy, he didn't think the armor was an evolutionary trait. The creatures had been designed and bred for war.

Someone grabbed his legs. After a moment of panic, he saw that it was Costas. The open blister was about the size of George Washington's eye on Mount Rushmore. He had sufficient room to stand uptight. The shadow and the deep ebony of the material made it difficult to place his feet properly while Costas unhooked him.

Grinning, Costas said, "Welcome to bug central, Doc. We'd better hump our asses before the residents come back." He now carried the heavy nuclear bomb strapped to his back, holding it precious as if it were filled with ice-cold beer and pretzels.

Evans dropped down behind him. The others were waiting inside the blister. Early radar imaging had indicated a deep opening behind the blisters. A quick visual inspection showed that the blister narrowed to a tunnel just large enough for him to move through while standing erect. One of his deepest fears had been of crawling through the creature's innards on his hands and knees. He quickly unpacked the LIDAR and released the four imaging drones. Each remote LIDAR drone was three inches in length, weighed less than three ounces, and maneuvered on two tiny rotating fans. Gyros balanced the scanner platform for a steady image. They fluttered aloft and dispersed into the tunnel. The drones began to paint a 3-D image of the interior on the screen,

"This tunnel continues for at least ten yards before intersecting with a longer tunnel running parallel to the creature's side forward and to the creature's rear," he informed Walker.

Walker waited impatiently while he stopped to take photos of the interior with his cell phone. Before they had traveled a few yards, the blister lid closed behind them, leaving them in total darkness. Gate experienced a brief moment of panic until the team switched on the powerful flashlights attached to their helmets, reminding him of his. He turned it on. The creature's dark crystalline material soaked up the light it cast, leaving him fearful of each step lest an undetected opening appeared in the floor.

He checked his cell phone for a signal.

"It's dead," Walker said with a frown, beating him to it. "I just checked mine."

"The ebony material soaks up energy, even phone signals. Thank God, LIDAR works."

"For now," Walker said.

At the branching of tunnels, they continued to the right, forward toward the creature's head. Fifty feet farther down the tunnel, they passed a second identical opening which he assumed led to another blister. The drone sensor indicated five such openings within range. So far, they had encountered no Wasps. They faced their first major decision when a large opening appeared leading to the left and deeper into the creature. The drones revealed a complex cavernous interior with numerous pockets or niches. Gate was eager to explore it, but Walker stopped him.

"Evans, take the doctor to the opening of one of the blisters and send all the data we have collected so far."

"I need to remain with you," Gate protested.

"Relax. Evans will bring you back. You can join us in the cavern."

Gate gave in. Walker was right. Their expedition was as much to collect data as to destroy the creature. "All right."

He watched Walker, Costas, Howard, and the taciturn Jackson enter the cavern opening; then dutifully followed Evans back to the surface. The blister was closed when they reached it. He fought down a growing claustrophobic panic. The air was stale and too thick to breathe, filled with alien odors and probably teeming with alien germs. It's the same air as outside, he reminded himself, but his mind had trouble accepting his reassurance. As Evans searched for some way to open the blister, he closed his eyes to shut out the darkness. It didn't help.

Evans discovered a bundle of thick gray fibers emerging from a small opening in the ebony material and attaching to various nodes on the blister lid. Smaller fibers wove intricate patterns across the blister's surface.

"Looks like a muscle," Evans said. "Maybe if I twitch it a little …" Before Gate could stop him, he raised his rifle and fired a burst into one of the nodes. As Gate suspected, the material was too dense to damage with gunfire. The bullets ricocheted off the lid, one barely missing Gate's head. Evans shrugged and offered him a slight apologetic smile. The bullets must have tickled the fibers, for the lid began to rise.

Staring out at the landscape moving past from the blister was dizzying, but the fresh air revived Gate. He quickly broadcast the photos, LIDAR images, and a few hastily scrawled notes to Colonel Starnes. He fell backwards, falling on his ass when a shadow darted past the opening.

"It's a Wasp," Evans called out. "Move!"

Gate crawled backwards just as the Wasp landed on the edge of the opening. It stared at them with its single alien eye, its mandibles clacking in agitation. Evans fired the rest of his clip into the creature's exposed abdomen. A stream of yellow ichor shot from the wounds, covering Evans, but the Wasp dropped away, injured or dead. Gate knew more would take its place.

"It's time to leave," he said with an urgency verging on panic.

They raced back to the point they had separated from Walker's team and entered the cavern. Walker and the others stood in a semicircle staring at the walls. He and Evans joined them in awe. The crystalline cavern was over eighty feet high and at least that large in diameter. The walls were covered with hundreds of shallow depressions. Each recess held an immature Wasp in a clear crystal, fluid-filled cocoon. Tubes pulsing with moving liquid ran from the wall to each cocoon. The lower tiers contained wingless larvae, while the upper levels held mature Wasps in suspended animation.

Through the soles of his boots, Gates felt the rhythmic pulsing of the creature's heartbeat and the flowing blood which succored the immature Wasps.

"It's a hatchery," he exclaimed. "The creature grows them inside itself."

"Are they baby behemoths?" Costas asked. "Do they lose their wings and grow enormous?"

Gate paused, examining the nearest creature. He wasn't sure of the answer, but as a scientist, the others looked to him for an explanation. That he was an astronomer and catastrophist didn't matter to them. "I don't think so," he ventured. "I think they're another species altogether, and Nusku is the host creature, like symbiosis. The larger creature nurtures them, and in turn, they feed it."

"What kind of screwed up alien planet creates shit like this?" Costas said, spitting at the nearest cocoon.

"I think it's no accident."

"Huh?" Costas said.

"Together, the two creatures make a formidable weapons system. I think the aliens designed them for that purpose."

"There must be hundreds here," Evans said. "There could be dozens of these nurseries."

A quick estimate of the number of blisters left a feeling of dread in Gate's stomach. "There are almost five hundred blisters. Even if there is a hatchery for every four or five blisters, the number is more like a hundred nurseries. For all we know there are more nurseries deeper within the creature."

"The important question," Walker said, "is do we place the bomb here?"

Gate shrugged. "I don't know anything about nuclear yields, but considering the propensity for this dark material to transfer energy throughout its body, I would say no. The deeper we go the better. Remember," he added, "I'm no xenobiologist. I'm just guessing."

"Hell, I don't even know what that is. You're the closest thing to an expert we've got." He looked at the others. "We go deeper."

Evans shook his head. "I knew I was going to die today."

Walker whirled on him. "No one dies on my watch, got it?"

"Hell, Evans," Costas said with a big grin. "Maybe they got alien dancing girls with two coochies."

Howard took out his knife and jabbed it in a groove along the edge of one of the cocoons. He slid the blade back and forth until a seam widened. Yellow ichor like the stuff oozing from the Wasp wounds spilled onto the floor of the cavern. He sniffed the tip of his blade, frowned, and wiped it off on his pants leg. The larvae in the cocoon wriggled for a moment as the seam began to reseal. Howard growled, ripped open the cocoon with his hands, and plunged his knife into the larvae's head. The larvae squealed and died. The ichor drained from the cocoon and formed a puddle on the floor.

"You shouldn't have done that," Gate said.

Howard sneered at him, wiped the blade on his pants leg, and shoved it back into its scabbard. "One less of the bastards to deal with."

"No, I meant that if the Wasps are a defensive system, the creature must have other defenses. We don't know how it might react to our presence."

Jackson knelt on the floor of the cavern, placed his hand palm down on the surface, and closed his eyes. After a few seconds, he said, "The blood is flowing from that direction." He pointed toward the creature's head. No one questioned Jackson's assessment.

"We go forward," Walker said, dismissing Gate's concerns.

"We might have company soon," Evans said. "I killed a Wasp in the blister that got too nosey."

Walker rolled his eyes at Evans' tardy report. "Lock and load."

Gate checked his M16 and was shocked to see that the safety had been off the entire trip. He made sure he pointed the barrel toward the ground, as he followed Walker. He didn't want to shoot someone accidentally. They ignored two more similar cavern openings they passed, but a third opening dropped sharply downward, promising access deeper into the creature. Walker checked his watch.

"We've been here almost half an hour already. We've got to hustle."

"You got a date, Captain?" Evans joked.

"In another hour, the creature will be at the outskirts of Groom Lake. If we can't stop it, they're going to attack it with everything they've got. I don't want to be here when that happens."

"How do we get down that?" Gate asked, pointing to the hole.

In answer, Evans removed the coil of rope Gate had been carrying wrapped around his pack. He pulled a short metal rod from his own pack, extended it, and secured the rope to it. Then he placed the rod across the opening.

"The same way we got here," he said.

Gate eyed the deep, dark hole with mounting trepidation. His adventure was beginning to look more like folly.

"What's the matter, Doc?" Evans asked. "Afraid of the dark."

He tried to smile, in spite of his fear. "No, I'm just afraid that this is its asshole, and that we'll wind up dropping like turds a couple of hundred feet to the ground."

Evans roared with laughter, but the tunnel absorbed the sound.

As Evans prepared the climbing gear, Gate looked at Walker. He didn't know much about the Special Ops captain, but one thing Costas had said intrigued him. He hesitated to ask a personal question, but needed to know.

"Costas said you are Muslim."

Walker narrowed his eyes. "Costas has a big mouth. It's true. I grew up in Dearborn, Michigan. I was raised Catholic but lost interest early. I knew about or at least thought I knew about Muslims, being around them growing up, but when I was stationed in Iraq, I found out that all I knew was wrong. Islam is an old religion, very peaceful, except for radical fundamentalists. The rituals reminded me of Catholicism."

"Do Muslims believe in aliens?"

"Do Catholics?" Walker replied with a grin. "The Koran says Allah created animals and placed them on Earth and in the heavens. I've never really given it much thought, but I suppose that allows for the possibility of aliens."

Gate nodded. "I don't know much about Islam except what I've read or seen on television."

"Islam presents a bad face to the world sometimes, but that's because of extremists. The religion is a personal one. I don't believe in all the ridiculous tenets, like subjugating women, killing infidels, or two virgins each with thirty handmaidens in paradise, but I feel how prayer affects me here." He made a fist and tapped his chest. "I guess it's the trappings of any religion that come between the worshipper and God, or Allah."

"But you kill Muslims. How do you reconcile that with your beliefs?"

"I'm a soldier defending my country. Hopefully, I only kill bad Muslims, dangerous ones. Men that use religion, any religion, to further their ambitions or to enslave another people are evil and deserve to die. I'm black, but if I was sent to Africa, I wouldn't have a problem killing people the same color as me if they were evil or a threat to my country."

"So you believe in evil?"

"Don't you?"

Gate considered the question before answering. "I didn't until these creatures landed."

Walker nodded. "Welcome to my world."

ISHOM

17

Saturday, August 11, 9:40 a.m. (PDT) San Luis, Obispo, California –

After the destruction of San Francisco and Oakland, Ishom turned south, a dreadnaught on legs. The Sierra Madre Mountains to the east directed its course southward toward Los Angeles. If its intention was to join its brother in Las Vegas, as some believed, it would have to wait until Bakersfield to turn east through Death Valley. Admiral Lloyd Trent Grayson believed the creature's destination was Los Angeles. If anything, Nusku would join it in Los Angeles after demolishing Las Vegas. He had seen videos of what the creatures were capable of, and he doubted Nusku would require any help in dismantling Vegas.

Los Angeles made a tempting target for an alien invader. Through its docks flowed the goods that fed a nation and facilitated the export of manufactured goods abroad. It was one of the economic hubs of the country. The Greater Los Angeles area had a population of almost eighteen million, a tempting target for a creature that consumed its enemies. Unless he could stop Ishom, LA would be destroyed.

Aboard the aircraft carrier CVN 81, *U.S.S. Monitor*, two miles off the coast of San Luis Obispo, Grayson commanded a fleet consisting of five cruisers, two destroyers, and six missile frigates. For three hours, they had been launching Tomahawk Cruise missiles and sorties by FA-18 Hornets and AV-8B Harriers at the creature in an attempt to slow it down. Their attacks had proven as futile as those against Nusku and Girra. Now, radar detected a swarm of Wasps headed in their direction.

He turned to the young lieutenant standing beside him. "Contact the Air Boss. Tell him to launch all available aircraft. I don't want anything with wings caught on the ship where it does no good. Inform the fleet to prepare for an attack."

As the officer relayed his order, Grayson leaned against the rail on Vulture's Row, the balcony outside the flight bridge. He had abandoned the flag bridge three decks below for a better view of the coming battle. As the battle klaxon rang, he raised his binoculars and focused them on the mainland. Ishom was almost fifteen miles away and hidden by a range of low hills, but he saw the plume of dust and smoke raised by its passage. The creature was almost as long as his eleven-hundred-foot, 7.5 billion dollar aircraft carrier.

He trained his glasses higher and spotted the incoming swarm of Wasps, thousands of them, each a nine-foot-long lethal weapon with wings. The infrared-guided missiles were ineffective against a living creature with no heat signature. The Hornets and Harriers picked off the wasps along the outer edges of the formation, but too few dropped compared to the loss of aircraft. Soon, he would see if the ship's defensive armament was up to the task.

Between his carrier and the escort ships, he was responsible for the lives of over 7,500 men. Command and responsibility was nothing new to him, or he would never have risen to the rank of admiral. However, this was a different kind of battle, one in which human had so far come out on the short end of the stick.

The FA-18 Hornets and Harriers began dropping lower to provide a shield for the *Monitor*. The frigates and cruisers launched their Seahawk helicopters to join in the fray. More Wasps fell to the sea, but their numbers were startling. The giant creatures seemed to produce the Wasps within their bodies. How could one fight and defeat an enemy that reproduced so quickly?

When the Wasps were within the effective two-mile range of the Vulcan Phalanx 20 mm Gatling guns, the six close in weapons system cannons began firing at 4,500 rounds per minute, ripping into the massed Wasps. The other ships' Phalanxes cut loose as well, joining the booming of the MK4 five-inch guns on the cruisers and the 76 mm guns on the frigates.

Grayson smiled as the Wasps began to fall in greater numbers. Hundreds were killed by the withering gunfire, but these were not an intelligent enemy that would retreat at such an overwhelming display of firepower. They were more like the dreaded Kamikaze pilots of WWII, who instilled fear in the hearts of the American commanders facing their acts of human sacrifice. Too many of the creatures got through the cordon of steel. They descended on the ships, a deadly living cloud, attacking gun positions and individual sailors standing on the decks firing rifles, machineguns, and pistols at the creatures. They ripped into the stunned men with scythe-like mandibles that rent human flesh as easily as scissors through silk. Three-foot-long stingers delivered paralyzing toxins to human bodies. Screams rattled throughout the bowels of the ship, mixing with the metallic wail of the klaxon, as the creatures tore through steel bulkheads and dogged hatches with superhuman strength, seeking their prey and dragging their victims back onto the deck to fly away with their prizes.

One of the Wasps dropped from above and lunged at him over the railing. The mandibles slashed air just inches from his chest. He stared for a moment at the alien creature hovering on its twin pairs of wings. The single elongated eye stared back at him, as if studying him. Then, anger surged in him. He drew his .45 from its holster and emptied the clip into its head, but it took a burst from a Marine's M16 to kill it. Yellow blood splashed his camouflaged uniform.

"Go inside please, Admiral," the Marine said.

Grayson complied, taking cover inside the flight bridge, as the young Marine braced himself against the bulkhead, firing into the Wasps now attacking the carrier's superstructure. The Marine fought valiantly but soon went down, cut in half by a sweep of one creature's mandibles. The upper half of his torso, still screaming, plunged over the railing to land on the flight deck over a hundred feet below. More Marines and sailors swarmed past Grayson and onto the balcony to meet the winged assault with automatic weapons.

With hands shaking more from rage than from fear, he reloaded his .45. The helmsman stood at the wheel unperturbed by events unfolding around him, his eyes trained on the compass before him, steering the ship along its intended course. Only when a Wasp crashed through the window amid a hail of gunfire die he move away from the wheel. Even then, as soon as the dead creature stopped moving on the deck, he returned to his post.

The carrier was moving at close to its top speed of thirty-five knots. The slower frigates and Cruisers began falling behind the ship they were supposed to protect. He turned to the ship's captain, Drew McAnders.

"Reduce speed to twenty-eight knots."

McAnders stared at him, his face as pale as the white dress uniform he wore. "If we reduce speed, we'll be a sitting duck."

"We can't outrun these things, Captain. We'll have to reduce speed to recover our aircraft soon anyway. We're straying too far from our escorts. Our fields of fire need to overlap. These aren't aircraft trying to bomb us. They're paratroopers landing on the deck."

The captain swallowed hard and nodded. "Helmsman, reduce speed by two-thirds."

Grayson turned his binoculars to the nearest *Ticonderoga-Class* cruiser. Smoke billowed from the forward hatch, and the ship was dead in the water. The central radar mast was broken and lying across the electronic warfare suite just aft of the bridge. Wasps clung to the superstructure. Men jumped from the decks into the water, as they abandoned the sinking ship. He watched in horror, as one sailor was snatched mid-leap by a Wasp. Two other ships were on fire as well and slowing down. The fleet had suffered damage, but the number of Wasps circling the ships was much smaller. They were making headway against their alien enemy.

McAnders answered an intercom hail, turned even paler, and confronted Grayson.

"Radar picked up a second wave of these creatures headed in our direction. We can't withstand another such attack." He paused. "What are your orders, Admiral?"

Grayson wanted to keep fighting. Retreat was not an option, but as he stared into the faces of the men around him, he could sense their fear. It radiated from them, a stink that filled the air, along with the smell of blood. They were up against an enemy that defied their imaginations. Three ships were badly damaged and perhaps lost. He couldn't jeopardize his remaining ships in a useless attempt to save San Luis Obispo. The city was doomed no matter what they did. His ships would be needed to defend or to help evacuate Los Angeles, whichever option the Commander-in-Chief ordered. Thank God, he didn't have to make that decision. He only had to make the obvious one.

"Order the fleet to make to sea at top speed. We'll regroup fifteen miles from the coast and steam south. Advise all aircraft of our position and order our birds home."

The captain visibly relaxed, as he turned to the intercom. Grayson remained at the window staring into the sky. Around him, the battle still raged, as men fought Wasps in corridors, gangways, in the hangar, and on the flight deck. Teams of armed sailors surrounded one of the creatures and fired until it stopped moving. Then they went on to another enemy. Their tenacity and bravery under fire heartened him. He would not throw away their lives uselessly. He didn't know how far the second wave of Wasps would pursue them, but he hoped they would eventually give up and return to their host creature. For now, hope seemed to be their only weapon.

GIRRA

18

Saturday, August 11,   10:15 a.m. (CDT)   Des Moines, Iowa –

Amanda Gilbert checked her close-cropped auburn hair in her mirror, wiped a smudge of mustard from the sandwich she had just from eaten the corner of her mouth, and took a deep breath. Wally Nelms, her cameraman, counted down with his fingers. By his expression, she knew he wasn't thrilled with her idea, but he had stayed nevertheless. For that, she was grateful. At Nelms' last finger, she erased all traces of emotion from her mien and faced the camera.

"Good evening from atop the Marriot Hotel in downtown Des Moines, Iowa. It is a wet, dreary day with rain clouds hanging low on the horizon. A steady downpour most of the day has made the air sticky and humid. The air is also filled with electricity, the electricity of fear of the unknown. We do not know or understand these strange creatures that have invaded our planet, our country, our city, and we fear them. That is understandable. Faced with the unknown, fear is the obvious reaction. Perhaps by better understanding them, we might face them as we would any other enemy, with strength and character. We here at KCCL Channel 8 are ignoring the curfew and the mandatory evacuation order to provide a live visual and personal account of the creature Girra's approach to our beloved city in hope of bringing a better understanding of just what we face.

"Already, Chicago, San Francisco, Oakland, Santa Barbara, and numerous other smaller communities have fallen beneath the terrible onslaught of these enormous creatures from another world. Davenport is no more. Is our city destined to be next? Of the half million residents of the five county area, estimates run into the tens of thousands of people who have refused to leave in spite of the danger. Their reasons range from belief that the creature will not destroy our city to the fear that looters will steal their possessions, as if anything will be left after the creature passes. The National Guard just made its final sweep through the city a few minutes ago. Now, they too are gone."

The camera panned from the rooftop to the city streets below, nearly empty but for a few stragglers hurrying through the streets. Abandoned and wrecked automobiles, looted storefronts, and overturned trash containers give the once beautiful city the look of a war zone.

"As you can see, we are almost alone in this city of two hundred thousand souls. Girra, that horrible monster that crashed to Earth two days ago with its companions, Ishom and Nusku, has lived up to its image of the Babylonian god of fire from which it was named, leaving behind a wake of flame and death. Now, Girra is less than five miles from the outskirts of the city. You can see smoke rising from the ruins of homes and businesses trampled beneath its enormous feet. Earlier, jets attacked the creature with missiles and bombs, but they were driven back by hordes of the flying creatures known as Wasps.

"Estimates run into the hundreds of thousands of people killed or devoured by the creatures. So far, all of our weapons have proven ineffective. Why not use nuclear weapons, some ask? Uncertainty of their effectiveness is one reason. A reluctance to destroy American cities and contaminate American soil with radioactive fallout is another. But if cities are so vulnerable to these creatures, doomed to fall one-by-one, why not sacrifice one city to prevent the destruction of others?" She paused to allow her words to sink in. "Would you, ladies and gentlemen, want to sacrifice your city, confine Des Moines to a smoking heap of radioactive rubble?"

In the distance, a loud explosion startled her. The camera quickly panned toward the east. A curtain of smoke draped the city like the folds of a blanket.

"Girra is getting closer. I can see its enormous dark body glinting through the pall of smoke hanging over the city. Flashes of light dance along its body, as the jets fire their missiles at it, without effect, I'm sad to say. It seems unstoppable, as the black tentacles surrounding its enormous mouth writhe in the air, darting at times into buildings to withdraw something, perhaps people, from the ruins. The ground is shaking from its heavy tread. It is standing just across the Des Moines River from me, waiting. I don't believe our namesake river will prove any more of a barrier to it than the great Mississippi River did at Davenport. The creature can swim or simply wade through shallower water. The creature Girra seems intent on destroying the heartland of America. If so, it will soon achieve its goal, as we seem unable to stop it."

She stumbled as the building shook, bracing herself on the roof wall to keep from falling.

"Around me, you see the Ruan Center, the Financial Center, and 801 Grand, all magnificent skyscrapers giving our city its beautiful skyline. Will they go the way of the skyscrapers of Chicago or San Francisco? Des Moines is, or was, the insurance capital of America. When the multi-billion dollar bills come due from these creatures' rampages, I wonder if any insurance company will remain soluble. The creatures have cost us more than dollars and cents. They have cost us human lives. They have cost us misery. They have cost us our sense of security. Once, we complained about long security lines at airports. We went to great lengths because of the possibility of a plane going down at the hands of an enemy. That enemy is among us now and no security checkpoint, no body scan, or no metal detector is going to bring that sense of security back.

"Oh, my God!" she gasped. "Thousands of Wasps are pouring from holes in the creature's sides, darting to the ground. I just saw a woman snatched into the air by one of the winged creatures. Their rapidly moving wings are filling the air with the sound of flags popping in a strong wind. You can hear them over the sound of collapsing buildings. They are drawing nearer." She motioned frantically to her cameraman. "We will leave the camera running, but we are going back inside and down to the basement in hope that we might survive this attack.

"This is Amanda Gilbert, KCCL Channel 8 signing off."

"Let's get the hell out of here," Nelms said.

"Make sure we're still broadcasting," she said.

"The camera's running and now so am I."

The power was off and Nelms had the only flashlight. She followed the glow of the light in the dimly lit stairwell. She took the first few flights of stairs in her heels before kicking them off to move faster in her bare feet. By the time they had descended the twenty-six floors to the basement, she was breathing hard. The building shuddered constantly, as the twelve legs of the creature pounded the ground. A tremendous crash sent her reeling through the doorway and onto the floor. The entire building shook as if it was collapsing.

"That was the Ruan Center, I think," Nelms cried out. "It's getting close." He turned to Amanda, shining his flashlight in her eyes. "This is your fault," he shouted. "You wanted a damn Emmy Award."

"You were just as eager to make a name for yourself as I was," she shot back at him. "You could have left. I know how to operate a camera."

The building shook again. Dust cascaded from the ceiling. A water pipe burst overhead, showering them with cold water. She coughed as she choked on the dust filling the room.

Nelms eyed the Emergency Shelter placard on the wall and snickered. "It might protect us from a tornado, but not from some alien hell."

Nelms was near hysteria. She tried to calm him down. "Close your eyes and imagine yourself somewhere else – Tahiti maybe." He had always wanted to go to Tahiti. It didn't work.

"We're going to die!" he shouted, and raced for the door just as the building began to fall apart around them. The wall around the doorway collapsed. A steel beam fell across Nelms, pinning his body to the floor. Cinder blocks and sheetrock fell on top of him, burying him in a pile of debris. Illuminated by the beam of his flashlight, a glistening stream of blood ran across the floor to pool at her feet. She knew he was dead.

She crawled into a corner, brought her knees up to her chest, and began to cry. Then, the floor rose beneath her and darkness took her.

NUSKU

19

Saturday, August 11,   8:10 a.m. (PDT)   Inside Nusku, outside Groom Lake, Nevada –

To Gate, the descent down the rabbit hole was as terrifying as the paraglider descent onto Nusku's back. Alien sounds and alien smells drifted up the yawning chasm in gusts of hot air. His headlamp illuminated only the wall around him. Staring down into the dizzying blackness below him birthed a panic that urged his hands to clamp down on the brake of the descent rope and remain fixed where he was. Only the scuffling sound of Costas above him forced him downwards.

Whatever his plight, Costas had it worse. On his back, he bore the heavy weight of the W54 nuclear warhead. His heavy breathing, magnified by the enclosed space, reverberated up and down the opening.

"How far?" Gate asked.

"One-hundred-ten feet so far," Evans called up to him. "We're almost out of rope," he added.

The LIDAR scan indicated that the shaft continued another fifty feet to the bottom, but branch openings should be nearby. They might not have enough rope to reach them.

Before he could imagine the long climb back up the rope, Walker yelled up from below, "I found an opening."

The hole continued into the depths, but a large opening on either side reminded Gate of bronchi of a lung. Inside the opening, the ebony crystalline structure gave way to a substance more resembling sedimentary rock. Up thrusts in the floor and wall revealed layers or bands of different colors and textures.

"I think this is muscle," Evans said, as he poked the material with the blade of his knife.

"Whatever it is, it's not as hard as the outside material," Walker noted. He placed his hand against the wall. Gate did the same. The wall vibrated in pulses. "Maybe the creature's heart is somewhere around here." He turned to Gate. "Anything on the LIDAR?"

Gate shook his head. "The drones have spread out. I have scans of tunnels above and below us, but not one of this tunnel."

Costas dropped his heavy load on the floor of the cavern. "Let's set the timer on this thing and get the hell out of here."

"We have to be certain we pick the right spot," Walker said. "We'll only get one chance."

As eager as Gate was to leave, he didn't want anyone to have to make a return trip to finish the job they started. "Let's follow the tunnel and see where it leads."

The tunnel was twice as tall as a man was, and three times as wide. Smaller openings in the walls and ceiling were too small for cithcr Wasps or humans. Gate could only guess at their functions. If his lung analogy held true, they were bronchioles leading to alveoli, or air sacs, but they could just as easily be structural elements like the openings of spongy bone.

Howard had been trailing behind them to cover their rear. After a few minutes, he rushed forward with bad news. "I think we've got company."

"Wasps?" Gate asked.

Howard shook his head. "No, they're smaller and wingless, but they look as if they mean business. They came out of those holes we passed."

Walker glanced at Gate, and then at Costas. "Jackson, you remain here with me. The rest of you continue. When you find a spot that looks as if it will cause some damage, set the timer and run."

Like the others, Gate had come to the conclusion that thirty minutes would not be time enough to negotiate the route safely through which they had entered the creature before detonation.

Jackson hesitated. "No way, Captain. I came along to protect you and Costas. Howard and I can handle this little job. You're needed with the nuke." He looked at Evans. "Sorry, Evans, looks like you might live through this one after all."

Before Walker could object, Jackson and Howard trotted back down the tunnel the way they had come.

"Time's wastin', Captain," Costas reminded him.

Walker took one last look at the retreating backs of his two men, looking as if he wanted to order them back, and motioned the others to follow him. "We double-time it," he snapped and set off at a fast trot. Costas and Evans started out after him. Gate, already exhausted by the journey, had trouble keeping up. Then, realizing that he probably needn't save any strength for the return trip, he reached down inside and tapped into his reserve energy.

The air became hotter the deeper they ventured. Gate decided that his lung analogy was incorrect. The air didn't travel both directions, as in breathing. The heated air originated from deep within the creature and moved outward. The tunnels functioned as ventilator shafts, cooling the creature's interior. The hotter the air, the closer they were to an energy source. At first, he thought thousands of tiny cilia he had noticed in the walls were simply swaying in the breeze, but then decided that they were actually moving the warm air outwards like millions of tiny fans.

His hand scraped the wall, as he caught himself after stumbling. He jerked it away in surprise. The wall was hot enough to blister the skin on the palm of his hand. Walker noticed his reaction and stopped running.

"I've noticed it's getting hotter," he said. "Is that significant?"

"I think we're nearing the creature's energy source."

"Then that would be a good place to leave the device, right?"

"I believe so. If we can disable it, it might die of overheating."

Costas laughed. "We're talking about a nuclear bomb here. It should rip its guts out and leave an empty shell, like a damned road kill armadillo lying on the side of the road."

Gate didn't share the large burly sergeant's enthusiasm, but he was certain it should cripple the creature at the very least and destroy most of the Wasps, especially the immature ones. The muted sound of gunfire behind them interrupted the conversation.

Evans growled, as if he wanted to rush back to help his friends. Gate was more worried about what they were shooting at.

Walker's face turned hard. "We came to do a job," he said with a low growl. "Howard and Jackson are buying us the time we need. Come on."

Ten minutes more at a fast trot left them standing at the edge of an enormous pit in a chamber almost a twenty yards across. Twenty feet below them, a cauldron of the yellow ichor the creature used for blood bubbled and boiled, heated by the creature's body heat. As Gate peered over the edge, air hot enough to singe his eyebrows stung his cheeks. The smell was appalling, a mixture of ammonia and rotting fish.

Costas pinched his nostrils with his fingers. "Good God, that stinks. It smells like a whore I knew in Calcutta. Only charged five-hundred Rupees, though, so I guess at ten bucks it was a bargain."

Keeping a safe distance from the edge of the pit, Gate examined the chamber. The curved walls rose fifty feet above them until they met to form a dome overhead. The walls were crisscrossed by vein-like tubes that formed a mass in the roof of the chamber, sending hundreds of tubes as thick as a man's arm into the pit. Each tube pulsed with a life of its own.

"Is this its heart?" Costas asked.

"No, I think this is an organ designed to cool the blood before pumping it throughout the creature." He pointed to a series of thin ebony crystal baffles rising from the center of the pit. Each baffle was a honeycomb of small chambers filled with the yellow liquid. The blood rose up the center of the baffle and cascaded like a fountain down the honeycombs into a collection pond, where it disappeared into small tubes at the base. "Wind passing over the baffle cools the blood by heat exchange," he explained. "The hot air exits the creature and the cooled blood is re-circulated – efficient but odd for a living creature." He studied the LIDAR image, and then pointed to an opening in the wall opposite the pit. "That shaft leads to what could be the heart. It's difficult to tell, but the air is cooler."

"That's where we go," Walker said.

The pit took up most of the chamber's interior, surrounded by only a narrow ledge. Gate kept as close to the wall as possible, but staring into the boiling depths below made him feel as if he was balancing on a tightrope. As he neared the far side of the chamber, Jackson and Howard burst from the opening through which they had entered. Howard stopped and fired a burst from his weapon back down the tunnel, and then, spotting the others, limped over to them with Jackson's aid.

"They're coming," he shouted, as he slammed a fresh clip into his rifle. His uniform was ripped, and he bled from half a dozen wounds on his leg and chest.

"You're wounded," Walker said.

"I'll live," Howard replied. "We had a dispute with the new neighbors."

Before he could elaborate, dozens of new creatures poured through the opening. The only resemblance to the Wasps was their large mandibles and multiple legs. Each mottled gray creature was the size of an English bulldog, but bloated and rounded like a tick engorged on blood. Their mandibles made a clacking sound as they advanced. As soon as the Ticks emerged from the tunnel opening, some of them began scurrying up the walls, while others charged directly across the floor toward them on thin legs tipped by deadly looking pincers.

Gate hurriedly raised his M16 and fired. His first burst missed, but he managed to correct his aim and kill one of the Ticks as it crawled along the wall. A dark liquid squirted from its wounds. The odor the liquid emitted made the yellow ichor in the pit smell like a flower garden.

"My God," Costas yelled. "If the jaws don't kill you, the stench will."

The others were much better shots than he was, quickly eliminating several of the creatures, but more Ticks joined the first group. He could see that they would quickly be overwhelmed. Howard joined them on the narrow ledge, knelt, and fired into the mass of creatures. Howard stumbled as he rose to his feet, caught himself, and braced his back against the wall to steady his aim. He emptied his clip and reached for a fresh one. He failed to see one of the Ticks crawling down the wall from above. Before Gate could warn him, the creature fell on Howard, sinking its deadly mandibles into the flesh of his shoulder and severing his right arm. Howard's agonized scream filled the chamber. As he yanked at the creature still perched on his shoulder with his other hand, he slipped from the ledge and toppled into the chasm. Gate watched horrified as Howard landed on his back across one of the baffles, instantly snapping his spine. He rolled down the baffle into the boiling liquid and sank from sight. His body clogged several of the intake tubes, for those nearest to where he fell began thrashing wildly from side to side of the pit. One tore loose and whipped over Gate's head, almost decapitating him, spewing hot yellow liquid from its tip.

Walker grabbed Gate by the collar and forced him through the opening behind him. Costas brushed up against his back and shoved him deeper.

"Move it," Costas yelled in his ear.

"What about the others?" he protested.

"They'll be along as soon as they tidy things up."

Gate felt badly about deserting the others, but he knew Costas was right. His gun would do little good. Their task was to place the nuclear device and set the timer. Nothing else mattered. Escaping before it detonated now seemed unlikely. The idea of sacrificing his life didn't bother him as much as it should have. After all the death and destruction he had witnessed, including Howard's, his life meant little to him if by spending it he could save others.

The gunfire continued behind him as they ran; a sign that Walker and the others were still alive. The sound faded as they trotted down the winding tunnel. The slope soon became steeper as it angled upward. They were forced to crawl along the floor on hands and knees. Costas was having a hard time with his heavy pack.

"I can help you with your pack," Gate offered. "Many hands make lighter work, they say."

"This is one burden I have to carry myself," Costas gasped between breaths. "Besides, it ain't so heavy. I once carried a Volkswagen Beetle up two flights of stairs."

"You're a God-awful liar, Costas."

"It's my only virtue."

The tunnel leveled off and opened into a chamber unlike the other chambers. Gate stopped and played the beam of his flashlight around, but the walls retreated beyond the range of the beam. It seemed to extend the entire length and width of the creature. Black columns ten feet in diameter rose from floor to the ceiling, a black forest filling the entire chamber.

"What is this place?" Costas asked breathlessly, as his lungs fought to suck in air. In spite of his protests to the contrary, transporting the heavy nuclear bomb was taking its toll on him.

While Costas rested, Gate examined the columns. Overlapping plates of the same material as comprised the creature's exterior ran their entire length. The room shuddered. He reached out to steady himself against the column and jerked his hand back just in time to avoid losing it, as some of the plates slid together and then back to their original positions.

"I think they started the attack early," he observed. He noted that the column radiated more heat after the movement. He attributed it to friction, but other mechanics might be at play.

"Maybe they gave up on us and started the attack early," Costas said. "I hope they blow this thing to hell."

Gate didn't share the sergeant's wishes. He turned his attention back to the columns. "These columns serve as shock absorbers, like our spine. They're composed of the same ebony crystal as the exterior. There must be muscles inside, protected by the armor. That's why the tentacles around the mouth are so prehensile and so invulnerable."

Costas grinned. "Maybe we should have brought along some Kryptonite. Can we break its back?"

"We might cripple it," Gate conceded, "but the bomb probably won't kill it. Even immobile, it could still produce more Wasps."

"Damn." Costas resettled the heavy pack on his shoulders and took a deep breath. "Let's push on."

They threaded their way through the chamber, weaving around the columns. The small pools of light cast by their helmet flashlights did little to dispel the darkness of the cavernous room. Distant scraping sounds behind them could have been from more ebony plates sliding together, but Gate's vivid imagination conjured images of horrible monsters crawling toward them. The two drones that had followed paths toward the rear of the creature were no longer broadcasting. As he watched, the remaining drone forward of them ceased functioning. They had no more views ahead. They were now moving blind.

"The drones are disappearing," he told Costas.

"Ah. Must be this damned heat," Costas said, as he wiped his forehead with his hand. "I'm about to conk out myself. It reminds me of this little whore I knew in Bangkok. She used to…"

"Later, sergeant," Gate replied. He conceded that the increasingly debilitating heat could have damaged the drones, but he worried more about the Ticks or some other as yet unseen creature lurking in the darkness being the culprit for their demise. If they were treating the tiny drones as interlopers, how much more effort would the creatures put into expelling the human invaders.

"Let's get this over with. I want to sit down and rest a spell. Just keep moving forward."

Gate stopped walking. "Which way is forward?" In the darkness, he had become turned around.

"It must be that way," Costas said, but then stopped and scratched his head. "It all looks the same. What does your gizmo say?"

Gate pulled out the LIDAR and turned it on. The machine mapped the immediate area, but the irregular rows of columns blocked the Laser scanning beam. He tried walking around with it, but it produced the same results. It was like trying to see through a forest. To make matters worse, the image was blurry as if the columns were moving, which he knew they were not.

"We're lost," he admitted.

Costas snorted. "Maybe we should have left a trail of breadcrumbs. Let's go back to where we came in."

"Which direction is that?" Gate asked him.

Another shudder ran through the creature, this one stronger than before. The columns nearest them ground together to absorb the shock. Either the creature was doing calisthenics or someone was attacking it. The scraping sounds grew louder, this time coming from behind and off to one side of them. Costas dropped the pack with the nuke and unlimbered his weapon. Seeing the wary look in Costas' eyes, he checked to make sure his M16 was ready and played his flashlight along the rows of columns.

Thinking in two dimensions almost cost him his life. When the clicking and scraping sounds continued to grow louder with no sign of the creatures making them, acting on a hunch, he turned his light toward the ceiling. At first, he thought his eyes were playing tricks on him in the poor light. The tops of the columns around them seemed to shimmer. Then, to his amazement, a dinner plate-sized creature the exact color as the columns launched itself across the space between two columns, giving Gate a view of its lighter underside, which bristled with a mass of tiny appendages that allowed it to grasp the columns. Nestled in the center of the legs, a mouth lined with tiny sharp teeth opened and closed menacingly. The thin, pancake-like creatures had no eyes, but Gate was certain they were aware of their presence.

"The place is crawling with them," Costas shouted. He didn't wait to see if the creatures were attacking or simply doing their jobs. He fired a burst at the nearest pancake. The 5.56mm bullets tore holes through the flimsy skin, but did little apparent damage. The creatures backed away a short distance and continued to study them.

"Just my luck," Costas said, "to be attacked by a stack of pancakes. They even secrete their own syrup. Look."

Gate looked to where Costas was pointing and noticed the glistening spots of liquid left by the creatures as they moved away. Their function became a little clearer.

"I think they lubricate the columns," he suggested.

"Then they're harmless?" Costas asked.

"With those teeth?" he shook his head. "No, I think they're quite capable of defending themselves."

"Well, they ain't bulletproof."

To prove his point, Costas fired another burst into one of the pancakes. This time, he hit a vital organ, for the creature dropped to the ground, writhing as its edges curled and uncurled. A clear liquid seeped from its body. The teeth gnashed together several times before it stopped moving. As if in response to the murder of one of their brethren, the other pancakes began lifting one edge of their bodies and tapping the columns rhythmically in unison. The sound echoed through the columned chamber like a marching drum corp.

"Jesus, I think I made them mad," Costas said.

Gate had reached the same conclusion. "I think you did, too. Perhaps we had better run."

"Which way?"

"Any way," he replied, as one of the pancakes launched itself toward them. Costas shot it mid leap, knocking it aside with a stream of bullets, but more began preparing to launch themselves at the intruders. "Now," Gate urged.

Costas sprinted away, weaving a dizzying path through the columns with Gate close on his heels. He risked a glance back at their pursuers and wished he hadn't. The pancakes couldn't fly, but they made good use of the columns, leaping from one to the other, barely touching the surface before leaping again. If the creatures got ahead of them, they would have to stop and fight, a prospect he didn't find encouraging.

They ran blindly with the pancakes in close pursuit, trying to keep to a straight line, an impossible task in the cavernous dark maze. The entire creature was less than a thousand feet in length, but his body ached as if he had run twice that distance. The hot air he sucked into his lungs was starved of oxygen. His injured ribs throbbed with each labored, gasping breath. He fought the urge to stop long enough to try to suck in more air. Costas with his heavy pack was tiring too, his steps faltering. He pushed himself along using the columns to remain upright.

Finally, the columns disappeared and they were surrounded by a reddish-brown material resembling limestone. Gate stopped long enough to take photos and to bury the tip of his knife into the soft wall before Costas yelled for him to keep up. The blade sank several inches before hitting a more resistant layer. A network of tiny tubules lay between the soft material and the hard. Slicing open one tubule, he discovered a network of miniscule threads bundled together.

"I think these are nerves," he said. "The softer material must be insulation."

"Not interested, Doc," Costas called out. "We need to get out of here."

The sound of pancakes clicking behind them punctuated Costas' words. He didn't think the pancakes would pursue them beyond the range of the ebony columns, but he didn't want to put his theory to the test. Suddenly, they were blocked by a ceiling-high wall. Unlike the black columns or the creature's exterior, the wall was composed of dark crimson-colored flesh covered in a fine filigree of tiny black lines.

"It's a dead end," Costas snapped in irritation. "What now?"

"I don't know. We're traveling blind."

Costas narrowed his eyes and stared at him. "Great! You mean we're lost."

"We've been lost," he reminded his companion.

Costas sat down with his back against the wall. "I guess I can rest now. At least it's cooler here."

Gate had noticed the drop in temperature as well but couldn't account for the sudden change. Backing away from the wall, the air quickly grew warmer. He walked along the wall, hoping to find some seam, some gap that would indicate a passage beyond. The mosaic of whorls and spirals made no sense to him. They served no purpose that he could deduce other than decorative. The pattern was random.

"There has to be a way through," he said, running his hand along one ridge.

"You could try saying abracadabra," Costas replied. "Give it up. We gave it a try and we failed. I say we set off the nuke and hope for the best."

The thought of death by nuclear incineration didn't appeal to Gate. He studied the wall again.

"Not yet. Just give me a few minutes."

"Take your time. We're not going anywhere." As Gate studied the walls, Costas dropped his backpack and uncovered the bomb. The small cylinder didn't look lethal – just a black metal canister eleven inches in diameter and five inches long with five-inch-diameter hemispherical protrusions at each end – but inside a deuterium core needed only a slight explosive shove to cause a chain reaction, producing a 250 ton TNT explosion. "Just in case," he commented to Gate's troubled expression.

"Don't do anything hasty," Gate urged.

Costas laid his M16 across his lap and faced the maze of columns from which the pancakes would emerge. He patted the nuke. "When I run out of bullets, I press the trigger."

Costas' eagerness to detonate the nuclear device spurred Gate to search harder for an opening. He retraced his steps along the wall. He played his flashlight up and down it, growing more frustrated by the minute. If it was a language, it made no sense to him. The lines had to serve some function. The wall separated them from something. Everything he had so far discovered about the creature intrigued him. If the aliens had set about designing a creature to use as a weapon, they couldn't have produced a more perfect product. He began pacing back and forth, paying less attention to the wall and more to a question that continued to nag him, to tickle the back of his mind. He was missing something important but couldn't lay his finger on it. He had been so set on finding the creature's weakness that he had failed to see its strengths.

The creatures were combination tank and aircraft carrier, armored and powerful. They housed an air force of Wasps and manned with Ticks serving the functions of security personnel and Pancakes as oilers. Like a ship, its sections were separated by bulkheads. He was treating Nusku as a monster to kill. Perhaps, he should think of it as an organic machine and search for a method of disabling it.

As he paced, he saw it, a brief shadow high above, visible only at a certain angle. It was an opening thirty feet above the floor of the chamber barely wide enough for a person to crawl through, but he was certain it went through to the other side. Cooler air spilled from the opening.

"I found it," he called out to Costas.

Just as he spoke, the distant sound of an explosion echoed down the chamber of columns. A ripple of flesh raced across the floor, knocking Gate down. He looked up just as the edges of the opening above him closed tightly.

"No!" he cried.

Now, they were truly trapped.

ISHOM

20

Saturday, August 11,   10:50 a.m. (PDT)   El Segundo, California –

After completely destroying San Luis Obispo, the alien behemoth Ishom took to the water again, marching into the Pacific Ocean to become a floating base of operations for the swarms of Wasps laying waste to the surrounding countryside. The men and women stationed at Vandenberg Air Force Base, home of the 30th Space Wing and a center for military satellite launches, waited breathlessly for the creature to descend on them, obliterating them, but they never came. Santa Barbara was likewise spared. This abrupt shift in the creature's tactics mystified officials even as they breathed a sigh of relief. However, the respite was short lived, as Ishom sailed down the coast at twice its walking speed, coming ashore at El Segundo less than two hours later.

Corporal Elias Matheson, twenty-two, from Cape Hope, Missouri, squatted behind his .50 caliber machinegun atop the I-405 overpass at I-105, trying to keep his hands from shaking. He and his fellow members of the 40th Army Infantry had arrived an hour earlier from Los Alamitos, hastily set up a defensive perimeter, and waited. Rumors were rampant about the monster's capabilities, but he didn't see his pop gun of a weapon doing much when jets and missiles hadn't. He was cannon fodder, and he didn't like the feeling. His buddy, Tracy Hayes, a California native, sat beside him smoking a joint. Matheson didn't mind marijuana as a recreational drug. He wasn't above taking a few tokes himself, but he wanted his loader to be clear headed.

"Stay frosty, damn it," he snapped at Hayes. "Don't get all weirded out on me."

Hayes laughed. "Weird? Man, how weird do you think this shit is?" He waved his joint toward the beach. "That mother-humper is going to stomp our asses like it was police payback time at a riot. We're sitting here like chumps when we should be hauling our sorry asses out of here." He took another drag and exhaled slowly. "Hell, we should go where it's done been, not where it's coming."

"If we don't stop it, it'll flatten LA," Matheson countered, though Hayes's words made sense to him. So far, nothing had slowed any of the creatures down. He didn't think their pitiful line of machineguns and mortars would make much difference.

"Screw LA, man. I'm from San Diego. LA sucks! This place don't mean shit to me. I'm here just like you are, another dumbass jarhead following orders."

"If we abandon our post, that's desertion. They'll shoot us."

"You got that right, but when everyone's running east, what say we run north? I got me a friend up in the mountains. She's real fine. Maybe she's got a friend for you. Sure beats dying."

Hayes's grip on the .50 caliber tightened. He glanced away from Hayes so his buddy wouldn't see the indecision in his eyes. His body urged him to run, but he was a soldier. He had a duty. His father hadn't run in Vietnam, had he? *Maybe he wanted to as badly as I do.*

"No, I'm staying."

Hayes shook his head slowly. "You're a fool, man. I'll hang here with you, but as soon as I see someone run past me, I'm out of here so fast you'll call me the Flash."

Matheson nodded. "Okay. We stay. Afterwards ... I don't know yet."

Hayes's grin widened. "That's all I'm asking, man. We do our bit for king and country, and then we haul ass for parts unknown. Hell, man, we'll be heroes, standing up to the big bad monster that ate LA."

The sound of heavy gunfire from Point Mugu Naval Air Station filled the pit of his stomach with acid. He could just make out the jets overhead, as they dove down toward the sea, firing their missiles. The monster was almost upon them. He noticed a dark cloud low to the horizon.

Great, we're going to fight in the rain.

Then, the cloud broke apart, became individual dots, and he knew it was Wasps. He had heard about them. They were something he could fight. The Wasps made quick work of the jets from Point Mugu. Then he watched in horror as they changed directions. He knew it was simply matter of perspective, but it looked as though they aimed directly at him. A group of AH-1F Cobras and UH-60 Blackhawk helicopters roared over the interstate low to the ground, aiming for the center of the alien formation. He was so engrossed by the battle that at first, he failed to see Ishom, as it rose from the sea and strode ashore at the Chevron refinery.

"Look at that mother humper," Hayes exclaimed. "It must be a hundred and fifty feet high."

Matheson's throat had suddenly become too dry to answer. He nodded instead.

Hayes stood. "We gotta get the fuck out of here."

"Sit down," Matheson shouted. He looked again at Ishom striding ashore, crushing buildings in its path like a rampaging crab. The urge to flee was on him too, but he resisted. "We'll run when the others do."

To his surprise, Hayes resumed his position holding the belt of .50 caliber ammunition prepared to feed it to the machinegun as Matheson fired.

The helicopters flew straight into the swarm of Wasps firing their Gatling guns and cabin-mounted .50 caliber machineguns. Their maneuver divided the swarm into two separate sections. Learning from earlier failures by other attack groups, each chopper's fire covered the other, creating an impenetrable field of fire. He took heart at the number of creatures falling from the sky. Then, almost as if closing a fist, the two halves of the cloud closed in. He watched one gunner yanked from his chopper and left flailing in midair. Before he hit the ground, a Wasp grabbed him and jabbed him with its stinger. The gunner immediately went limp.

Helicopters began spiraling to the ground, as Wasps dove into their rotors in a kamikaze assault. Two out-of-control Blackhawks collided and exploded. Pieces of metal and burning men rained to the ground. A few helicopters managed to slip away from the melee, but Wasps swarmed after them. Within minutes, no helicopters remained.

His attention was drawn back to Ishom when the first oil tank exploded in a ball of orange flame. A cloud of black smoke shot high into the air, as a million gallons of burning oil spilled across the earthen dike built to contain it, spreading the flames to the surrounding tanks. One of the creature's massive legs smashed a second tank, flinging a sheet of fire over a nest of pipes running from the tank farm to the refinery. Within minutes, the entire tank farm and connecting pipelines were ablaze. Ishom stood unscathed in a lake of fire, a black demon from hell.

A steady breeze blew from the ocean, fanning the flames and dispersing clouds of smoke and oil droplets inland. Tiny drops of hot oil splashed around Matheson and Hayes. Matheson wiped oil from his forehead, as it ran into his eyes, blurring his vision. He could barely see the creature through the wall of smoke and flames, but when the guns around him began chattering, he pressed the trigger on his .50 caliber and held it down. He poured his anger and his fear into each round that sped its way to the creature. He didn't realize he was screaming until the gun went silent as ammunition ran out. He looked over at Hayes. His loader's eyes were glazed and his jaw slack. A dribble of spittle ran down his chin, washing a clean path through the sheen of oil.

"More ammo!" he yelled at Hayes to snap him out of his trance.

Hayes fumbled with the ammo can, pulled out another belt, and fed it into the .50 caliber. As he stared at Matheson, his eyes blinked rapidly. For the first time since he had known him, the wisecracking Californian was silent.

The first of the Wasps reached the row of defenders scattered along the interstate. A gun crew fifty yards away disappeared beneath three Wasps. Two of the creatures ripped one man in half with their terrible jaws. He watched a second soldier carried aloft by one of the Wasps, dangling beneath it impaled on a stinger. One Wasp rose from beneath the overpass directly beneath them and hovered in front of his position on its two pair of wings like an alien Angel of Death. He pressed the trigger and held it until the creature's head exploded. A second took its place. It, too, met the same fate. He was in a killing frenzy. His heart raced as it pumped blood and fire through his body. He willed his rage into his trigger fingers, using it to keep them there, pouring lead into the Wasps.

The sky overhead filled with the creatures. He swept the machine gun from side to side, firing into their midst. He didn't know how many he killed. He was no longer protecting the city. His mind was fixed on keeping them away from him. Around him, more gun emplacements went silent. More screams filled the air. He paused in his killing spree just long enough for Hayes to change ammo belts, and then returned to his orgy of destruction.

The gun clicked on empty. He turned to look at Hayes. His loader stared at the Wasps, slack jawed and whimpering. Hayes had had enough. He jumped to his feet and darted across the overpass, ready to climb down an overhead streetlight to escape.

"Come back here, you fool," Matheson yelled at him, as he grabbed his last ammo belt and threaded it into the .50 caliber.

Hayes, in his fright, ignored him. As he began shimmying down the metal pole, a Wasp rose from the far side of the interstate, hovered above him for a few seconds, and then dove at him. He didn't see it coming. The Wasp pulled him from the pole, stabbed him with its stinger, and attempted to fly away with its prey. Matheson swung the .50 caliber around and fired a burst into the creature's wings. It fell to the asphalt, dislodging Hayes from its stinger. Injured but not dead, the Wasp crawled toward him. He continued firing even after the creature's head disintegrated under a hail of bullets.

Hayes was still alive. He struggled to his feet, bleeding from a hole in his upper right side. He stumbled toward Matheson with one of his arms outthrust, while the other hand clasped the wound. He took two steps before falling to his knees. Matheson abandoned his gun and went to his friend's side. Hayes was breathing rapidly, his face pale. A crimson froth discolored the edges of his mouth.

The stinger had punctured a lung. He pushed Hayes hand aside and examined the wound. A tracing of fine black lines radiated from the hole left by the stinger. Hayes' hand grasped Matheson's.

"It hurts, man," Hayes gasped. "God damn it hurts."

"I'll get you to a medic," Matheson promised, knowing it was probably too late for his friend. The alien poison was coursing through his veins.

"Get the hell out of here. I saw a jeep below the overpass." He gritted his teeth and doubled up in pain. As soon as the spasm faded, he continued, "Take it and head north to Castaic Lake. Ask for Julie. She's a Park Ranger. Everyone knows her. She'll put you up." He began coughing blood. He saw the red liquid on his chest and smiled.

"We'll both go," Matheson said. "I'll get you out of here."

Hayes shook his head. "No way, man. I feel that shit shooting through my body. It burns like fire. I …" he grabbed Matheson's shoulder and pulled him toward him. "Promise me."

Matheson shook him when he stopped talking, but it was already too late. The blackness had spread over Hayes' entire side and chest. The poison was moving too quickly to stop. He watched the life slowly fade from Hayes' body, listened to his last bloody, dying gasp, as his chest heaved and his body shook.

"I promise, man," he said.

He continued to grasp Hayes' hand for several minutes until the ground began shaking. He looked up to see Ishom standing in the middle of the refinery, tossing separator tanks and cracking towers around like toys. It would be upon him in two more strides.

He gently laid Hayes' body on the ground, closed his friend's eyes, and leapt for the light pole. He slid down, paying little heed to the friction burn in his hands. The jeep was where Hayes said it was. The keys were in it, but the driver was nowhere to be seen. Perhaps he was a victim of the Wasps. Matheson didn't want to join him. He cranked the jeep and headed north away from the flames and death. He didn't look back.

NUSKU

21

Saturday, August 11,   9:05 p.m. (PDT)   Inside Nusku, Nevada –

Walker watched Howard's death in horror, but he didn't have time to dwell on it. The Ticks filled the chamber, pouring through the opening at an alarming rate. Three weapons weren't enough to stem the tide. Ticks crowded the narrow ledge and crawled along the wall and ceiling. The only place they avoided was the pit itself. One part of his mind considered this for a moment, as his well-trained fighting mind continued to aim, pull the trigger, and fire into the mass of Ticks. The germ of an idea began to take shape. He had no time to weigh the pros and cons. If he didn't want to lose his entire team, immediate action was called for.

"Retreat to the passageway," he yelled. He didn't know if his hastily contrived plan would work, but he saw no other option.

At the tunnel entrance, he said, "Shoot the nearest tubes," as he fired a burst into one of the overhanging tubes.

Not as dense as the black material, the tubes still required several bursts before spilling their contents. A stream of boiling yellow ichor sprayed the ledge and wall, dripping down the sides of the pit. The creatures completely drenched in the liquid stopped moving, while Ticks caught in the golden shower hissed and scampered away licking their wounds. The sprayed Ticks clinging to the walls released their grip and fell in piles of wriggling, dying creatures that blocked the ledge. Jackson cried out in pain when some of the hot liquid splashed onto his left arm, but he retained his grip on his weapon and fired one-handed. Now, only a handful of Ticks remained. Carefully aimed bursts from the M16s quickly eliminated them as a threat.

However, Walker's glee was short-lived, as more Ticks appeared from the tunnel. The creatures spread out and surged across the chamber, a new wave of assault. They would soon be overwhelmed.

"Back into the tunnel," he ordered. He stopped to watch as Ticks clambered over each other in their haste to enter the chamber. It gave him an idea. As Jackson rushed past him, Walker removed a grenade from Jackson's pack strap. He also unclipped the grenade he had been carrying and pulled the safety pins on both. He didn't know how much damage the grenades would do to the creature's flesh, but he was certain it would kill Ticks.

He double-checked to see that Jackson and Evans were still running down the tunnel, and then waited for the Ticks. Just as they had while entering the chamber, they jammed together in their eagerness to enter the smaller tunnel. He shot the creatures at the leading edge to slow the others' advance, and then released the strike levers of both grenades and dropped them just inside the passage in front of the creatures.

He caught up to Jackson and Evans, urging them to move faster, while counting down quietly. He hoped the twists and turns of the tunnel would dampen the blast.

"5, 4, 3, 2 … Everybody down!"

The concussion of the blast swept over them, as they hugged the floor with their arms covering their heads. After the explosion, he pointed his weapon back down the tunnel and waited. After a couple of minutes, no more Ticks appeared.

"Let's go."

When they entered the chamber of black columns, he didn't stop to consider their purpose. He saw it only as the perfect place for an ambush. He knew they were being watched. The fine hairs were crawling up and down the back of his neck the same way they did just before an attack. He peered into the darkness but saw nothing. He sniffed the air and caught the faint scent of WC 844, the smokeless gunpowder used in 5.56mm rounds.

"Stay alert," he cautioned.

He detected slight sounds in the darkness. The echo made pinpointing them impossible, but he knew they were closing in. Almost by instinct, he moved aside as something brushed his right cheek. He shined his light on the underside of a small creature just in time to see the row of razor teeth on its underside before it landed on a column and almost disappeared. He reached up to touch a trickle of blood on his cheek.

"We're surrounded," he shouted and dropped to his knees.

The three pointed their flashlights in different directions to illuminate their field of view. Hundreds of the small creatures clung to the black columns.

"Fire," he ordered.

Three streams of bullets tore into the creatures, killing some and driving others to the far side of the columns. The almost constant shudder running through the creature made aiming difficult. Walker watched the plates on the columns sliding over each other and reminded himself not to lean against one. He knew the shudders meant that Nusku was under attack from Groom Lake and Creech Airbase. The colonel had given up on them. He hadn't failed in a mission yet and was determined not to fail at this one. He admitted to himself things looked bad. He was surrounded by flying hubcaps in a black forest and Costas and Gate were missing.

He could still see the tunnel by which they entered the cavern and knew that Costas would be headed forward toward the creature's head. He motioned for the others to lay down a field of fire and follow him. He led the way at a fast trot, firing at anything that moved. The creatures had grown wary, deciding the intruders were dangerous. They launched attacks from ambush. One of the critters landed on Evan's back. He screamed in pain until Jackson skewered the creature with his knife, lifting it off Evan's back. It left a long gash that spilled blood down Evan's back, but he shook off the pain and continued firing.

They fought off attacks for twenty minutes, but the creatures had gotten ahead of them. Their perfect camouflage made it impossible to see them until they moved. Each of them had received various cuts and slashes from the creatures' attack and retreat tactics. It was almost as if they were attempting to delay the intruders. He suspected that the closely packed columns would make it impossible for the Wasps to negotiate the chamber, but Ticks or some as yet unseen creature could manage nicely. They didn't have enough ammunition to sustain a massed attack.

"We're going to have to run the gauntlet," he said.

Evans looked at him and shook his head. "I'm too tired to run. Just leave me here."

"Screw that, Evans," Walker snapped. "I don't leave anybody behind. You know that. Now, haul ass, or I'll stick my foot so far up your butt you'll learn to enjoy it."

They raced headlong down the chamber, firing only when a target presented itself. He hoped they were headed the right direction. He had an excellent sense of direction, but dodging and twisting through the columns was confusing.

"We've got company," Jackson called out.

Walker glanced over his shoulder. Just at the edge of Jackson's flashlight beam, the floor was covered with tiny, pale creatures the size of mice. They weren't moving quickly, but their numbers made shooting them all impossible, even if they had enough ammunition. Luckily, the flying hubcaps had fallen back upon the arrival of the mice.

"Evans, toss me your grenade."

Evans removed his grenade and lobbed it underhanded to Walker, who deftly pulled the pin and dropped it at his feet.

"Run faster," he told his companions and put on an extra burst of speed.

Behind them, the grenade exploded, thunderously loud in the chamber. The columns shielded them from flying shrapnel, but he hoped it put a dent in the horde of mice. He spotted a light flashing ahead of them and directed the others in that direction. He was relieved to find Costas and Gate on the far side of the chamber; then noticed the downcast expression on Gate's face.

"What's up?" he asked.

"Your explosion set off the creature's defense mechanism. We're trapped."

Walker glanced down at the nuclear device sitting by Costas's side and guessed at what Costas was thinking. Had they really failed in their initial mission? If so, he couldn't let a perfectly good nuke go to waste. The mice would be arriving soon. "We can't go back and we can't go forward. I guess it's time to call the game."

Gate was visibly shaken. "No, not yet," he pleaded. "It won't do any good here."

"So you say, but I don't see that we have much choice. We don't have much time."

"We're so close."

"Close won't cut it, Doc," Costas said. "This ain't horseshoes."

"Shhh!" Gate replied. "I'm thinking."

Costas shrugged and looked at Walker. Walker nodded.

"We don't have much time. Jackson, take care of Evans' back."

Evans removed his shirt, revealing a long, bloody gash. Jackson worked slowly, favoring his burned arm. Evans winced as Jackson slapped an adhesive pad on the wound and began wrapping gauze around his chest. Walker watched Jackson work. Jackson's long-fingered hands were too gentle for a man whose job entailed killing.

He looked down at his own hands. They were large and calloused, weathered by the desert sun. When he was young, he had considered building things with his hands – a carpenter or a woodworker. In the army, they had filled his hands with a weapon and pointed him at an enemy who looked much like the people he had known growing up. Their religion was the same as his adopted religion. They worshipped the same god as him. Their only difference was that they wanted to kill all non-believers or Muslims who didn't follow their strict tenets. He had done his job. Now, his job was to kill a monster, and for the first time, he had failed in his mission.

As eager as he was to do something, he didn't want to detonate the device except as a last ditch effort. If Gate could find a way to get them deeper inside Nusku, the chances of killing it improved greatly. He checked his watch.

"You've got ten minutes to figure out something, Gate, if those mice don't get here first."

He sat down beside Costas to rest. His body ached and his mind felt like mush. He had seen too much, had been forced to accept too much in too a short time. Twenty-four hours earlier he hadn't even heard of aliens, didn't believe in them. He thought they were myths, like fairies or leprechauns or jinn. Now, he was crawling around inside one's guts lugging a nuclear bomb.

He checked his watch. It was past time for his *Asr* prayer. He didn't have his *musallah*, but a prayer rug wasn't necessary for prayer. It was to provide cleanliness. How could a man feel clean inside the guts of an alien creature? He tried to clear his mind before *wudu*, absolution before prayer, but the death of Howard made it difficult. Howard's death lay heavy on his soul. Asking for absolution seemed too self-serving. Instead, he accepted his responsibility and asked for Allah's mercy. He spoke the words of the *Asr* silently so that he would not disturb the others. After a while, a sense of peace began growing inside, tiny at first, like the first gasping breath of a newborn. He grasped it with his mind and breathed it to life, allowing it to sweep through him like a calming wind.

He felt the presence of the others around him, but they were shadows imposed upon a cloud, insubstantial and fleeting. He could also feel Nusku around him solid and unyielding, and knew that it did not belong. It was not part of Allah's universe. It was a thing of evil, a demon from a dark place, *Jahannam*, the Abyss. It was his duty as a Muslim to destroy it, but how?

A hand shook shoulder. He opened his eyes and looked up into Gate's grinning face.

"I think I've found it," he said. "I need your help."

Gate worked as he explained his solution to Walker. He ran his hands along a curved line raised slightly from the surrounding flesh. "These ridges are really seams, openings in the wall. I think the creature sealed the openings after it detected us, a kind of internal defense mechanism, like the Ticks. It left one open, the one up there that the LIDAR drone went through." He pointed above his head. "Your explosion closed it."

"So how do we get through?" Walker asked. "We're out of rope."

Gate smiled. "We don't have to use that one. Maybe I can figure out how to open one of these."

Evans raised his M16. "Maybe it's like the blister cover, Doc. A little lead ought to do the trick."

"No!" Gate shouted, but it was too late. The ever-impatient Evans fired a burst into one of the seams. At first, nothing happened. Then, a section of flesh as large as a garage door folded upwards like an accordion blind, revealing a dark opening beyond. A blast of cooler air poured from the aperture, bringing with it the putrid smell of decay.

Evans turned to Gate, smiling. "See, Doc. I told you –"

He never finished his sentence. A Wasp flew from the dark opening, skewering him through the chest with its three-foot-long stinger. Gate stared in frozen horror, as the Wasp lifted Evans from the floor, circled once, and then dived back through the newly revealed exit. Evans lifted one hand in the air, his eyes pleading to Gate for help, but he and the Wasp disappeared into the darkness before any of them could react.

Gate's numbness evaporated, replaced by a surge of anger. He rushed toward the opening, firing his rifle blindly into the darkness. Walker tripped him with his foot before he could enter the tunnel. He skidded across the floor and rolled over, glaring up at Walker. He held his M16 across his chest and was almost angry enough to use it on the captain.

"We've got to save him," he snarled.

"It's too late for Evans. We can't charge blindly into an unknown situation. You still have the LIDAR. Use it."

Gate's anger ebbed, replaced by embarrassment at having forgotten where he was and why he was there. Even without the drones, the LIDAR could sweep the opening and reveal what lay beyond. He nodded.

"You're right. I just …"

"I know. Evans was my friend. Even in my business, we don't like losing friends."

While he set up the LIDAR rig, Jackson, Walker, and Costas guarded the opening. As he worked, sounds carried by the foul breeze stoked his imagination. He heard the raspy breathing of a dozen dragons with their long, sharp claws scraping stone and their scaled tails slithering along behind them as they approached the opening. His hands fumbled with the instrument.

"Focus, Doctor Rutherford," Walker urged. "We need you."

Gate took a deep breath, held it for a few seconds, and released it. He willed his heart to slow its jackhammer pounding in his chest. Then he flicked the on switch.

The LIDAR projected a low-intensity Infrared Laser into the tunnel, sweeping it both vertically and horizontally across the opening. Using only micro joules of energy, its range was limited, but by switching between IR and UV scanners, it slowly built up a 3-D image of what lay beyond. The image on the screen was frightening.

The chamber was over a hundred feet in length and almost as wide. It rose from a level twenty feet below them to a height seventy feet above their heads. Crisscrossing the chamber at various angles were hundreds of thick fibers or support structures. Movement indicated hundreds of Wasps flying through the chamber. More creatures crawled along the walls and internal structures. The chamber was alive with alien activity.

More disturbing was the smell of decomposing flesh emanating from the chamber. As he looked up from the screen, a vertical slit opened at the far end of the chamber, flooding the chamber with outside light. He shielded his eyes from the unaccustomed brightness, but not before it revealed the true purpose of the chamber. They were in the creature's mouth. The crisscrossing structures were giant muscle bundles used for opening and closing the enormous mouth. They were encased in the ebony crystal to protect them, operating like the shock absorbers in the columned chamber. Rows of ebony teeth lined the slit. Two ebony tentacles thrust into the mouth, releasing their burden of captured humans. The still struggling people fell onto the rows of razor-sharp teeth, which began grinding against each other, reducing them to pulp. In the brief flash of light before the mouth closed, he saw that the bottom of the chamber was a feeding ground. Wasps, Ticks, and creatures they had not yet encountered lined the pool of thick liquid at the bottom, devouring the ground, partially digested food, which consisted of thousands of humans. He turned away, repulsed by the scene of horror, but not before coming to the conclusion that the pool was for feeding Nusku's host of creatures. Nusku drew sustenance from another source. He was willing to bet his life, if he hadn't already, that its power came from the crystalline armor. Each attack only served to strengthen the creature. It was the perfect fighting machine.

"It's the mouth and stomach," Walker said with undisguised rancor. "I thought you were taking us to its heart."

Gate shook his head, unable to respond to the captain's accusation.

"It's all made of the black crystal material. The nuke won't do much here. We didn't come all this way just to give it heartburn," Walker continued. "We came to kill it."

Walker's anger struck him like betrayal. Hadn't he risked his life with them? "I don't know," Gate answered. The horrors he had seen wouldn't release him. Walker was right. He had failed, but it wasn't his fault.

Walker shook him hard. He didn't resist. He fought the hysteria building up in his chest, threatening to erupt into maniacal laughter. "God damn it! I brought you along because you said you could help us. We could have detonated this nuke an hour ago and been long gone. Now, I've lost two of my men and for what? For what?"

Surprisingly, it was Costas who came to his defense. The big sergeant's voice was calm and collected, as he grasped Walker's arm. "Let it go, Captain," he said. "Can't you see he's had enough? We all have. He's broken."

Gate finally found his voice. He was still numb inside. He felt no anger toward Walker. He understood the soldier's frustration. "No, I'm not broken. I'm tired and hungry, and I've seen too much death, but I'm not broken. Not yet." He stared at Walker. "I don't know where we go from here. I don't know where the creature's heart is. I don't know if it has one. It moves blood through this massive body, but maybe it uses constricting vessels instead of a heart. Maybe it's a mechanical pump. In case you haven't noticed, Nusku isn't a natural creature. Evolution didn't make this, this … thing."

His statement brought a look of despair to Walker's face. "What do you mean?"

"The aliens manufactured it. They designed and built an impervious shell of the crystalline armor and filled it with organic constructs to meet their needs, using some tissue culture they cobbled together in one of their labs or factories, or what do you it call it – arsenals. It may even be different creatures each serving a different function. They added more horrors as defenses and turned it loose on us. Nusku and the others are tailor-made constructs designed to kill humans and destroy our civilization."

He felt no satisfaction at seeing Walker's face blanch at his revelation. The truth had been hovering at the edge of his consciousness all along, but he had been unable to accept it. The truth was too horrifying. He was no biologist, so he overlooked the obvious signs of alien manufacture. The aliens were far more advanced than he had even considered. They had designed weapons especially suited for Earth's environment. That spoke of a purpose beyond just one planet. They had done this before, raided worlds, perhaps many times for thousands of years. Mankind was just the latest victim.

"So we've lost?" Walker asked. "We just give up and try to go home?"

"Through that?" Jackson asked, pointing toward the openings high above them. A line of Wasps flew from the openings to the feeding pool of food and back. "Uh-uh, not me. Not through that shit."

"Let's blow this radioactive mother and end it," Costas said. "I'm tired of lugging it around. The radiation has already dried up all the little wrigglers in my nut sac. Let's do it already."

Gate noticed movement on the LIDAR screen. "We had better do something soon. I think it knows we're here."

"Find us another way out of here," Walker demanded.

Gate moved the LIDAR around, seeking a means of escape. The tunnels above them led to the blisters, but they were too high to reach and filled with hungry Wasps. Finally, he spotted something. "I see a series of small openings just below us. I don't know where they lead."

Walker sighed. "We know where the one we came through goes, and we can't go back that way. Let's move it."

As Costas picked up the nuclear device, Jackson stopped him. "You look tired, old man. Let me carry it for a while."

"You're injured."

"One arm," he replied, looking offended at Costas' accusation. "I can carry more with one good arm than you can carry on that big back of yours."

Costas glared at him, but replied, "Suit yourself, sonny boy. You've got more muscles than brains anyway."

He handed the pack to Jackson. Jackson slipped it over his shoulder with his one good arm and smiled.

"Hell, Costas. I've taken dumps that weighed more than this."

"That's because you're full of shit, Jackson."

Gate stowed the LIDAR in his pack and picked up his weapon. As he entered the cavern, the stench was almost enough to knock him to his knees. The odor of the abattoir pushed into his nose and mouth, triggering his gag reflex. He fought the impulse to vomit. He stopped long enough to take a sip of water from his almost empty canteen, but the taste and odor lingered. Walker seemed oblivious to the stench, as he played his flashlight along the ground, searching for some way down to the opening below them.

The floor sloped sharply to the lake of digested food at the bottom. Slipping and sliding into that pit of stomach acids would kill a human immediately, dissolving flesh from bone in seconds. Tiny creatures the size of the palm of a hand scurried from small openings in the wall down to the pit and back up, like a trail of foraging ants. Occasionally, one of the creatures they had named Ticks raced down, seized one of the Palm Ants in its jaws and raced away to feed. In turn, Wasps plucked up Ticks and other similar-sized creatures and delivered them to the acid pit. Even inside Nusku, the viciousness of its creators was evident.

"I see a narrow groove in the wall that descends to one of the openings," Walker said. "We can shimmy down it like a rock face chimney."

"I've never rock climbed," Gate reminded him. The thought of missing the tiny opening and sliding all the way to the bottom troubled him.

"I'll go first," Walker replied.

With that, Walker began backing down the channel. Jackson stood at the top, guarding his descent. Walker reached the bottom, pulled his M16 from around his shoulder, and yelled back up.

"Costas, you come next, then the doctor. Jackson, bring up the rear. All three of you remove your belts and give them to Jackson. He can connect the belts and lower the pack to reach the opening."

"If I drop my trousers, don't peek," Costas joked, as he unbuckled his belt.

He let go of the edge and slid down on his ass. After Costas safely reached the ledge below, it was Gate's turn. Rappelling by rope had been uncomfortable enough for him, and he had a brake and carabiner as a safety precaution. Now, he had nothing. Lowering his legs over the edge, he eyed the steep slope with trepidation. He spread his legs to brace himself and wriggled down the groove, keeping one eye on the space around him for uninvited guests. Halfway down, his right foot slipped. He frantically dug his hands into the rough material as he slid. He stopped after a few heart-wrenching seconds, clinging to the side of the groove while he caught his breath.

"Come on," Walker urged.

Gate sighed and continued his descent. When he was standing next to Walker and Costas, he said, "No more of that please."

He examined the opening with his flashlight. It was more of a triangular slit in the muscle tissue surrounding two bundles of tubes secreting acid into the pit below. He blanched at the tiny enclosed space, but he had no choice but to see where it went.

Above him, Jackson lay flat on his belly and slowly lowered the pack with the nuclear warhead. The pack swayed from the strain on his wounded left arm. Costas and Walker waited ready to grab it, while Gate stood guard with his M16.

"A little farther, Jackson," Costas urged. "Don't make me come back up there and take it from you."

The first notice they had of any danger was Jackson's frenzied scream.

"The mice … they're all over me," he yelled. The pack jerked wildly as it dangled from the interlocked belts. "Grab it!"

"Drop it. We'll catch it," Walker ordered.

Gate shined his light back up the slope. Tiny creatures the size of mice covered Jackson's head and shoulders. Blood streamed down his cheeks. "They're like little grinders," he yelled. "They're ripping off my skin."

One of the creatures crawled across Jackson's right cheek, leaving a livid trail of raw, bleeding flesh. He shook his head to dislodge it. The pack swung like a pendulum five feet above Walker's outstretched arms. Walker leapt up, barely brushing the bottom of the pack with his fingertips, almost losing his balance with the effort. If not for Costas, he would have fallen backwards off the ledge.

"Drop the pack and get down here," Walker urged.

As Gate watched, one of the creatures crawled down Jackson's bandaged arm. In spite of the agonizing pain he was experiencing, he refused to relinquish his grip. He stretched farther over the edge to lower the pack. However, his screams had drawn other predators. Two Wasps appeared from the darkness and hovered just above him. Gate fired a burst into one's abdomen, praying he hit it instead of Jackson. It veered sharply, crashed into the slope, and slid to the bottom. He watched it slide slowly into the vat of acid.

Another scream from Jackson drew Gate's attention back to him. The second Wasp had landed on Jackson's back. The massive mandibles opened wide, engulfed the top of Jackson's head, and clamped down. The pincers dug through flesh and sliced bone, as the creature flapped its four wings and lifted the hapless soldier from the ledge. With a loud crack, the pincers sliced through Jackson's skull. The top of his head and a piece of brain fell away. Blood sprayed Gate's upturned face. Now dead, Jackson released his grip on the heavy pack. It tumbled end-over-end, struck the slope a few feet to the side of the groove out of reach, and careened down the slope to the pool below. Gate watched it disappear into the darkness with a sickening feeling. All their efforts had been for nothing. The nuclear device was gone. They had failed.

"No!" Costas screamed, as he poured a stream of gunfire into the Wasp bearing away Jackson's corpse, but in his anger, he missed. The creature and Jackson disappeared from sight.

"That tears it," Walker said, slamming his fist into the side of the pit. "We've lost the nuke."

"Won't the acid detonate it eventually?" Gate asked.

Walker's words poured out like the acid churning below them. His eyes were cold and hard – a man on the edge of despair.

"No, it takes an explosion to drive the two halves of deuterium together. The acid will eventually dissolve the case, releasing radiation. No explosion."

"We might as well piss on this creature for all the damage we can do now," Costas added.

Gate sat down on the edge of the ledge. He saw no need to push himself farther. He was tired and emotionally drained. They would never make it back to where they had entered the creature or to the gliders, if they still remained on Nusku's back. At the sound of slithering, he glanced back up the slope. Hundreds of the mouse-like creatures that had attacked Jackson poured down the slope toward them. Their snail-like pace was deceiving. They would reach the ledge in less than five minutes. Behind them, they left a trail of polished ebony crystal. The creatures were cleaners, scouring the interior of Nusku, removing any growths or alien contamination.

And we're alien contamination, Gate mused.

He, Walker, and Costas had nowhere to go except the narrow unknown slit before them. He didn't know if he could face more of the same. Moreover, this time the space was so small that he would have to crawl through it.

"We've got to keep moving," Walker insisted, seeing his hesitation.

"Why?" he challenged.

"Yeah, screw that," Costas joined in, pointing to the tiny opening. "I'm tired of plodding through this beast's innards." He raised his M16. "Let's go out in a blaze of glory."

"We have intel others might need. We need to get it out."

"How?" Gate demanded. "We can't go back the way we came. We can't escape through the mouth." He pulled out his cell phone. "I've got no signal. We can't wait for it to open its mouth again." He pointed back up the slope. "We'll probably be dead by then. Just what do you expect us to do?"

"I expect us to keep moving. A means of transmitting the data will present itself eventually. Until then, we stay alive. There has to be some way to defeat this creature. I won't give up. I can't give up. Come on."

Reluctantly, Gate got to his feet. He knew he was going to die, but he didn't want to die being rasped to death by the cleaners. He watched Walker crawl into the tunnel, took a deep breath, and followed. The sides were damp and brushed against him. He tried not to examine his environs too closely. Behind him, Costas roared, "Fucking monster! My mother always said I'd come to a bad end. I should have listened to her and become a pimp."

GIRRA

22

Saturday, August 11,   1:20 p.m. (CDT)   Omaha, Nebraska –

Paige Collins was elbow deep in grease. It smudged her right cheek and forehead. Dabs of marine grease and oil dotted the locks of dirty blonde hair escaping from beneath her Corn Huskers baseball cap. She worked frantically on the starboard outboard 250-horsepower engine. The single remaining engine could propel the forty-foot work barge downriver, but only at a snail's pace. To escape Girra, they needed speed.

"For God's sake, hurry," urged one of her passengers, Michael Cosgrove, an infuriating man she was quickly growing to despise.

She turned on him in fury, the screwdriver in her hand shaking with the effort to keep from plunging it into his heart. He had been nagging her for an hour, as she tried to repair the engine. "Shut the hell up. If you're in a hurry, get the hell off my boat and walk."

Cosgrove's wife, Jenny, snickered. She, too, was tired of her husband's tirades.

"Girra's just a few miles away," he said.

"You think I can't hear the bombs? If it turns down river, we'll be sitting ducks with only one engine."

Her business ferrying personnel to and from passing barges and tugs and hauling freight up and down the river was on hold until the threat of Girra was over. Everything she owned, every penny she had was tied up in the old barge. Before evacuating the city, she had agreed to take on passengers, ten of them at two hundreds dollar a head. She would need the cash for fuel if she wanted to head downriver to Saint Louis or even farther to New Orleans to start over. Now, she was regretting her decision.

At thirty-two, life on the river was all she knew. She had learned under the tutelage of her father, a former tug captain. She knew the river like a book. She had been daughter, lone crewmember, and chief cook and bottle washer her entire life. Upon his death, she had become sole owner and operator of Collins River Freight, LLC. She had also inherited his debts. She lived in a small cabin below decks to save money.

She slammed shut the engine housing. "Maybe that did it," she announced to her nervous passengers.

"Thank God," Cosgrove said, wiping sweat from his brow with his sleeve.

She walked across the deck to the cabin, crossed her fingers, and pushed the start button. The engine coughed and sputtered, kicking out a cloud of smoke, but it started. She cranked the second engine and smiled as it hummed to life.

"Now we get the hell out of here. Someone kick off the fore and aft lines."

"What?" a young man asked. He wore tan slacks and a white Izod shirt. The backpack on his back contained all he owned.

She sighed. "The ropes at the front and the back of the boat. Take them off the metal cleats on the dock."

He nodded and rushed to remove the ropes.

She watched a small Cessna fly low overhead as it took off from Eppley Airfield, barely missing the roofs of buildings and tops of trees. She marveled at the pilot's lack of intelligence or his daring. The sky was filled with military aircraft and missiles. The pilot had to fly at treetop level to avoid the jets. *That small Cessna must be the last plane out of the city*, she thought. She hoped he made it. She hoped *she* made it.

Council Bluffs had already been smashed by Girra and by the bombs dropped by the B2 bombers flying out of Offutt Air Force Base. Smoke blanketed the eastern horizon, a sign the creature was close. If the jets circling like vultures were any indication, it was now crashing through the neighborhoods of the West End headed toward the river. Clouds of dust rose from each of the massive creature's twelve legs as it smashed into homes. A rhythmic thunder marked the creature's steady pace, as it continued it western trek. She had watched the live broadcast of the ebony alien destroying Des Moines, sitting transfixed to the television until the camera went dead. That had been terrifying enough. She didn't want to witness it up close and personal.

As the boat pulled away from the dock, she gunned the engines. No Coast Guard would force her to follow the No Wake rules. The Coast Guard had moved their boats downriver. Six B2 bombers from Offutt Air Force Base darkened the sky. Seconds later, they dropped their loads of bombs on Girra. The explosions were dramatic and generated a lot of sound and fury, but did nothing to slow Girra's steady march toward Omaha. For eighteen hours, it had resisted all attacks as it brought massive devastation from Indiana to Omaha. It seemed strange that the world could change so dramatically in so short a time. With the arrival of Ishom, Girra, and Nusku, the debate over alien life was finally settled. Mankind was not alone in the universe. Unfortunately, his neighbors were not friendly. Now, the debate of methods of survival had taken its place.

More than the strange, ugly alien monster, she feared the Wasps that poured from its belly, spreading out across the countryside, killing and capturing humans and feeding them to the creature. She eyed the .45 automatic on top of the control panel. She wouldn't let them take her alive. She glanced at her passengers. They were from all walks of life – businessmen, homemakers, professionals. They all had one thing in common. All were frightened and shell shocked, uprooted from their homes and familiar lives. She needed to occupy their minds.

"You two." She pointed to two women huddled close together, a woman and her daughter. "Go to the galley below and make some sandwiches and coffee. You," she called out to a young boy of about fifteen wearing a Led Zeppelin tee shirt and shorts. "Go to the bow and watch out for trees or debris in the water. Sing out if you see anything."

The heavy rains had caused massive flooding to the north, raising the river level and washing dead trees and abandoned automobiles from the banks. A collision could penetrate the aluminum hull or shear off a propeller blade, leaving them dead in the water. During the flooding of 2011, she had seen entire houses floating down the river like half-submerged houseboats. On the plus side, the fast current added speed to her barge. She pushed the engines for every knot she could urge from them. She aimed for the fast flowing current in the middle of the river to avoid any obstructions in the backwater along the banks.

Ahead, the twin pylons of the Bob Kerry Pedestrian Bridge rose like a fairyland gateway across the river. The spider web display of suspension cables supporting the three-thousand-foot span was a stirring sight, or would have been if she had time to consider its beauty. Now, she only used the bridge to mark her passage down river. The I-480 Bridge came next. She glanced at the hundreds of cars and trucks on the bridge abandoned when an eighteen-wheeler jackknifed the day before, blocking three westbound lanes. Heartland of America Park was empty of sightseers.

The two women returned from below decks bearing a tray of sandwiches and a pot of coffee. When a loud explosion ripped the air off to their left, the daughter dropped a coffee cup to the deck, shattering it. A plume of smoke and flame shot up from West End, as grain elevators exploded from the rampaging fires sweeping across the city.

"Be careful," she snapped at the daughter. "Those cost money."

She regretted her hasty words when she saw the look of horror on the girl's face. She realized that she was short tempered, because she too, was frightened.

Beneath the Union Pacific railroad bridge, she spotted a body suspended by a rope, a suicide unable to face the alien apocalypse. She wondered why anyone would bother going all the way out onto the railroad bridge when so many trees were available. She supposed people did strange things when faced with death. She hoped she didn't face such a challenge.

"I wonder why he did it?" one of the women asked her. She held a sandwich in her hand, but she hadn't taken a bite.

Paige glanced at the woman, unable to remember her name, and then turned back to the river before her. "Who knows? Maybe he just gave up."

"I'm not giving up," she said.

The woman sounded so determined that Paige studied her more carefully. Her clothing said well-to-do, but her speech and mannerisms spoke of a humbler background, as if she had married well. She hadn't bothered with references or background stories when accepting passengers. She only noticed the color of their cash.

"Is that why you decided to travel by river?"

The woman's face colored briefly with embarrassment, or perhaps it was shame. "I waited on my husband, Steve. He was on a construction job in Papillion just south of here. He finally called this morning and said he would wait for me there. The bastard didn't have the balls to drive back here to pick me up."

"Maybe he couldn't make it," Paige suggested. "The roads are blocked."

She snickered. "No, he's a coward. I've always known he was. He was simply looking out for his own skin. Well, I'm not going to Papillion. I'm going as far as you'll take me. Screw him."

Faced with an alien invasion, Paige supposed families were either growing stronger or disintegrating all across America.

"Good for you," she said. "We'll drink Hurricanes together in New Orleans."

"I'm looking forward to it." The woman walked away sandwich in hand, still untouched.

Once past the I-80 Bridge, Paige began to relax. The parking lot of Harrah's Casino on the Missouri side of the river was empty for the first time she could remember.

As the river curved east in the big bend around the marshlands south of West End, she caught her first glimpse of Girra. Her heart pounded so hard she had difficulty breathing. The creature's head rose almost two hundred feet above the house rooftops. Each stride carried it a hundred yards. Though the city had been evacuated, many residents still lingered, either too frightened to leave or left with no transportation out when the roads closed. The creature's tentacles dipped into the rubble, extracting struggling people, and delivered them to the yawning maw that opened vertically along its face, making it appear even more alien. The ebony carapace seemed to suck in light from the sun and reflect darkness, lending an aspect of evil to the creature. It raised two of its six sharply pointed front legs into the air and brought them back down on the roof of a hotel, ripping away part of the structure. Concrete dust billowed into the air, as the wall collapsed. Within seconds, the hotel was a pile of rubble.

Girra crossed the river just below the I-80 Bridge, generating six-foot waves that soon reached the barge, rocking it wildly. She fought the wheel to keep the barge straight. The creature strode into the riverfront park like a Brobdingnagian among the Lilliputians, towering over church steeples and office buildings. Old Market, Rosenblatt Stadium, and Henry Dooly Zoo disappeared beneath its heavy tread. She forced herself to watch, as a swarm of Wasps bearing their human prey from Council Bluffs delivered them to the open mouth, and then flew away toward downtown Omaha. She wanted to imprint the grisly image in her mind in case the creatures came for her. She would need unquavering resolve to pull the trigger on the .45 when that happened.

With a final chatter and a puff of smoke, the engine she had just repaired stopped working. The barge immediately slowed to a crawl. She yanked Cosgrove over to the wheel.

"Here, keep it in the middle of the river while I fix the engine."

"I can't ..." he protested.

She picked up the pistol. "You drive or I'll toss you and your two hundred dollars over the side to lighten the load."

To her relief, he didn't call her bluff, but grabbed the wheel and held on tightly with both hands. She jammed the pistol down the front of her jeans, and amid the frightened stares, raced to the rear of the barge. The engine was on fire. She ripped the fire extinguisher from the cabin wall and sprayed the engine. Once the fire was out, she tossed the empty extinguisher over the side, and then yanked the cover from the 250-horsepower Johnson engine. The damage was easy to spot. A pinhole fuel leak had started a fire, melting the electrical wiring. The engine was finished, beyond her ability to repair.

"Damn," she cursed, slamming the cover back down.

"What now?" the young man in the Izod shirt asked, following her back into the cabin.

She pushed Cosgrove aside and took the wheel from him. "We keep going," she said. "That thing is too busy destroying Omaha to bother with us."

"What about them?" Cosgrove's wife asked.

Paige followed her pointing finger, turning pale when she saw the swarm of Wasps headed down the river. They could never outrun them, even with both engines. There was only one thing she could do.

She killed the other engine. In the sudden silence, she shouted, "Everyone below decks. We'll try to bluff them."

"Are you crazy?" Cosgrove questioned. "They'll tear through this hull like it was paper."

"What choice do we have?"

Cosgrove became belligerent, coming over to stand right in front of her, glaring down at her. "Take us to shore. We can hide in the buildings."

He towered over her by almost a foot and outweighed her by seventy pounds, but she was used to dealing with tugboat captains and river rats. She didn't back down.

"We don't have time."

"I demand …"

She had had enough. She pulled the .45 from her jeans and jammed it in his belly. "Either go below or over the side. Nobody's staying on deck."

Cosgrove's wife pulled his arm until he backed away, still snarling. "Don't be a fool dear," she said. "I think this young lady means it." Cosgrove glared at his wife but didn't resist.

"Go below," she yelled and waited as everyone filed down the steps to the galley.

She rushed over to the five-gallon can of gasoline she had used to prime the engine and began splashing fuel onto the metal deck. She was careful to avoid the wooden parts of the cabin. She splashed a liberal amount on the tires tied to the gunwales as bumpers. The Wasps were exploring buildings along the banks of the river, but they were getting closer. They would be upon the barge in less than five minutes. As she retreated to the hatch, she removed a flare gun from its cupboard and fired at the deck. The flare struck the deck and bounced over the side. The gasoline burst into flames. As she watched the black smoke rise from the burning tires, she hoped the fire would dissuade the Wasps from investigating before the fire engulfed the entire barge. She closed the hatch and faced her passengers.

"Now, we wait," she said.

23

Saturday, August 11,   2:15 p.m. (CDT)   **Mission Control, Houston –**

Director Caruthers fiddled nervously with the ink pen, tapping it on the desktop. Lack of sleep, lack of food, and a feeling of abject helplessness had made him irritable. Except for the sound of his tapping, Mission Control was eerily quiet. He had snapped at so many technicians in the past few hours that they were afraid to venture near his desk or start an idle conversation. The stink of a score of unwashed bodies permeated the room. He knew he stank as well. His shorts were riding up his crotch, making him uncomfortable, but he didn't have time to shower or to change clothes. He ripped off the old nicotine patch on his arm and applied a fresh one. Then, he shoved a stick of gum into his mouth for good measure. Neither the patches nor the gum were doing much to alleviate is cigarette craving. He wanted nothing more than to walk out of the room and have a smoke, but he didn't have the time for that either.

Pegasus was currently on the far side of the moon, out of radio communication, *Lunar One* was on a slow death spiral into the moon, and the *Armstrong*, the lunar lander not meant to land, was currently on its way up from the moon's surface with Commander Langston and Crenshaw aboard. On top of everything else, his friend, Gate Rutherford, was currently incommunicado inside the creature Nusku with a nuclear warhead. Everything had slipped beyond his control. He was a mere spectator in events unfolding around him unable to affect any changes or to offer any sage advice. He didn't like the feeling.

When the radio link with *Lunar One* crackled to life, he jumped from his seat, knocking over a cup of long cold coffee. He ignored the trickle of coffee dripping off the desk and rushed to stand beside CAPCOM's desk.

"*Lunar One* to Houston. Come in Houston."

Caruthers recognized Langston's voice. It sounded as tired as his was. He nodded to Tray Davis to reply. Davis, who had not abandoned his post since the change in *Lunar One's* mission, kept his voice calm as he spoke.

"This is Houston control, *Lunar One*. Glad to have you back, Langston."

Caruthers snatched the microphone from Davis' hands. "Caruthers here, Langston. *Pegasus* is silent at the moment, but they are on course and should arrive shortly. I highly suggest all four of you remain where you are."

He had pondered Langston's earlier cryptic message and hoped Langston hadn't done anything stupid. The one-and-a-half-second delay seemed to last forever before *Lunar One* replied, "We appreciate all the effort directed toward our rescue, Director. The logistics must have been a nightmare."

"We have a great team here, Commander Langston. They all pushed maximum effort to bring you all back safely."

"We haven't detected *Pegasus* yet. It might not make it in time."

Caruthers gripped the microphone tighter. *In time for what?*

Langston continued. "We've reached our decision. I'm transferring my crew to the *Armstrong* to await *Pegasus'* arrival."

"I repeat. Hold on as long as you can. Pegasus should be arriving shortly."

"Negative, Houston. The crew of *Lunar One* will board *Armstrong*, facilitate a stable orbit, and await rescue by *Pegasus*. I will take *Lunar One* to the surface and make maximum contact with the alien object. With luck, I can bury it beneath fifty meters of regolith and cut off communications. At the very least, I can prevent it from taking off and achieving lunar orbit, as it's now attempting."

Caruthers knew his suspicions had been correct. After a moment of stunned silence, he replied, "The odds are against you, Commander. Don't waste your life. Wait for rescue."

"My decision has been made, Director. The others have agreed with my decision. It's what I want to do. I've seen that thing down there. I've … felt it inside my head. I have to stop it, destroy it if I can. It's now or never. I don't have enough oxygen for another orbit."

He recognized the desperation in the commander's voice, but he was still a member of NASA. "Langston, if I was in your position, I might do the same thing, but I urge you to reconsider. Your expertise …"

"I'm certain that teardrop on the surface controls the creatures. I can … feel it. If I can create a landslide and cover it … well, it might shut down the signal."

"If it can signal from the moon's far side, it must be directing a signal through the moon. I doubt a few meters of regolith will stop it."

"I've thought about that. You remember that Chinese rover they sent up here three years ago. I believe the teardrop is relaying messages through it to our communications satellites."

"I'll contact Wenchang launch facility in China. If you're right, maybe we can jam the signal. If the nuclear device works on Nusku, we might have the means to stop them here."

"It's too risky. The Chinese haven't been very cooperative lately. Besides, you and I both know I'm too old to fly again. I don't want to spend the rest of my days behind a desk. If there's even a small chance of success, I think it's worth it."

He had no way to stop Langston, and Langston knew it. The commander was asking for his blessing, not his permission.

"I say again, Commander. I recommend that you await *Pegasus* for transfer and return to Earth."

"Negative, Director."

Caruthers' gaze slowly scanned everyone in the room. By their expressions, they knew he was wasting his time. So did he. If he were in Langston's place, he would do the same thing. A person could accept just so much before the need to strike out outweighed common sense. He sighed into the microphone.

"I can't stop you, Commander. We'll take good care of your crew." He paused. What more could he say. "Good luck, Commander. Houston out."

He handed the microphone back to CAPCOM and returned to his desk to wait, feeling much too old for his years.

* * * *

As soon as Langston switched off the radio, Mahall said, "God wouldn't let us die like this. We'll be rescued. I know it."

"God didn't do so good a job on the Christians down there," Crenshaw shot her, jabbing her finger out the porthole toward Earth. "What makes you think you're any better than them?" She laughed. "Maybe God is willing to kill you to take me out."

"You don't believe in God," Mahall snapped at her.

"I didn't believe in aliens either until a couple of days ago. Maybe I'll find God yet, but I don't think he'll give a rat's ass if I die up here or down there."

Ingersall cleared his throat. He had remained out of the fray that had erupted when Langston had presented his proposal. His quiet reserve had seemed out of character and worried Langston. This was the doctor's first trip. He was young and impressionable. He hoped Ingersall hadn't given up hope.

"It seems to me that our choices are limited. Numbers might mislead, but they don't lie. In about an hour, we'll crash on the moon. Even if by some miracle we don't crash, in another two or three hours at best we'll be out of oxygen. Help might come or it might not. I want to live, but I don't want to live badly enough to ignore the facts." He glanced at Langston. "You could have ordered us to take the lander and wait for rescue, and then crash the Orion, but you wanted our vote." He paused. "We voted."

Langston nodded. "So you did, and I'm proud of you all. You're a fine crew. It's been my honor to serve with you. I'm leaving you enough oxygen for two hours if you remain in your suits. If a rescue hasn't taken place by then, it's not likely to. I'm taking what's in my suit and enough LOX to cause an explosion."

He looked at each of them, gauging their reaction to his decision. Ingersall smiled. Mahall had tears in her eyes, but she didn't argue. Crenshaw stared at him as if he had kicked her in the gut. She wanted to accompany him, but an extra person wouldn't improve his chances.

"The *Armstrong* has enough fuel left to reach a stable orbit. We'll be in position to impact the crater in forty-five minutes. We'll separate the two vehicles then. There's time for each of you to make personal calls if you want." He smiled at them. "Is anyone hungry?"

As they had before their disastrous encounter with Girra, they had one last meal together. Crenshaw tried to make it as festive as possible with cake and wine she had sneaked aboard, or at least thought she had. Langston had personally inspected and weighed every kilo of baggage loaded. He had allowed the wine for a celebration. Now, it would serve a different purpose. His meal – roast beef, potatoes, and gravy – passed through his lips but left no impression on his taste buds. His thoughts dwelt on his impending death. Looking back on his life, he felt a twinge of guilt at what he had missed, but was proud of what he had accomplished.

His wife had left him early on during his astronaut training. The dedication and long hours had been too much for her to endure. He didn't blame her. It had been a conscious decision on his part, selfish and motivated by his desire to become an astronaut. That goal superseded his marriage. He had no children to mourn him, and his close friends were involved with the program. They would understand.

One personal goal, setting foot on the moon, had been unexpectedly met. It had taken an alien invasion to do it, but he was satisfied with his lot in life. Sacrificing his life for his country was no more than one might expect of anyone in the military. So many had died already. His life meant nothing in such an overwhelming context.

As they were clearing up the dishes, sipping wine through straws from pouches, Crenshaw began singing a song. Her Australian city accent slipped into Outback Stine, making some of the words difficult to recognize, but the melody was soothing and the few lyrics he did recognize spoke to Langston of quiet nights with soft moonlight, lovers, and hope for the future. It was a fitting song. In the silence that followed, no one stirred for several minutes for fear of breaking the magical spell she had woven.

Closing the hatch on the *Armstrong* was the most difficult thing he had ever done. As he sealed it, he peered through the glass and into the subdued faces of Mahall, Ingersall, and Crenshaw. Part of him wanted to remain with them. They were his crew, and he was responsible for them. However, leaving them improved their chances for survival, and he had a task to perform.

The Orion craft shuddered once as the *Armstrong* broke free and drifted away. When it reached a thousand meters distance, Crenshaw fired the engine to boost it into a stable orbit. With a wistful feeling, he watched it grow smaller. The tiny craft had carried him to the moon and back. *Pegasus* would be in radio range within fifteen minutes. Allowing thirty minutes to match orbits and for docking, his crew would soon be safely on their way home, and the *Armstrong* would be space junk orbiting the moon. Crenshaw had all the photographs and telemetry of the alien teardrop aboard. He hoped some of it might prove useful.

The Orion had no more fuel for the main engine. He could maneuver only with the Vernier thrusters. Once he broke orbit, gravity would do most of the work. He had carefully worked out the precise position to drop from orbit and the trajectory he needed to follow, but it would be seat of the pants flying, the kind at which he excelled as a Navy pilot.

"*Pegasus* to *Lunar One*."

Langston grabbed the radio. "*Lunar One* here. Is that you, Gilbert?"

Gilbert Hastings, pilot of the *Pegasus* answered, "Copy that Commander. We have *Lunar One* and *Armstrong* on our radar. No visual yet. ETA sixteen minutes with *Lunar One*."

A sense of relief swept over Langston. "Copy, *Pegasus*. Negative for *Lunar One* rendezvous. Make rendezvous with *Armstrong*. I'm sitting out this dance. I have a prior engagement."

He understood Hastings' confusion when Hastings said, "I don't understand, *Lunar One*. Repeat."

"Rendezvous with *Armstrong*. I'm taking *Lunar One* out for a spin."

Crenshaw's voice from the *Armstrong* broke in. "I'll explain, *Pegasus*. We have you on our radar. I'll flash our outside lights."

After a moment of silence, *Pegasus* answered, "Copy that, *Armstrong*."

There was no need for further conversation. *Armstrong* was aware that rescue was minutes away. He had already said his goodbyes to them. His part in the *Lunar One* mission was over. He redubbed *Lunar One*, the *Avenger*. His new mission was military, not exploration.

He watched the shipboard clock, counting down the minutes, and then the seconds until he would fire his thrusters, sending him in his slow death dive. He had time to contemplate his life, but chose not to do so. He had regrets and he had successes. Each life was a measure of both. His life was no more or no less precious than another's was. Sometimes life called for sacrifice. This was one of those times.

When the clock hit zero, he pressed the button but felt nothing. He fought the thought that the rockets had failed, taking heart as the altimeter began to drop. He was falling toward the moon like a rocket from hell. There was no atmosphere to heat the vehicle, no buffeting to shake it to pieces. The *Avenger* fell smoothly and silently. Ahead of him, the wide expanse of the *Mare Moscoviense* glowed softly in the harsh sunlight. He imagined that he could see the ebony teardrop of the alien ship in the crater like the dark pupil of an alien eye glaring at him.

He wasn't sure if it was his imagination or the teardrop feeding them into his brain in an attempt to stop him, but chaotic images bombarded his mind as he fell. He glimpsed one of the alien monsters, a black behemoth stalking the landscape. He sensed a mind compelling it onward. Behind the mind lay nothingness – no joy, no beauty, no marvel. It was a mind devoid of any of the attributes so innate to humans, a mind devoted to chaos and destruction. The image strengthened his resolve. He knew the creatures were being directed by an alien presence through the teardrop.

The *mare* was large enough to cover the entire horizon now. The moonscape swept by at a dizzying speed. The long, dark length of the rille with the rim of the crater beside it loomed larger. He willed the *Avenger* toward the rim above the teardrop, feeling like Slim Pickens as Major 'King' Kong riding the nuclear warhead in *Dr. Strangelove*. He resisted the impulse to yell, "Yahoo!"

He checked his watch – 3:45 p.m. (CDT).

He knew he should not have been aware of the crash, but some part of him had melded with the presence within the teardrop. Through alien eyes, he saw the Orion looming larger as it neared the crater. He saw the blast when the ship crashed into the rim of the crater, watched the tower of rock collapsed and slide in slow motion to cover the teardrop with tons of regolith. Instantly, he no longer sensed the creatures on the Earth's surface, only the rage of the alien mind. That part of him that remained smiled at their confusion. He sensed that they had never known defeat or even resistance in their long lifetimes. The loss of control of the creatures was a new and frightening thing for them.

The alien mind withdrew, and he was alone in the void.

NUSKU

23

Gate felt like a morsel of food passing through Nusku's gut, crawling and sliding through the slippery tunnel that led God knows where. Several times, he jackknifed his body to maneuver around particularly sharp turns. His arms were lead weights, and his legs throbbed from heel to hip. Every muscle in his body protested his acts of contortion, and it seemed as if the passageway was growing smaller the deeper they progressed. If they reached a dead end, he wasn't looking forward to the task of backing out.

Behind him, an equally disheartened Costas kept up a running litany of complaints. "I'm too big for this shit." "I'm stuck." "I can't see behind me." "Are we there yet?"

Gate sympathized with the big sergeant. Both he and Walker were tall and slim, whereas Costas had to force his way through the tight confines. Even so, Gate was ready to call a halt. They had crawled for thirty minutes and he was exhausted. Worse, he was thoroughly soaked with whatever foul smelling liquid the passage walls secreted. Some had gotten into his mouth, almost gagging him. He was just glad it wasn't acid, but even that might be better than whatever fate awaited them at the other end.

"Hold on," Walker called.

Gate shined his light on Walker's legs and saw that he was standing with his upper body thrust into another opening above them.

"This looks promising," he said, and then disappeared up the new tunnel.

Gate followed, pleased that the new tunnel was less confining. It was also drier and cooler. The passageway sloped upward at a steep but manageable angle. He emerged behind Walker into an illuminated circular space that reminded him of a carousel. Behind transparent crystal walls, rows of glowing red and green spheres floated a few inches above the surface of their ebony crystal hemispherical bases. The orbs rotated rapidly, scattering a dizzying, scintillating pattern of light around the room.

"This isn't biological," he said. As he watched, some of the spheres moved up and down. He guessed at their purpose. "They're gyroscopes."

Walker looked at him with disbelief.

"Feel the room jostle as the creature moves? The spheres are responding to that movement, keeping the creature upright and oriented."

"But it looks mechanical."

"I think it is, at least in part. If, as I believe, the creature is a mechanical construct filled with biological organs, each designed for a specific function. The creature probably has no real brain, just a neural network located throughout its body. The gyroscope orients it."

"Then we can destroy the gyroscope," Walker said.

"I believe we can. At the very least it will render it directionless."

"If we only had the nuke," Costas said, as he joined them.

"We'll have to make do, Sergeant," Walker said. He reached out and pressed his hand against the clear crystal. He quickly withdrew it. "It's cold."

Gate nodded. "I noticed that. The aliens probably use some super-cooled liquid to cool whatever magnetic forces are at work. If we could find the source and stop it."

"We could heat the creature up," Walker finished.

Gate smiled. "Exactly."

Costas tapped the transparent panel with the butt of his rifle. "If it's as hard as the black stuff, we're out of luck."

"We're deep inside the creature," Gate countered. "I think its only purpose would be to serve as an insulator."

Walker slid the bolt back on his M16. "There's only one way to find out. Stand back."

His weapon clicked on an empty chamber. He tossed it to the ground. "I'm out of ammo."

Gate handed him his M16. It was the only thing that had had made it through the tunnel with him. His pack and helmet were gone. "Here, you're a better shot than I am."

Walker fired a burst into the transparent wall. It shattered like glass. Frigid air poured from the opening, forming a dense fog on the floor as it heated. The cold air climbed up Gate's leg, making him shiver, but it didn't immediately freeze his skin.

"It must be compressed carbon dioxide gas. Liquid nitrogen would be at minus 346 degrees Fahrenheit and liquid oxygen at minus 297 degrees. Both would freeze our skin immediately."

"Thanks for the heads up, Doc," Costas said.

"Carbon dioxide is about minus 108 – freezing but it warms quickly."

Walker didn't seem concerned what gas it was. He stepped through the opening he had made. As Gate followed him, the hairs on his arms and head stood on end.

"Static electricity," he noted aloud. "The spinning orbs in a magnetic field create an electrical charge."

"How do we interfere with them?"

"The coolant draining off should heat them up quickly," Gate replied.

He held his hand experimentally over one of the orbs. He could almost feel the energy field the spinning orb created. He tried to shove one of the orbs off its base, but his hands refused to make contact with it. They moved aside as if pushed away by an unseen hand.

"It has some kind of force field protecting it. The spheres may be constructed from the same material as the crystal."

He searched the room for some sort of radio, anything that might receive a signal from the aliens and direct the creature's movements but found nothing. For all he knew, the entire crystalline structure of Nusku could act as a gigantic receiver.

After a few minutes, he noticed that the room was growing colder. So did Walker.

"The system is pumping more liquid carbon dioxide into the walls. The creature must be stripping it from our atmosphere. It's weeping from the walls. It's repairing itself," he said with disgust.

"Damn," Walker cursed. "We're getting nowhere."

"Shoot out all the glass," Gate suggested. "Maybe we can outpace its ability to produce coolant."

Walker and Costas fired at the transparent crystal. The walls shattered and the room grew warmer. Within seconds, Costas began choking.

"I can't breathe," he gasped.

"It's the carbon dioxide buildup," Gate realized aloud. "We can't stay here."

Walker removed his knife and plunged it into the wall behind the row of orbs. The blade sank into the flesh up to the hilt. He began hacking until he had enlarged an opening wide enough for him to step into. He continued carving away at the alien flesh, ignoring the fluids that seeped from the wound. Gate glanced at Costas, who shrugged and plunged into the cavity after Walker, joining him at slicing a passageway out of the spherical room with his knife.

The air became hard to breath. Gate became dizzy and disoriented, stumbling along behind Costas. The only sounds he heard was his labored breathing. He reached out his arm to locate Costas, and stepped into nothingness. He had the unnerving sensation of falling just before he blacked out.

* * * *

He awoke with Walker gently slapping his face and shining his flashlight in his eyes, blinding him. "Are you okay?" Walker kept repeating, punctuating each question with a slap. Gate raised his hand to ward off another blow.

"Where are we?" he asked.

"I think it's the power source," Walker replied.

Gate looked past Walker's shoulder. What he had thought to be Walker's flashlight were flashes of lightning high above them arcing between clusters of crystals protruding from the roof in an irregular pattern and a crystalline rod running the length of the chamber. The crystals glowed faintly, pulsing rhythmically. He sat up groaning from his aches.

"How long was I out?"

"Oh, two or three minutes. I cut through the wall of this chamber, and we slid down the side for about twenty feet. No bones broken?"

"No, I'm okay." Gate stared at the electrical interaction between the crystals. "It could be the power source. I think those crystals are the ends of the columns we saw. The energy absorbed by the armor is transferred here. An attack helps power the creature."

"So is it a machine or a cyborg?" Walker asked.

Gate shared Walker's confusion. It had taken him a while to grasp the enormity of the alien's technology. "It's a living, breathing creature designed to fit inside an artificial shell, like a hermit crab."

"We could boil the bitch, but we don't have the friggin' nuke," Costas said. He tossed his M16 to the ground. It clattered on the floor of the chamber and slid to Gate's feet. "And I'm out of ammo for the rifle. All I have is my .45 and two clips. I can't do much damage with that."

Gate sympathized with Costas' frustration and understood his anger. He had lugged the heavy nuke through Nusku for four hours only to lose it before reaching their destination. Along the way, he had also watched three companions die. The sergeant was eager to strike out at something. He wanted payback.

"I've still got my pistol," he said. He didn't want to part with it, but he offered the two extra clips to Costas. "You take the ammo."

"We're not done yet, sergeant," Walker said, as he scanned the crystal matrix running the length of the chamber. "We're where we wanted to be. All we need is some way to cause a bit of trouble. You're good at starting trouble, aren't you, sergeant?"

Costas grinned. "I've been known to start a ruckus or two."

"Then find me a way to kill this beast."

Gate shook his head as he listened to the conversation with growing disbelief. "You two amaze me. The entire U.S. military hasn't been able to stop this thing, and you think two practically unarmed men can do something. You're delusional."

"We have an advantage, Doctor. We're inside it, and the last time I checked, there were three of us. Are you giving up on me?"

Walker's accusation stung. "I don't know what I'm doing yet. I'm just tired."

"We all are. Look, I don't know a damn thing about aliens, but you say this thing is part machine. I do know machines." He grinned. "Costas and I have thrown a few monkey wrenches in quite a few pieces of machinery over the years. It's what we do. You point out the most likely spot to cause the most damage, and Costas and I will find some way to break it."

Gate sighed. Walker was right. If he gave up, he would simply die inside Nusku. Being enclosed in the alien monster made him realize just how much of life he had been missing. Maybe his friend Joe Palacio had the right idea – a wife, a family, a life outside NASA.

"Okay, let's kill this thing, but I warn you, you'll have to dispose of the other two on your own."

Gate drank the last of his water, barely enough to wet his lips. Walker saw that his canteen was empty and offered him a sip from his. Though his thirst was strong, he refused. "You'd better save it. You must be low too."

"Take it. I learned to get by on very little water in the desert. You need it more than I do."

"Thanks," he said.

As he took the canteen, he noticed that his hand was shaking, a sign of dehydration. The chamber they were in wasn't as hot as the blood pit, but it was warm enough, well over a hundred degrees. The heat was slowly baking the moisture from his body. He took a sip and handed the almost empty canteen back to Walker.

"Too bad the condemned don't get a last meal."

"There's a couple of protein bars in your pack. They'll help take the edge off."

"I lost my pack back there," he jerked his thumb toward the narrow slit, "With my helmet and flashlight."

As Walker rummaged through his pack, he said, "You did quite well, Doctor, much better than I expected."

"Despite getting us lost?" Gate questioned.

"It's an unusual situation. Honestly, I didn't think the LIDAR would work inside the creature. I'm surprised the drones lasted as long as they did."

"If we could only transmit the data we've gathered," Gate lamented.

"We're not dead yet," Walker said, handing a protein bar to Gate.

"You really believe that, don't you?" he asked, as he tore open the wrapper and took a bite of the bar. "Not only does the ebony armor absorb the kinetic energy of the attacks, it also absorbs solar energy. The entire creature is one vast solar cell. Its alien designers did their job well. If Area 51 attacks, those crystals up there are going into energy production overtime. We'll be fried in here. It'll be like the inside of a microwave oven."

"Maybe we should leave," Costas suggested. "I wouldn't want to end up a microwave *Hot Pocket*."

"Where do we go?" Gate asked. He finished the bar in two bites. It left him hungry for more. "We're out of options."

"We dug our way in," Walker said. "We can dig our way out."

Gate couldn't fault Walker's logic, but he didn't share the captain's optimism. "We've gone from one dangerous spot to the next. What makes you think any place we go will be better?"

"Hope."

Gate shook his head. "You're crazy."

"Perhaps, but I don't feel like giving up." He took out his knife and pointed toward the wall behind them. "Let's try that way."

Reluctantly, Gate joined him. After half an hour's labor, both men were drenched with fluid from the gash they were carving in the creature's flesh. Gate wiped his eyes and examined their progress. They had excavated a six-foot-deep tunnel in the creature, but they had no idea how much farther they had to go or where they would come out. The task looked daunting. As he paused, Gate massaged his throbbing right arm. He turned and shouted to Costas.

"Costas, can you spell me?" No answer. He peered out the hole and looked around. No Costas. "Where's Costas?"

"Maybe he walked off to take a piss."

"Costas," Gate yelled again. He glanced at Walker and saw signs of concern in his eyes. "He can take care of himself."

"Well, he couldn't have gone far." Walker looked up at the hole from the gyroscope chamber. "There's only one way out of here."

Such an expression of trepidation came over Walker's face, that some of it rubbed off on Gate. "What?" he demanded.

"The fool has gone back after the nuke."

"I thought it fell into the acid pool."

"Costas wasn't sure. He couldn't remember a splash. I told him it wasn't worth the risk. I guess he thought otherwise."

Now, Gate was becoming alarmed. "If he finds it, will he set it off?"

Walker's dour expression was all the incentive Gate needed. He continued carving alien flesh, expecting nuclear incineration at any moment. He braced himself against the side of the pocket and dug frantically, using both hands to jab the knife into the wall and hack away chunks of flesh. A clear liquid dripped from the wounds they were inflicting on the creature. The smell was an atrocious mélange of musty old books and bad dog breath. He suspected it was some type of lymphatic fluid and hoped it wasn't deadly. He worked blindly, trying to keep the liquid out of his eyes. He was so intent on his labors that he would have fallen through the opening that suddenly appeared in front of him if Walker hadn't grabbed the back of his shirt. For a terrifying moment, he stood leaning precariously over the edge of a precipice, a black chasm with no bottom that he could see. His heart began hammering his chest hard enough to start his injured ribs aching. Then, Walker yanked him back in.

"Dead end," Gate groaned. "We can't go any farther."

Walker thrust his head through the opening to verify Gate's observation. He snapped a glow stick to activate it and dropped it. As it fell, it revealed a bundle of muscles below them expanding and contracting to the rhythm of the creature's movements. The glow stick was barely visible when it hit liquid at the bottom and sizzled out.

"It must be fifty or sixty feet down."

Gate pointed to a large structure sliding back and forth in the opening, resembling an upside-down pendulum. "That's one of the creature's legs," Gate said. "We're in some kind of hip joint cavity. The liquid must be a lubricant." He glared at Walker. "So what now?" He didn't hide his bitterness. He was bone tired. His arms ached, his side throbbed, his eyes burned, and his enthusiasm for continuing was rapidly waning.

"I see something like a strut or a brace just below us. It looks flat and level enough to cross over to the other side. It's narrow, but we could make it." Walker paused, as he shined his light on the moving strands of muscle sweeping across the open space. Any attempt to cross the strut would end in decapitation. "But we could never make it through that." He turned to stare at Gate. "I guess we're stuck here,"

"It appears so," Gate said. "I was more comfortable back there." He jerked his thumb toward the power chamber and started back.

As they entered the chamber, an object tumbled down the slope from the gyro chamber, followed by Costas. Walker shined his light and picked out Costas' head. A long, bloody slash marred the right side of his face, and his uniform was soaked with blood, but his injuries didn't suppress his wide grin. He pointed to the bomb at his feet. The backpack was missing. Costas had rigged a sling from several of the belts they had used to try to lower it.

"I found the bomb lying at the edge of the pool. The backpack was eaten away, but the nuke was okay."

"You look a bit worse for wear, sergeant," Walker said. Gate detected the obvious relief in the captain's voice at seeing Costas. He was also glad to see that Costas had made it. He had come to like the big, gruff soldier.

"I had an argument with a few of the residents over possession of the nuke, but I won." He looked at the new opening. "Is this a way out?"

Gate shook his head. "I don't think we're getting out." He glanced up at the dark crystals. The power surges had grown stronger. Brilliant flashes of light danced along the ebony rod and poured into the floor of the room. He could feel the energy through the soles of his boots.

"Then I suggest we set this baby off."

He looked first at Walker, and then at Gate. Walker nodded. After a few moments deliberation, Gate nodded as well. It looked as if they weren't getting out of Nusku alive. Quick immolation by a nuclear blast beat slow cooking by microwaves.

"Five minutes?" Costas asked.

"Five minutes is good," Walker replied.

Gate found his voice frozen from fear. He nodded his consent.

Costas set the timer and sat down beside the bomb with his arm draped casually over the device. "I lugged this thing all through this beast. Now I get to put it to good use."

To Gate's surprise, his fear melted away at the inevitability of death. Since he could do nothing about it, a sense of tranquil acceptance came over him. He sat down and allowed the rhythmic cadence of Nusku to relax him. He looked over at Walker, who had his eyes closed, toying with his knife. His lips were moving. Gate wondered if he was praying.

"It's been a pleasure, captain," he said.

Walker opened his eyes and smiled. "I hope you learned what you came for."

"I only wish I could transmit the information somehow."

"It seems both our missions were only partially successful."

The power surges increased. The entire ebony rod now glowed from within with a deep purple light. A high-pitched hum filled the air.

"Three minutes," Costas called out.

Gate wondered which would kill them first the bomb or the energy discharges. As he glanced up, the light disappeared, as did the humming sound. In fact, the entire chamber had gone silent. Then, he noticed the lack of movement.

"What happened?" Walker asked, as he leapt to his feet.

"I don't know. I think Nusku has stopped moving."

He and Walker looked toward the tunnel to the leg at the same time.

"Stop the nuke," Walker yelled.

Costas struggled to disarm the device, as Walker raced to the tunnel. He emerged a minute later and said, "The leg isn't moving. I think we can make it."

"What's going on?" Costas asked.

Gate shook his head. "Something has happened. If we're ever going to get out of the creature, now's the time."

"Set it for thirty minutes," he told Costas. "We're leaving."

They wasted none of their precious time. Walker went first, lowering himself to the strut below them, a narrow ebony structure barely two feet wide. Balancing with his extended arms like a tightrope walker, he reached the halfway point, where he had to wedge himself into a narrow space between two muscle bundles. Gate held his breath, fearful that the creature would start moving at any second, crushing Walker. He released his breath only when Walker made it across safely.

"Careful, it's slick," Walker warned. He played his light around the wall. "The wall is honeycombed with openings," he called out. "We won't have to dig."

Gate went next. As he hung suspended by his fingers and toes, he regretted his decision. Dying clean and quick in a nuclear blast would be better than falling. When he reached the strut, Walker's light shone on the narrow beam to mark his way. He could see nothing below him, but he knew he was hovering over a chasm. His fear of heights kicked into overdrive, threatening to tip him over the edge. Walker's comment about the strut being slick was an understatement. Mounds of a wet substance dotted the strut. He tried to avoid the larger piles, but each step was precarious and filled the air around him with the stench of rotting blood.

When he reached the muscles, he threaded his way through them as quickly as he could, hoping that whatever had stopped the creature would last a little longer. As he stepped off the strut onto the ledge on the other side, a sense of relief swept over him. He still might die in a nuclear blast, but he had conquered the chasm.

He examined the wall. Some of the openings were just small cavities in the ebony material. After examining a few, he decided that they served to strengthen the creature's structure while reducing weight. Two openings that they could reach were as big as the first passages they had encountered. He hoped one led somewhere safer than where they had been.

"Here I come," Costas called out.

Costas chose to crawl across the strut on his hands and knees, bitching aloud as he smeared stinky goo all over his hands and his uniform. "It's like pigeon shit."

Gate's stomach tightened. That's exactly what the goo reminded him of. "Hurry," he yelled, trying to keep the rising panic from his voice. He didn't know how much time they had. Costas had a difficult time squeezing through the tight opening between muscles. Gate checked his watch. Costas was moving too slowly. They had less than eighteen minutes left.

"Hurry!" he yelled to Costas. Then, he heard a familiar droning sound – Wasps.

Costas heard it too and put on a burst of speed, but he was too late. Two Wasps appeared, one on each side of him, illuminated by Walker's flashlight. Gate drew his pistol and fired at the nearest creature, but he only had a shot at the creature's back, and the bullets bounced harmlessly off the armor plating. One of the Wasps dove at Costas. Costas swatted it away with his hands, but couldn't avoid a savage slash of its massive jaws. They sliced into his right shoulder, almost dragging him off the strut. Gate emptied his clip, and then realized that he had given his extra ammunition to Costas. He stood helplessly, as Walker continued to reload and fire, keeping the creatures at bay until Costas could cross safely. Then Costas, ignoring the deep gash in his shoulder, joined in, firing until they finally brought down one of the monsters. The other one backed away, but didn't leave. Uncharacteristically, the Wasp continued to hover out of range. Knowing that the creatures were usually ruthless and suicidal in their attacks, he wondered what it was doing.

The droning sound grew louder. Walkers shined his light upwards. Gate swallowed against the lump in his throat, as the light revealed hundreds of Wasps using the struts as perches. They were in the equivalent of the Wasp nest. Most seemed dormant, but the closest ones, aroused by the gunfire, were dropping toward them.

"Run!" Walker yelled.

To Gate's immense relief, the tunnel led to a passageway running parallel to Nusku's side, perhaps the same tunnel they had explored upon entering the creature. That meant they were near one of the blisters. They only faced two problems – they didn't know where their ropes were, and Wasps were chasing them.

Costas, clutching his useless arm and bleeding like a stuck pig, stumbled often. Gate tried to support him, but the heavy sergeant was a handful. After he had pulled Gate to the ground for the third time, Costas groaned in pain and yelled, "Leave me, damn it! I'll take a few of these bastards with me."

Walker helped them both to their feet. "No one gets left behind," he said.

"I'll be in good company," Costas said. "Maybe you can say one of them Muslim prayers for me. A quick one, mind you," he added with a big grin. "I don't have time for a lot of that pagan gibberish."

"Come on, sergeant. I'm still giving the orders."

As he ran, Gate wondered why the Wasps weren't attacking. Something had happened to change the way the creatures acted. Before his mind could dwell on it, he saw light ahead from an open blister. They stumbled down the short tunnel to the blister. He was surprised at just how much he had missed seeing the sun. He had been inside the creature for only a few hours, but it seemed like days. He held onto the side of the blister, as the creature shuddered from an explosion. A jet swept by less than a hundred yards away.

"An *F-35 Lightning* from Nellis Air Force Base outside Vegas," Walked called out. "It's carrying *Storm Shadow* cruise missiles and *Sidewinders*."

"Looks like we got here just in time to die from our own friendly fire," Costas said, collapsing on the ground. His face was pale from loss of blood, but he didn't give an inch. He clutched his .45 in his good hand and faced the tunnel in expectation of Wasp company.

Another shudder ran through the creature.

"Look at the Wasps," Walker yelled.

Walker was right. The Wasps weren't attacking. They're just hovering in the air as if confused. The pilots of the flight of *F-35*

Lightnings had noticed as well. The jets swept down on the Wasps with guns blazing, dropping them like clay pigeons. It was a massacre, this time on the good guys' side.

"Yeah!" Walker yelled in encouragement.

"What stopped it?" Gate asked, confused. "Nothing we've tried so far has stopped it."

Walker was barely paying attention. His gaze was fixed on the jets mopping up the confused Wasps. They fell to the ground, riddled with machinegun bullets.

"Allah willed it," he said.

Gate's phone rang, startling him. He yanked it from his pocket.

"Doctor Rutherford," Colonel Starnes said. "You're alive."

"Nusku stopped moving," Gate yelled into the phone.

"All three creatures stopped moving at the same moment. We don't know what happened. Do you have any idea?"

"Can we have this discussion later? We just activated the nuke. We have less than twelve minutes. Get us the hell out of here!"

"I'll advise the authorities."

"In the meantime," Gate said, "would you please contact Nellis Air Force Base and tell them not to shoot any more missiles at us. I would like to go home now."

The colonel chuckled. "Sit tight. I'll get help to you as soon as I can."

"We're not going anywhere. You might tell them to hurry up. These Wasps might get restless again, and we're damn low on ammo."

"And tell them to send a pretty nurse to tend to my wounds," Costas reminded him.

Gate sat down beside Costas, suddenly exhausted by his ordeal. He checked his cell phone. The time was 1:55 p.m. (PDT).

Five-and-a half minutes later, a Blackhawk helicopter hovered just outside the blister. The pilot nodded to them, pointed up, and then rose above the blister. A cable with a sling dropped from the chopper. Walker grabbed it and pulled it inside the blister. He insisted that Costas go first. Costas was barely conscious, as Walker tightened the harness around him. When it was Gate's turn, he insisted that Walker go up with him.

"We don't have much time," he said.

Walker nodded and held onto the harness with both hands. As he rose up the creature's side, Gate wondered if it was dead or merely sleeping. Soon enough it wouldn't matter. As soon as they were aboard, the helicopter took off toward Nellis.

Less than two minutes into their flight, the bomb exploded behind them. It wasn't a large explosion with a blinding flash and a mushroom cloud. Fire and smoke belched from each open blister and from the creature's mouth. The ebony armor absorbed much of the blast, but the more sensitive internal organs were vaporized, as were most of the Wasps still hovering nearby. Nusku's legs collapsed and folded and as Goliath felled by David's stone, the creature fell to the ground head first, pushing up a giant mound of dirt as it slid forward. It lay there a smoking, dead hulk. The helicopter pilot cheered. Gate was just too tired to yell. He was ready to go home.

GIRRA

24

Saturday, August 11, **4:30 p.m. (CDT)** **Omaha, Nebraska –**

The sounds of the Wasps on the deck had quieted, but as Paige Collins started for the hatch, her passengers cast looks of disbelief in her direction. Michael Cosgrove, a constant thorn in her side since he came aboard her work barge, led the throng.

"They might still be out there," he warned.

She caressed but didn't draw the .45 in her waistband. "It's been long enough. We haven't heard anything in half an hour. If that fire gets out of control, we'll burn in here."

Cosgrove crossed his arms over his chest and assumed a smug expression, trying to look intimidating. "It's too dangerous. We need to wait."

Her patience was wearing thin, but she didn't want to have to shoot him to prove that she was captain. "If I don't repair that engine, we'll be paddling down river. We're up against the bank now, or can't you tell?"

A brief look of uncertainty crossed his face.

"If Girra decides to move south," she continued, "I don't want to be here. Do you?"

Cosgrove's wife, a woman of infinite patience, walked up beside her husband and took his arm. "Leave the nice lady alone, Mike. It's her boat, and I agree with her."

He fumed but nodded.

Paige drew her pistol and opened the hatch slowly, peering out the narrow slit. She saw no Wasps, and the barge wasn't on fire. *So far, so good.* She pushed the hatch open wide and stepped out onto the deck. Two of the tires were still smoldering. She kicked them over the side. The barge was rocking gently against the Iowa side of the river, caught in the shallows. Despite her assurances to her passengers, she doubted she could repair the starboard engine. It needed a complete rewire job. However, she could continue down river on one engine and hope she came across an abandoned boat with an engine she could borrow. *Oh, hell, steal,* she reminded herself. *No time for semantics.*

A pall of smoke hung over the river from still fires raging in Council Bluffs. She could barely see Omaha in the distance. She removed a pole hook and began to push the barge into deeper water.

"It's not moving," the young boy said.

"Then grab a pole and help," she snapped at him.

"No, I mean Girra. It's standing still."

She glanced toward Omaha and saw that he was right. Girra was motionless. She stopped pushing and looked at it, as the rest of her passengers filed slowly onto the deck. Most of Omaha was in rubble. Only one or two skyscrapers remained standing. She recognized the Woodmen Tower and One First National center. Two of the creature's front legs were impaled in the top five floors of the partially collapsed Northern Natural Gas building. Jets continued to fire missiles at the creature and to attack the swarm of Wasps hovering near the creature.

"What's going on?" one of the women asked. "Is it dead?"

Paige wondered how she had graduated from boat captain to sage of all things concerning Girra. "I don't know. I don't want to wait around and find out."

She cranked the engine, maneuvered the barge into the center of the river, and headed south. She glanced back one time to assure herself that the creature wasn't following her. She wasn't a religious woman, but she felt like saying a prayer of thanks.

ISHOM

25

Corporal Elias Matheson sat on the ground in Chino Hills State Park and watched Ishom march closer to Los Angeles. It had destroyed El Segundo and Inglewood and was now an angry Goliath striding through Los Angeles Memorial Coliseum, swinging its twelve massive legs like war clubs, smashing buildings and toppling towers. Los Angeles appeared doomed.

After Hayes' death during the Wasp attack, his plans to take the jeep north had ended at the first snarl of abandoned vehicles along I-110. Realizing that he would never make it through Los Angeles ahead of the creature, he backtracked to Highway 91, just minutes ahead of Ishom's rampage. He pushed the jeep as fast as it would go east toward Anaheim, dodging abandoned military vehicles and automobiles. He had not been the only soldier to desert his post. He ignored the frantic pleas of fellow soldiers and civilians along the road desperate for a ride and focused on the hills to the east. He took the Orange Freeway into the Chino State Park, but had to leave the car outside the park because of the traffic.

He was not alone on the hill. Thousands of evacuees had chosen to seek refuge on higher ground rather than face the hundreds of thousands of people still fleeing south and north out of the LA basin. Some, with typical California aplomb, had set up tents, treating the invasion and imminent destruction of LA as an event. He was surprised some entrepreneur had not hit upon the idea of selling tickets. He noticed several military uniforms in the crowd, but they discreetly chose to ignore each other. A deserter could not denounce another deserter.

The crowd was hushed, expectant, and perhaps even eager to witness the coming destruction. The carnival atmosphere struck him as macabre, but then it was human nature to appreciate a disaster, as long as you were not personally involved. A few of the crowd were on their knees praying, but most were merely spectators, glued to their seats.

It was several minutes before he noticed the lack of motion in the creature. It was difficult to tell through the smoke and dust, but it quickly became obvious that something had happened. He doubted it was because of the mosquito-bite stings of the jets worrying the creature. The Wasps also seemed confused, hovering around Ishom as if waiting for instructions. A few people cheered, but most, like Elias, simply waited to see what would happen next.

After ten minutes of inactivity, a spontaneous cheer erupted from the crowd. Despite his misgivings, Elias joined in. Whatever had happened, Los Angeles had been spared, at least for now. A sergeant walked over to him.

"Do you think it's dead?" he asked.

"Maybe, I don't know, but something happened."

The sergeant glanced nervously at the patch on Elias' uniform and saw that it was the same as his. "Are you going back?"

He hadn't had the time to let events sink in. "Maybe. You?"

The sergeant nodded. "I think so. Most of my squad was killed in the first few minutes of fighting. I wasn't the only one running," he said defensively.

"No condemnation here. I ran as fast as my ass would go."

"They may need us. Even if it's over, things are going to be bad for a while."

"I guess it beats looking over your shoulder for the MPs the rest of your life."

"Yeah, I've got a wife and kid."

"I've got a jeep," Elias said.

"Maybe I can round up a few more men. It won't look so bad if a bunch of us show up, you know, like stragglers."

"Yeah, good idea. If things get bad, food shortages and such, being in the army might not be so bad. As long as we don't have to fight more of these things," he added.

As the sergeant walked through the crowd rounding up stray military personnel, Elias looked back at Ishom. It remained motionless, as jets continued to fire missiles at it.

"Fuck you, aliens," he yelled, as she shot the creature a bird. The simple gesture made him feel better.

26

Saturday, August 11,   2:30 p.m. (PDT)   Nellis AAFB, Nevada –

The medics rushed Costas to the hospital as soon as the helicopter touched down. Safely away from Nusku, his spirits had improved dramatically. In spite of his severe injuries, he was hitting on the female stretcher-bearer, as they unloaded him from the Blackhawk helicopter. He gave a thumbs-up signal to Gate, as they closed the doors of the ambulance. Gate didn't doubt that the burly sergeant would recover quickly. He was too stubborn not to.

All three creatures remained immobile. Aircraft were busy mopping up the Wasps still in confused turmoil outside the creatures. Los Angeles still survived, as did most of Omaha. The radiation count around Nusku was above a safe level, but the authorities had evacuated most of Las Vegas before the blast. The levels would drop rapidly with dispersing winds.

Gate was glad he was free of the creature. His initial curiosity had turned to reflection on his life. He had survived when many hadn't. He had tempted fate, while hundreds of thousands eager to get away had died a horrible death. He didn't know if it had been luck or divine intervention, but he was still alive.

As he sat in the mess hall sipping coffee and nibbling on a sandwich, he decided to call Director Caruthers. He still stank of alien blood and guts, and his uniform was filthy, but none of the men and women sitting at nearby tables said anything, though a few glanced at him questioningly. He appreciated their discretion. He was a sorry sight.

The Director answered on the second ring. "Gate, are you all right?" His voice was full of excitement, quite different from their last conversation.

"Yeah, I made it out okay. The creatures stopped moving. Why?"

"The object that damaged *Lunar One* was some kind of communications drone. The collision sent it crashing to the moon. Commander Langston took the lander to the surface and examined it."

"They're alive. I'm glad to hear it."

Caruthers' long pause made him wonder if his relief was too early. "I'm afraid Langston is dead. He decided to crash *Lunar One* into the object. That's what stopped the creatures."

Gate was crestfallen. Their mission, the men Walker had lost – all for nothing. *No,* he thought. *We didn't know about the communications drone. We did what we had to do.*

"Then the crew of *Lunar One* … all gone?"

"No, only Commander Langston. The others are safely aboard the *Pegasus* on their way back home." He paused. "Langston died a real hero."

"That's something anyway. After all this, I imagine there are lots of heroes out there."

"The military is chomping at the bit for a peek inside one of these creatures. They smell an opportunity to learn from the alien technology."

"They'll be disappointed. It's mostly biotech."

"I'm sending some technicians to Girra after the military cleans out the Wasps. Do you want to go?"

Gate smiled. "No, I've had my fill of aliens. Tell the military that Wasps aren't the only things to watch out for."

"I'll relay the information to them."

Gate dreaded the next question, but he had to know. "How many dead?"

"Estimates are between ten and sixteen million, but no one's certain. It could be twice that number, but survivors are popping up from the ruins everywhere. It was costly, but we won."

"No, we won a battle. There's still a war on. They won't give up. We just got a breathing space."

A long silence followed in which neither man spoke. Gate realized that his ordeal had left him physically exhausted and mentally anesthetized. It would take time to digest all that had happened, time to realize the full horror of the carnage. The world had changed, and he would have to change with it if he wanted to survive.

"I have to go now," he said. "I'll call later."

He hung up abruptly before Caruthers could reply.

Walker crossed the room and sat down across the table from him. Like him, Walker still wore his soiled uniform, but he had washed his face.

"It's over," he said.

Gate looked at him and raised an eyebrow. "Do you really think so?"

Walker glanced away. "No, not really. I think they'll try again. They strike me as a determined species."

"So are we," Gate countered. He took another sip of coffee, marveling at how it tasted so much better after his ordeal. Even the stale ham and cheese sandwich tasted like manna from heaven. "Mankind knows we're not alone and that not everyone out there is our friend."

Walker chuckled. "We're used to that. I'm sure lots of countries were smiling as they listened to the news about America."

"They may be next. If they are, they'll need our help. This invasion might just make a real world out of us, united and determined to be free."

"Allah willing, but I wouldn't hold my breath. It never stops."

Gate studied Walker's face. It bore a look of hardness he hadn't seen during the entire Nusku operation. "What's up?"

"I'm headed back to Iraq. The natives are getting restless. They think America is down for the count. I have to remind them we're not."

"So soon? No vacation?"

He shrugged. "I go where they send me. I'm finished here."

"But your ..." He stopped. Walker didn't need reminding of the men he had lost.

"I'll work alone for a while, at least until Costas gets off his lazy ass. Then I'll build a new team. What about you?"

What about me? "Maybe I'll take a short vacation on some beach somewhere, soak up some sun. Then, I want to go back to Houston. What I learned might be of some use for the future."

Walker stood and offered his hand. "It's been a pleasure, Gate. If you're ever in some Godforsaken desert, look me up."

"Allah willing," he replied with a smile, as he shook Walker's hand. He considered the captain a friend. "You're leaving now?"

Walker shrugged. "You know the army. I'm catching the next flight out of here."

Gate nodded. "Good luck."

As he watched Captain Walker stride away, he wondered how he coped with it – the loss of lives, the daily tension, and the guilt. His own guilty feelings were few, but they nonetheless weighed heavily on his mind. How much more so for a man whose commands sent men to their deaths? Being a catastrophist was better, though maybe it was time for a change in profession. Looking at the stars through a telescope again might reconnect him with the universe. Even then, he wouldn't be able to forget that one of those specks out there might just be the aliens coming again.

He repressed a shudder and finished his coffee. For now, at least, they were safe.

The End

CHECK OUT OTHER GREAT KAIJU NOVELS

MURDER WORLD | KAIJU DAWN
by Jason Cordova
& Eric S Brown

Captain Vincente Huerta and the crew of the Fancy have been hired to retrieve a valuable item from a downed research vessel at the edge of the enemy's space.
It was going to be an easy payday.
But what Captain Huerta and the men, women and alien under his command didn't know was that they were being sent to the most dangerous planet in the galaxy.
Something large, ancient and most assuredly evil resides on the planet of Gorgon IV. Something so terrifying that man could barely fathom it with his puny mind. Captain Huerta must use every trick in the book, and possibly write an entirely new one, if he wants to escape Murder World.

KAIJU ARMAGEDDON
by Eric S. Brown

The attacks began without warning. Civilian and Military vessels alike simply vanished upon the waves. Crypto-zool-ogist Jerry Bryson found himself swept up into the chaos as the world discovered that the legendary beasts known as Kaiju are very real. Armies of the great beasts arose from the oceans and burrowed their way free of the Earth to declare war upon mankind. Now Dr. Bryson may be the human race's last hope in stopping the Kaiju from bringing civilization to its knees.
This is not some far distant future. This is not some alien world. This is the Earth, here and now, as we know it today, faced with the greatest threat its ever known. The Kaiju Armageddon has begun.

CHECK OUT OTHER GREAT KAIJU NOVELS

KAIJU WINTER
by Jake Bible

The Yellowstone super volcano has begun to erupt, sending North America into chaos and the rest of the world into panic. People are dangerous and desperate to escape the oncoming mega-eruption, knowing it will plunge the continent, and the world, into a perpetual ashen winter. But no matter how ready humanity is, nothing can prepare them for what comes out of the ash: Kaiju!

RAIJU
by K.H. Koehler

His home destroyed by a rampaging kaiju, Kevin Takahashi and his father relocate to New York City where Kevin hopes the nightmare is over. Soon after his arrival in the Big Apple, a new kaiju emerges. Qilin is so powerful that even the U.S. Military may be unable to contain or destroy the monster. But Kevin is more than a ragged refugee from the now defunct city of San Francisco. He's also a Keeper who can summon ancient, demonic god-beasts to do battle for him, and his creature to call is Raiju, the oldest of the ancient Kami. Kevin has only a short time to save the city of New York. Because Raiju and Qilin are about to clash, and after the dust settles, there may be no home left for any of them!

mpliance